the WIDOW'S GUIDE to SECOND chances

VALERIE PEPPER

For all the second-chancers.

1

DEVON

6 MONTHS TO GO

MY GRANDMOTHER GIGI always said in order to succeed, you have to know your strengths. And while I wasn't successful by pretty much anyone's definition, I *was* good at travel. The rock star of road trips. Mistress of miles. President of packing and pit stops.

Planning to live out of a backpack for a month? I got you. I was capsule wardrobing before Pinterest launched. Want a list of the best gas stations on I-40? Most impressive selection of snacks on I-95? Tips on which roadside attractions in middle America are really worth it? Me. I'm your person.

Which is why it was not at all okay for my brother Rick to stand in front of me and declare that we would be driving straight home to Talladega. No pit stops. No looking for the world's biggest balloon animal installation or anything else remotely approaching fun and adventure on my way to months of forced stillness. My skin itched at the thought of it.

"We can't make it to Talladega in twenty-five hours." I glared at him as we stood on opposite sides of his SUV.

My beloved Highlander had given up the ghost in Arizona,

where I'd had a gig leading hikers around Antelope Canyon, and Gigi herself had died a week later. I'd already flown in and out of town for the funeral, unwilling to stay in Talladega any longer than necessary, but thanks to Gigi's will, Rick was here to drag me back home for at least six months after years of near-constant road-tripping.

Home. It wasn't really home. Not anymore. "It's impossible."

"We can if we drive straight through," he said.

"Rick!" I gestured at the air, as if it could help. "You know how I feel about this." I learned to drive on a road trip to Tarpon Springs, Florida; got my first period standing in the room where the Declaration of Independence was signed; and had my first crush over a boy in the other family on our walking ghost tour of Charleston, South Carolina. It was a road trip through Mississippi and Louisiana in search of the perfect tamale that made my husband and I fall in love. "This is ridiculous! If Gigi were here—"

"She's not." He said it softly, like he was testing how far he could push me.

I wouldn't let his gentleness sway me. Not this time. "I know, Rick. She's been dead for weeks. You're also aware we've lost our parents, and my husband's dead, but I'm not so fragile that I'm going to fall apart."

He held his hands up in surrender. I wasn't letting up. "So yes, she's gone, *and* she is rolling over in her grave, she is literally churning in that coffin at the audacity of us driving straight home to Talladega. Who does that?"

He narrowed his eyes. "We do that," he said flatly, clearly done handling me with caution. "Because we spent all day yesterday walking around." He opened the door and got in.

I gaped at him, then opened my door to make sure he heard me. "Rick, we spent yesterday hiking Antelope Canyon. We weren't just 'walking around.'"

"And now we need to go home." He gestured for me to get all the way in. His expression was firm, his jaw set in a familiar line that I could still see even underneath the salt and pepper beard he sported these days.

I made one last swing. "You do realize that this no longer qualifies as a road trip—it's just miles and miles of road. No trip."

"Sorry, little sis. I never said it was going to be one. Ceci needs me home. The twins—"

"Are absolute angels and should not be used as an excuse."

"Are a lot of energy for one person to handle," he hedged. "They're awesome kids, but tell me the last time you hung out with a pair of three-year-olds."

"Angels. They are angels." I was adamant on this point, despite my brother guffawing. "They are angels and you two just don't appreciate their…their…angel-ness."

He kept laughing. "Sure I don't. I also can't wait to leave them with you while I take my wife away for a weekend. On a road trip."

I gave him the stink-eye. "That was low."

He grinned and adjusted his baseball cap. "Ah, man, that was better than all of last year's dad jokes combined." He started the ignition.

I shook my head. "How does Ceci put up with you?"

He waggled his eyebrows. "Wouldn't you like to know?"

"Oh god. Stop. Stop right now." I gagged and pushed the image away before it solidified in my head.

His face got serious. "Devon, we really have to go. You're only prolonging the inevitable, and Ceci made it real clear my ass was due home with a quickness."

I scowled and looked at the sun rising on the horizon. I didn't want serious. Serious made me think, and thinking wasn't helpful. Especially for me. So I took a breath and focused on the deep oranges and pinks pricking at the dark blue sky above.

Rick got out after a minute, rounding the front of the SUV to stand beside me. I leaned in, and his hug was sturdy and comforting, just like him. He was the best man I'd ever known; my own husband never hurdled the bar Rick set. No man ever would, because there was no one like my brother. I cleared my throat to loosen the emotions that clogged it. "I still can't believe Gigi did this, you know?"

"I can," he answered. "The whole time you were gone, she wanted you home."

"But forcing me back like this..."

He didn't speak.

Defeated, I bent to grab my backpack and small suitcase and nudged the larger suitcase toward Rick. "Let's go."

RICK SHUT THE SUV. "IS THAT EVERYTHING?"

I nodded.

I didn't plan on a nomadic life. I'd done the basics: fallen in love with Jason, a sweet boy who loved me back, knew I wouldn't find anyone better, and married him right out of college. We road-tripped in the Highlander during my summers off from teaching school to reach my goal of visiting all 50 states by the time I was 40.

Then he went on shift after a stupid argument. The middle school caught fire and Jason returned to the building for an unaccounted-for teacher. I could still smell the smoke on Chief Suarez as he held me while I screamed at him.

Despite everyone's pleas to stay and process my grief, I upended my life after the funeral, put everything in storage and headed for the East Coast. As far as I was concerned, there was nothing to process: my husband was dead. I'd lost my parents, and now my husband. Staying in one place and opening my heart only brought heartache. So I started over, vowing to never depend on anybody ever again. For five years, I'd done it, moving from gig to gig, never settling down with anyone or anything.

I shut the passenger door. "We're eating a real breakfast before we hit the road." I crossed my arms.

My patient brother didn't flinch. "Sounds good."

Once there, we ordered stacks of blueberry pancakes, scrambled eggs, and an unholy amount of bacon to go with the coffee I sucked down like my life depended on it. We'd head straight home to the twins, without delay, per my now-boring brother. And if I so happened to need a pee break at the exact exit where an awesome installation of, say, yarn art stood, then I guess we'd just have to stop. I was getting my adventure in whether Rick liked it or not.

"You know, despite the way this is going down, I'm glad you're coming home," Rick said.

Not by choice. Gigi's will mandated I physically live in it for at least six months to keep it and fix it back up, or it went to the local historical society. The very society helmed by her decades-long arch-nemesis. Gigi would flat-out haunt me from the beyond if I allowed that woman to get her grubby hands on the house, and honestly? I'd haunt me, too.

It never occurred to me that it wouldn't stay with us, but I'd assumed that Rick would be the one to get it. He was the one who lived in town. He was the one with a family.

"Well, when my time is up and the house is officially in my name, I'm handing it straight over to you. You can do whatever you want after that." I shoved a bite of syrup-drenched pancake in my mouth and chewed. "As long as it stays in the family."

He polished off his bacon and shrugged. "We'll see. Gotta say, I didn't know the house meant so much to you."

My mouth dropped open. "Seriously? Rick, the house was

my sanctuary after our parents died. Our whole lives are in that house. Every bit of sunshine and rain. Think of all the stories she told us as she tucked us in. How she taught us to cook, and how we nearly burned our eyebrows off trying to imitate Iron Chef. Epic hide and seeks. Remember when I scared you and your friends so much you ran next door because you thought a ghost was in the house?" I grinned, happy to see the scowl it earned me. "All those school dances and first kisses." And first other things, too. "We can't let that go."

He leaned back in the booth and appraised me. "Huh."

"What?" I took a sip of coffee.

"It's nice to see you so riled up. I've missed it."

I scoffed. "You've missed seeing me pissed off?"

He nodded, a grin tugging at his lips. "Absolutely."

I rolled my eyes.

"You should stay. Beyond the required six months, I mean. The twins would love it. You know Ceci would love it. And I miss my little sister."

"You just want free babysitting."

He smiled. "I wouldn't hate it." He pointed a fork at me. "But I really miss having you around."

I looked away. "You'll be sick of me by the time the six months are up."

"Never."

I slid out of the booth, needing to break the seriousness, and he signaled for the bill.

In the restroom, I washed my hands and used the water to tame my dirty blonde hair, pulling it into a loose top bun.

Ten minutes later, we were pointed east. Rick took first shift and I looked at the flat road ahead of us, already squiggly with heat, the bright blue of the sky an exclamation point on the beauty of the surrounding canyons.

We stayed quiet. It was one of my favorite things about Rick: we could go for hours without a word between us, both of us perfectly content. I'd call him from the road or whatever town I'd landed in for a bit, and we'd throw our phones on speaker and just...be. He'd always known what I needed, and he'd never failed at giving it to me.

Too bad he couldn't wave a magic wand and keep me from having to go home and face the past.

2

AARON

I ADDED THE cooked sausage to the pasta sauce I'd made and tasted it. Needed more oregano. I was in the last twelve hours of my three-day shift, and I'd grown tired of the probies' pathetic attempts at food. Turns out, most new firefighters were shit at cooking. One guy's efforts at "spaghetti" (microwave ramen with heated ketchup and Italian seasoning) were a crime against both food and humanity. I added more seasoning to the sauce, tested it again, and let it simmer while I pulled the noodles off the heat.

"You're not rinsing those, are you?" My oldest brother, Will, walked into the firehouse's kitchen with an eyebrow raised at the pasta. "Dad would have hated that."

"I wasn't, but now that you mention it..." I ran water over the noodles, delighted in how affronted Will looked.

"Asshole," he muttered.

I laughed. "It's not like we're some Italian family, Will. We're Southerners. Dad wouldn't have cared whether the pasta was rinsed or not; he just wanted to feed us."

Will grunted and pulled bowls down for the few of us eating. We ate in shifts, and naturally, first up had me with both my firefighter brothers and Mike, my partner in the ambulance and a fellow paramedic.

I chopped basil and sprinkled it on the finished dishes, wiping off any drips of sauce before handing them to Will. He rolled his eyes at my insistence on presentation—a person ate with their eyes just as much as their mouths—but said nothing.

"What a treat," Chief Suarez said as he sat down.

"Looks awesome, man," Mike said.

My other brother, Price, slapped me on the back as he took a seat. "Doesn't look as good as me, but then again, nothing ever does."

I shook my head. "Just say thanks, Price."

He tipped his chin at me and laughed. It was as good as he'd give and I knew it. Which was standard.

"Looks like Samson's working on a love connection with your Daisy," Chief said, shoveling a forkful of pasta in his mouth. Samson was a stray dog that'd ingratiated himself into the firehouse's neighborhoods' hearts, which basically meant he didn't miss a meal. He was a little thing, not quite knee high, with a dingy yellow coat and a crest of hair like a mohawk.

I took a normal-sized bite and shrugged. "Of course he is. Daisy is fully trained, up to date on all her shots, has a home, gets bathed regularly…she's a catch."

Chief laughed. "Sure wish someone would take Samson on. He's a great little dog. Ugly, but great."

Price looked up. "Have you had 'the talk' with Daisy? Made sure she knows her worth?"

I tried not to smile, but it was pointless. Daisy was my two-year-old brindle pit bull and the only woman in my life. She was my baby, and I wasn't apologizing for it. Besides, she wasn't going anywhere *and* she didn't give me grief about anything, both of which were nearly impossible to come by. "We've talked. Samson isn't good enough for her, but he sure does like her."

"Sounds about like the rest of you bozos," Chief said.

We all groaned. I prepared for his regular jab at me about needing to find someone. He was obsessed. I'd done the dating apps for a little while, but then I realized Chief was on there, too, trying to get women to swipe right on me.

Mortifying didn't begin to describe it.

The other day, he spent an entire hour telling me why I should take one of his nieces out on a date, despite her not being even twenty-three years old. Considering I'm thirty-three, I refused to listen to him. And maybe that was a mistake, but as far as I was concerned, that whole 'age is just a number' thing doesn't happen until both parties are thirty and above. I'm not saying I was some enlightened dude in my twenties—I was just as much of a self-centered asshole as the next twenty-something —but hitting thirty was different. Suddenly the under twenty-five set looked like middle-schoolers, and I figured they'd hang around about as long as a middle school crush. I wanted more than that.

"Which reminds me," Chief continued, sitting back and wiping his mouth with a napkin, "I found the perfect little lady for you, Will."

I smirked and kept my eyes on my plate, happy the spotlight wasn't on me for once. Chief was convinced he was the town matchmaker, but had yet to make anything happen. For one, he was a confirmed bachelor himself, and second, no one seemed ready to forgive him for the time he spent trying to match up the mayor with our local weather person. Yes, they were close in age, but the mayor was engaged, and Chief basically refused to acknowledge that in his quest to create a happily ever after for the weather forecaster.

"I'm going to stop you right there, Chief," Will said. "The fact you said 'little lady' is a problem. You can't talk about women like that."

I grinned. Will chapped my ass on the regular, but he was a feminist of the highest order. Not that anyone else really noticed, because it's not like he was walking around wearing a t-shirt proudly proclaiming his status, but he constantly did this sort of thing. That he did it with his signature scowl made it even better.

"Fine. Her name is Connie. Would anyone else like to hear about her?" Chief asked.

"Also not okay. She isn't a piece of cattle to be auctioned off. Have some respect."

Chief's eyebrows rose. "Remember who you're talking to. I'll have you on bathroom duty for a month if you keep it up."

"Fine. Tell me about this wonderful Connie," Will said, turning on a dime.

Everyone laughed. We all knew Will's hatred of bathroom duty, feminist or not.

While Chief rhapsodized about the woman he had in mind for Will, I opened my social media. As I scrolled, my eyes snagged on a gorgeous blue-eyed blonde.

Devon.

She smiled from the passenger seat, her brother in profile in the driver's seat, with the morning sun shining on them both. *My brother swears we're not on a road trip*, the caption read. *I say we are. We'll see who wins.*

I double-tapped to like the post before I could second-guess myself. Chief took that precise moment to look over and stick his nose where it didn't belong.

"Is that Devon Rayne?"

I blackened my phone and didn't bother answering. Chief never asked a question he didn't already know the answer to.

"You know she's coming back to town," he said.

I knew.

In fact, I knew way more about Devon than I ought to, thanks to my relationship with her grandmother Gigi. I'd been the paramedic on-scene a few years ago when Gigi fell down the steps and broke her arm. She'd had the same eyes as Devon, light-blue and sparkling, even in pain. When I checked up on her after she was back from the hospital, she invited me to sit on the porch for tea and cookies. That was all it took to make me a near-weekly visitor.

Gigi wanted Devon home for years, and was convinced we'd be perfect for each other. When she pulled out her phone and shoved Devon's social media photos in my face, demanding I follow her, I did, because I always did what Gigi said. Besides, Devon had so many followers I doubt she ever noticed.

In the dozens of times I sat on that porch, I never bothered to tell Gigi I'd been gobsmacked by her granddaughter from the very first time I laid eyes on her, when I was a know-it-all punk just starting out as an EMT. Devon was married, so I knew enough to keep my hands and thoughts to myself, but from the second she came by the firehouse, I was drawn to her. It sounded completely hokey and woo-woo, which wasn't really like me, but there was something about her energy, I don't know. All I could do was wish I'd met her first.

But now she was coming back. I assumed she'd stay at Gigi's, which was close enough to the firehouse that I was pretty much guaranteed to see her at some point. And while I'm certain Gigi would've loved to see a happily ever after with Devon and I, the chances of Devon sticking around long-term were probably slim. No one had—not my high school girlfriend or any after that, and certainly not my mom.

My mood darkened at the thought of my mother, and I swept it away. She deserved nothing from me, not even my thoughts.

"Sure you don't want me to give Connie your number?" Chief was asking Will.

Will sighed. "Chief, all due respect, no."

Chief shook his head. "You'll regret it, but okay. When you inevitably meet her, because this town is too small for you not to, you'll kick yourself. Be sure to let me know when that happens so I can know I was right."

Will chuckled, a look of pure relief on his face. "Sure thing, Chief."

"But you're still on bathroom duty this week."

The table erupted in laughter as Daisy came trotting in, tail wagging, no sign of scraggly Samson in sight. She made her way to us, then sat and waited, her eyes trained on me. Daisy knew she wouldn't get attention or food scraps while we were all at the dinner table. But dogs were nothing if not hopeful, so I let her stay while we ate.

I finished my bowl and stood up, and Daisy popped up with me. "Good girl." I leaned down to give her a scratch. She looked at the bowl and then me, her eyes wide.

I chuckled. "You can't lick the bowl, Daisy, and you know it."

She huffed and walked away. Because I was nice as hell and used to live with two brothers, I started tidying the kitchen as Chief and the rest of my table finished up, and the second round of guys started in.

Without a word, Mike stepped in to help me at the sink. We'd been partners almost since I started seven years ago, but he was in a completely different world than me. Married with three kids, all of them under age ten. Which, honestly? Kind of terrifying. I loved kids, but I'd never felt that urge to have them. I'd be perfectly content to be a doting uncle, but even that hadn't worked out yet. All the Joseph brothers were single, and some would say we were notoriously so. Maybe another product of dear old Mom, or maybe we were just built that way.

"That was some good pasta, man," Mike said. "Not as good as my wife's, but great."

I grinned. "Since Miranda hails from an Italian family, I'm going to take that as a compliment."

"You should." He burped.

I laughed. "You act like that at home?"

He smiled and handed me a plate to put in the dishwasher. "Hell yeah. Little man loves it. Wife? Not so much."

The station's siren went off, and we instantly shifted into work mode. Mike turned off the water, and we headed to the engine bay, Will and Price right behind us.

Mike pulled his phone out and checked the info that dispatch had pushed onto the app. "Possible gas leak, male unconscious, mid-forties. Let's go."

I hopped into the driver's seat of the ambulance and Mike took the passenger side, immediately throwing on the lights and siren. "Left," he said. "Head toward the racetrack."

I checked to make sure no one was about to walk in front of us, then punched the gas.

3

DEVON

LET THE COUNTDOWN BEGIN: 5 MONTHS, 29
DAYS TO GO

I STEPPED ONTO the front porch, took a deep breath, and
promptly sneezed.

Stupid summer allergies.

I'd stayed out of the southern United States these last five
years for many reasons, and the pollen count was absolutely one
of them. Guess I'd be swinging by the pharmacy later for some
meds.

Sneezing fit over, I looked around the big front porch. Like
the rest of the house, it needed work. The shiny gray paint on
the floorboards had dulled and was flaking, and white paint
peeled off the railing. The rocking chairs showed their age, no
paint or varnish to speak of, but I knew that hadn't stopped Gigi
from using them. I could see her so easily, tiny and plump, a
glass of sweet tea in her hands, chatting away to neighbors or
whoever.

I cleared my throat, blinking away the tears to continue my
inspection. The porch swing had seen better days, too, just like
the rocking chairs. I bet the twins loved that thing. Ferns hung
like sentries around the porch, lush and thriving. Clearly

someone had been taking care of them, because Alabama's
midsummer heat was nothing to play around with.

I stepped off the porch and moved down the walkway,
shading my eyes to get a better look at the house.

My heart hurt.

Gigi was so proud of this house. Built in 1890 by her grandparents and situated in the historic district, Gigi had been nearly
fanatical in her efforts to keep me and Rick involved in the
upkeep. Even though we were kids, the house was our responsi-
bility, she said, whether it was yard work or handling minor
repairs ourselves. I knew this house from the attic rafters down
to the dogwoods on either side of the front yard.

I'd loved taking care of the yard, bringing the flowers and
azaleas to life with care, and had handled it almost from the
minute we moved in. I'd been so angry at the world for taking
my parents, and once Gigi got us here from Portland, she
quickly saw I needed something physical to do. Seeing as how I
was crap at sports, she'd turned me toward the yard and set me
free.

Now I saw what five years of avoidance had done. The white
clapboards lining the house were...fine, but they needed a fresh
coat of paint. Weeds had nearly overtaken the beds lining the
front of the house, and where there weren't weeds, the once-red
mulch had faded to nearly white. The azaleas in the beds needed
a good watering, and the spots where I'd usually planted
annuals were barren.

In the years before I left, it'd been me and Rick and a contact
list of handymen taking care of the inside whenever Gigi let us
know something needed fixing. She was independent as hell and
stubborn as a mule, though. Something told me I'd find all
kinds of things that Rick never knew about.

Right now, the only thing needing attention was my desire to
shove caffeine in my body. I'd found some instant stuff in the
kitchen, and that flat-out wouldn't do.

Rick had brought me over last night after dinner, even though Ceci wanted me to stay my first night back in town with them. But I'd been eager to get over here, more to face the music than anything. Of course, I'd slept like absolute shit in my old room, unable to shake the memories.

I didn't have a car, but I knew good and well there was a coffee shop in the town square, about a ten-minute walk from here. A coffee shop that happened to be down the street from the firehouse where Jason had worked. A coffee shop now owned by Jodi, one of Jason's sisters. Who I'd all but ignored for years.

I swallowed the burn in my throat. It was just allergies, and I was being ridiculous. Maybe a little worried about Jodi's reaction when she saw me.

Yeah. No. I was *terrified* of what she'd say. Her family had fractured after Jason's death, and instead of reaching out to her, I ran.

In my years of marriage to Jason, Jodi had clung to me like a barnacle, as if sensing I wasn't really into being a sister-in-law but determined to hug me into submission anyway. When Jason was alive, she wore me down, but after I left I slowly stopped regular communication with everyone other than my immediate family. It got to where I really only sent Jodi happy birthday texts and liked all her Instagram posts. Which were prolific. So it felt like I knew what she'd been up to, even if maybe that hadn't gone both ways.

I headed inside to get ready, brushing my teeth, putting on a ton of deodorant to fight the early morning heat, and throwing on sunscreen. No make-up. I was in jean shorts, an old N-Sync concert tee, and Birkenstocks. I appraised my wavy hair in the bathroom mirror and took in the way it hung halfway down my back. I should probably get it trimmed and colored; I'd only paid attention to it maybe once a year these past five years.

Wait. You know what? Fuck it. If I was going to be stuck

here for six months, then I was doing at least one thing totally in my control.

Walking into Gigi's room, I diligently ignored the way my heart ka-thumped at the sight and baby-powder scent of it, and pushed open the ensuite bathroom door. I pulled open the left sink drawer, and sure enough, her cutting shears glinted in the light. I grabbed them and bolted to the other bathroom.

I fluffed my hair, considering. I'd always wanted chin-length hair, and had watched about a million videos on Instagram about how to do it, but had never been brave enough to make it happen. Well, today was the day.

I pulled up the video I'd watched the most and set to it, parting my hair into quadrants and carefully clipping, taking my time and making liberal use of the hand mirror that was still under the sink. Twenty minutes later, I'd cut off at least a foot of hair, and the rest hung thick and fluffy just below my chin. I looked like a totally different person.

Perfect.

4

DEVON

5 MONTHS, 29 DAYS TO GO

I STARTED toward the coffee shop, cropped hair already clinging to the back of my neck thanks to the humidity. The neighborhood hadn't changed at all, other than bushes getting fuller and trees growing taller. They looked good, with perfectly trimmed yards and flawless green carpets of grass winking at me as I passed, making Gigi's house look even worse by comparison.

I heard a yip, and a yellow dog trotted up, his scraggly tail wagging at full speed and wearing what I'd swear was a smile on his face. He was grungy, and he had a mohawk on his head. Cute. Ugly, but cute. Likely a stray, if I had to guess, but a well-fed one. I leaned down to pet him, and he stopped and planted his butt on the sidewalk.

"Aren't you a good boy?" I cooed, giving him a good scratch. It probably wasn't the smartest thing to be too nice to him, but it's not like I was sticking around.

As I straightened and resumed my walk to the coffee shop, the dog kept pace with me. I wasn't too mad about it, because the closer I got, the more my hands shook. I breathed deep.

Who knows? Maybe Jodi wouldn't be there. I hadn't *completely* ignored her like I had her younger sister Jess, but Jess hadn't seemed to care like I knew Jodi did.

The dog gave a little woof and went up on his hind legs, forcing me to a stop right as we got in front of the shop.

I smiled. "I'm being silly, aren't I?"

He woofed again and licked my hand.

"Guess I need to put on my big girl pants and go in there. Right?" My smile faltered.

He snuffled and woofed, then took off at a sprint. I watched him go, and then gasped as he hightailed it into the firehouse a block away.

Jason. I could see him sauntering out of there like he was invincible, a grin on his face as he made his way to me after a shift and wrapped me in a hug. I smelled his soap-and-fire-station scent, the memory of him suddenly, painfully physical. Nausea gripped me, my stomach roiling, and my mouth went dry. I bent over, my hands on my knees, and squeezed my eyes shut. *God, the last thing I said to him…*

This right here. This is why I didn't want to come back.

It'd been five years, but sometimes it felt like it was yesterday. Being here, in front of Jodi's coffeeshop and down the block from the station, wasn't helping.

Breathe.

"Hon? You okay?"

A set of orthopedic sneakers appeared in front of me, and I straightened, pushing everything down and blinking away the tears that'd nearly come. I couldn't think about Jason like that.

I took in the five feet of octogenarian wrath before me. "Mrs. Withers." None other than Gigi's mortal enemy since a fight over a boy. The very woman who would lead the historical society to take possession of Gigi's house if I weren't here.

She blinked back at me, her owlish eyes sharpening into a

hawk's behind her bottle-thick glasses. "Devon Rayne." Her mouth flattened and puckered like she'd eaten something foul.

Her mean-girl transformation was impressive enough to knock me back to as normal as I was going to get. "Nice of you to check on a stranger."

She sniffed and raised her chin, giving me a perfect view of the chin hair I could probably pluck out with my fingers. "Well, you *were* blocking the sidewalk."

I narrowed my eyes. "Right."

"I presume you're here because of Shirley's will." She barely managed to not sneer Gigi's name.

I wanted to roll my eyes, but Southern manners ran deep and Mrs. Withers had many, *many* decades on me. Even if she was committing so many fashion crimes it was a wonder someone hadn't locked her up. "News travels fast," I said sweetly.

"Well, I guess you'll be on your way." Her voice warbled a little, and normally I'd have thought it was almost melodic. Coming out of Mrs. Withers, however, it was as though one of Satan's henchwomen was screaming at me. "We'll take care of the house."

I cocked my head and gave her my best shit-eating grin. "Oh, now, Mrs. Withers. Where's the fun in that? No," I sighed, putting my hands in the back pocket of my shorts and really getting into the act, "I think I'll stay the whole time. Who knows? Maybe I'll run for Town Council."

Her eyes flew wide.

"Now if you'll excuse me." I sidestepped her and headed for the coffee shop, shaking my head as I went. That woman was unbelievable. I couldn't wait to tell Rick.

The smell of roasted coffee beans hit me as soon as I opened the door. The shop had undergone a massive transformation since Jodi took over, the overhaul of which I'd followed on Instagram. Overstuffed couches and chairs filled one corner, with a

counter and stools behind them. Tables were scattered through-
out, and around the cash register were carrells of jewelry, which
I'd bet anything were crafted by local artists. I couldn't help but
smile. She'd taken it over at twenty-three, right after college,
and turned this place into the exact kind of shop she'd always
wanted, and I was so proud of her.

But she still wouldn't want to see me. If I were her, I'd be
pissed at the way I'd all but ignored her for years.

I kept my head down in the hope no one noticed or recognized me, because even though this wasn't a super-small town,
it wasn't that big, either. I'd gone through enough emotions
already today, and it wasn't even nine o'clock.

Naturally, my luck ran out when I got to the counter and Jodi
herself came out of the back.

"Devon?" Her forehead crinkled.

Shit. I gave her a tentative smile as I handed over my card to
pay for the order. "Jodi. Hey."

A huge smile broke across her face. "Oh my goodness, it *is*
you! Get over here!" She beelined to me, wrapping me in her
arms before I could process what was happening.

I stiffened, surprised at the contact. But as she tightened her
embrace, I relaxed and and reveled in the familiar closeness. As
the hug kept going, I laughed. "You're not mad at me?"

She squeezed me closer. "Are you *kidding*? I could never be
mad at you. I'm so excited you're here!"

She eventually let go of me and pulled away, but kept her
hands on my arms. We stared at each other and smiled, and a
weight lifted off me.

"You look amazing." She'd been her brother's opposite their
whole lives: fair-skinned where he wasn't and redheaded to his
nearly black hair. Even their eyes were different, hers an almost
turquoise to his deep brown. Her red hair flounced in a ponytail
at the top of her head, and was tied back with a sky-blue

kerchief. She wore a chambray shirt and jeans with a simple black apron on top, and checkered red and white Vans on her feet.

She waved the compliment away, her eyes sparkling. "Oh my goodness, it's been so long! How are you? Your hair! Here, come sit." She grabbed my hand and led me to a table, waving at someone to bring my coffee over. "Tell me everything." She smiled broadly and gestured for me to speak.

"I—"

"I was so sorry when Gigi passed." She lay a hand on mine. "You know she came here every Sunday. She'd buy a hot chocolate and a lemon-raspberry scone and we'd catch up."

"Really?" I beamed. Of course Gigi did; it was exactly the kind of thing she did.

She nodded. "Yeah. She was a big help for me at first, helping me figure out what would sell here, that sort of thing." She squeezed my hand. "But go on."

"Well, I—"

"You know I bought this place, right?"

I laughed.

Jodi steamrolled on. "Like, that's why Gigi would come. She was always like another grandma for me, especially after you left. I think I reminded her of you, which is weird because we're nothing alike. Guess it was a grandmother thing. But she was great when my Dad left, and when Jess left...anyway." She gestured at me.

I tried not to wince at all the leaving Jodi had endured. "So it's just you and your mom here?"

She rolled her eyes. "Yes, but enough about me. We're talking about you!"

"Right. Gigi left me her house."

Jodi grinned as she nodded. "I heard! I didn't think you'd come back, though."

My smile dimmed at the stab of guilt her words shot through me. "The house has always been in my family, so...."

"Oh my gosh, that means you're moving in? That's amazing! It'll be like you never left and—"

I hurried to stop her. "Jodi, I'm not staying."

She went quiet and her expressive eyes searched mine. "You're not?"

I shook my head. "Not past the six months. It's too hard," I said, swallowing hard. "Even just now, outside...well. It's too hard."

Her shoulders slumped. "Oh."

My heart squeezed. She'd been like a little sister to me for so long, and when I bailed on this town, I bailed on her. And clearly I wasn't the only one. The fact that she was even being nice to me was proof of how wonderful she was. "How..."

She looked at me expectantly.

"How did you do it?" I looked around the shop to gather my resolve before turning back to her. "Move on, I mean."

"Ah." She reached for my hand and squeezed it. "One day at a time, Devon. I missed him—I still do—but I had to pick myself up and keep going. Especially after Dad took off and Jess went to Nashville. So, I didn't really have a choice."

"You could have fled like the rest of us."

She pursed her lips. "Someone had to stay with Mom and keep this town in line."

I looked at her in wonder and shook my head. "You're a badass, you know that? So much stronger than us mere mortals."

She shrugged. "Stick around, kid, and I'll teach you my ways."

I laughed. "I'm older than you, you know."

She waved a hand in the air. "Yeah, but I'm the one who's the most emotionally healthy. Not just in my family, either," she said pointedly.

I winced. "Damn, woman, you aim straight for it."

"Tell me I'm wrong."

"You're right. You're absolutely right." A piece of my heart clicked into place.

"So, six months?"

I nodded. "And judging by the look of the house, I'll be busy."

"Well, we'll have to make the most of it while you're here, right? We have so much to catch up on, and you can come to the weekly events here, and I'll introduce you to the regulars..."

She kept going, and my heartbeat kicked into high gear. This was too much, too soon. I lurched to a stand and grabbed my coffee.

Jodi stood with me, not seeing my distress. "Oh, you have to go. Lots to do at Gigi's of course!" she gushed. "I'll see you tomorrow morning, right?"

I nodded distractedly as she followed me to the door.

"Come earlier tomorrow, it's Sunday and you can have those scones Gigi used to have." She pulled me into another long embrace.

Finally, I pushed the door open and yanked myself out of her hug while still walking.

"Oh, wait!" Her eyes widened.

"I'm good, I gotta go!" I walked like a woman on a mission. Because I was. And the mission was to leave with all of my limbs and emotions intact.

"Samson!" she yelled as she reached for me.

Who was Samson? It didn't matter. I darted out of her reach like a ninja. "Okay, bye!"

I turned, and my foot promptly knocked into a tiny, grungy, four-legged terror.

Oh no.

I flailed and shrieked, losing my balance and hitting the pavement with my knees, then palms, then chin. "Owww," I moaned. In front of me, the coffee gurgled out of the to-go cup's lid as it rolled away.

It was really good coffee, too. Like, really good. *Damn.*

The demon dog—Samson, I gathered—woofed and licked my cheek, then scampered off.

And to think I'd liked him on the way here.

"Oh my gosh, are you okay?" Jodi asked.

I moaned and lay there another moment, trying to decide if I was hurt or simply mortified, when for the second time that morning a set of shoes appeared in my line of sight. Black work boots stopped the coffee cup from rolling any farther and a deep voice said, "Samson strike again?"

I propped myself up on my elbows and followed the boots up a pair of navy uniform pants, to a navy fire department t-shirt tucked into a trim waist, then on up to a blinding-white smile and cheerful blue eyes that crinkled at the corners.

"Something like that," I muttered, pain blooming in my jaw.

He held his hand out, his grip warm and certain as he helped me scramble to my feet. I tried, and failed, to keep the pain from showing on my face as I straightened.

"You okay?" he asked as he released me.

"Um, yeah, I think I am," I mumbled. Mortified. That was the winner.

"Wait a second. Devon?"

I finally took a closer look at him, and realization hit me like a punch. I knew him. Boy, did I ever. I winced, whether from the pain in my face or the memory of the man in front of me. His dark blond hair was cut close on the sides and back but a little long on top. Full lips were tipped into a gorgeous smile, and his eyes still seemed to see right into me, stripping away my defenses the same way they did before. I breathed out. "Aaron Joseph."

He smiled, and it was like being warmed by the sun. "Yeah. Can't believe you remember me."

There was no forgetting you. The man had always affected me. I'd done nothing about it, of course, but there was no denying the pull he'd had on me. I remembered him at Jason's funeral, the way his eyes had burned into me. As though he could unlock my secrets. I wanted no part of it. I had enough guilt over Jason as it was.

"Good to see you." I was shocked at how normal my voice sounded.

"You, too." He tucked his hands into his pockets and kept studying me.

Jodi appeared from my left and shoved a fresh coffee in my hand. "Here."

I grabbed it, grateful for the distraction, and took a deep sip. Immediately I had regrets, because of course it was as hot as the man standing in front of me and I could not, would not, let my face show it. I swallowed, taking the burn down the throat, and tipped the cup at Aaron. "Well, um, I should go. Nice seeing you."

"You sure you're okay? That was a heck of a tumble you had." Concern knitted his brow and he reached for my face.

Instinctively I jerked back. No touching. Not by him. Absolutely not. He would incinerate me. "I'm fine. Thank you."

He pulled his hand back, one hundred percent professional. "Of course. But your chin…."

"I'm sure it's okay," I interrupted. I needed to get out of here. Immediately, if not sooner.

He nodded, his eyes searching mine.

Fuck. I turned to Jodi. "Thanks for the coffee. I'll, um, I'll see you soon."

She smiled brightly. "Don't let Samson scare you off!"

I forced a smile and laugh, trying again to hide the wince at the stab of pain that shot through my jaw. "I'll do my best."

I turned and headed to Gigi's, coffee in hand, and kept my

eyes forward. I would not turn around to see if Aaron was still there.

By the time the house came into view, which took a while because my knees definitely didn't feel awesome, I felt a bit more like myself. Whatever happened back there was a fluke; it had to be. Because no way could Aaron Joseph have affected me like that. It was impossible.

5

AARON

I STOOD THERE like an idiot, watching the way her ass moved in those jean shorts as she fled. Devon Rayne. Wow. I didn't think I'd see her so quickly, or that she'd be so...I don't know. Intense? Amazing? Three-dimensional?

And she'd remembered me. More than that, maybe, because there was a look that flickered across her face for the briefest of moments.

Despite my best efforts, something in my chest unfurled.

Daisy nudged my leg and I reached down to pet her. She smiled like she had something to do with it, and beside her, like the absolutely wonderful saint of a dog he is, was Samson, who *definitely* had something to do with it. He grinned right alongside Daisy.

I shook my head and chuckled. "You two are really something, you know that?"

Samson woofed and took off after Devon. "Good luck buddy," I muttered. "Maybe you'll get farther than I did."

I went into the coffee shop, knowing Daisy would wait outside, patiently taking her pets from passers-by like the queen she was.

Jodi stood behind the counter, arms crossed, a knowing grin splitting her face in two. "Well?"

"Well what?"

"Did you ask her out?"

Heat flared on my neck. "What? No! I was doing my duty. That's all."

She crossed her arms and looked me up and down, and I knew she was about to call me out. "Bullshit."

Sometimes it was a real pain to still know the people you grew up with.

"Aaron, I see all the likes you make on her Instagram posts. And I can see the moony look on your face right now," she continued. "So. Make your move."

I rubbed the back of my neck. "Can I just get some muffins for the station? Please?" I pointed to the display case and avoided her eyes. "A dozen blueberry and a dozen banana nut." No way was I having a discussion with the little sister of the town's dead hero. Didn't matter that we had incriminating year-book photos of each other.

Jodi pursed her lips as if she was trying to decide how much she was going to torture me, then looked behind me and seemed to think better of it.

"Did I hear that Devon Rayne is back in town?"

Ah, shit. Cecilia Rayne, better known as Ceci, wife of Rick Rayne, mother of twins, sister-in-law to Devon, and Olympic-level meddler.

I turned. "Hey, Ceci."

She smiled up at me and winked. "Just kidding. I know she's back in town because Rick brought her back. You see her yet?"

I fought the urge to sigh. Based on that little sentence alone, I knew she was up to something. "Just a few minutes ago, after Samson tripped her."

A flash of concern swept across her face as she turned to

look around the coffee shop. "What? Is she okay? Where is she?"

Jodi piped up. "Seems like she's okay, Ceese. You here for your daily dose?"

"Can I get those muffins?" I reminded her. "I really am on shift."

Jodi rolled her eyes and grabbed a pastry box. "Fine."

Ceci laughed and turned back to me. She wasn't very tall, maybe five feet five inches, but you'd never know it the way she looked at you. "So, Aaron."

Here it came. "So, Ceci."

"I like you. You're young—"

"I'm thirty-three."

"Like I said, you're young, smart, nice, you look great in a uniform—"

"You're married!" I protested.

She shrugged. "Doesn't mean I can't appreciate how you fill out a uniform."

My neck blazed again. I needed out of here. "Jodi? Muffins?"

"Sorry, gotta get some from the back!" She waved and smiled as she backed away from the pastry case. The pastry case that *definitely* had enough muffins in it.

"Traitor," I said under my breath.

"I'm not sure you know my twins very well, but they can be a bit, shall we say, *much* at times," Ceci continued. "And their Aunt Devon knows exactly how to harness their energy for good."

I nodded warily. "Okay."

"And I want Devon to stay in town. For much longer than the six months she's planning on."

Six months? Why did that length of time seem so familiar?

Jodi emerged from the back. "I've got the muf—"

"Shht!" Ceci spat out the noise and held up a hand to stop Jodi in her tracks. Honestly, it was impressive. Not only did Jodi freeze, but so did I and the other barista. Those twins had no chance.

Ceci continued, her hand in the air, Jodi and I still in place. "Listen, Aaron, I'm going to get straight to the point. You need to ask her out. I like your chances," she waved her free arm up and down, presumably indicating me or my body, I wasn't sure which. And I didn't care for her to elaborate.

"Can I move?" Jodi squeaked.

Ceci smiled graciously at her and lowered her arm. "Of course." She turned her steely eyes back to me. "So you'll ask her out. Muffins are on me."

Ha. "Despite your generous pastry purchase, Ceci, I don't think she's interested." Although that look on her face…Either way, I didn't want yet another person—or two people, seeing as how Jodi and Ceci were both trying to tag-team me here—interfering in my life. "So thanks, but no thanks." I grabbed the muffins from Jodi, threw a couple twenties on the counter, and nodded at both of them. "It's been a pleasure." I turned and hightailed it out of there before Ceci could say another word, or at least before I could hear it.

Outside, Daisy popped up from where she'd been sitting and we headed back to the station.

Chief caught my eye as I sat the muffins on the kitchen counter. "Long line at the Daily Dose?"

I shook my head. He knew exactly why it took me so long. The meddler network's force was powerful. "Samson tripped someone."

Chief's thick eyebrows rose. "She okay?"

"Pretty sure you already know the answer to that, seeing as how I didn't tell you whether they were male or female," I grumbled.

He laughed, utterly unapologetic. "How was it seeing her? You like enough of her posts on social media."

I narrowed my eyes. Him, too? I'd been betrayed by Instagram. "She's not staying." Why would she?

"Hmm. Maybe she didn't post that part on the face feed," he mused.

"What are you talking about?"

"Six months."

"Six months?" Again with the six months.

"She has to stay for six months. Something to do with Shirley's will." He said it like he was talking to a toddler.

I stared at him as it hit me. Holy shit. Gigi had really done it. *"Just think about it, Aaron,"* she'd said, *"I'll write it into my will and she'll have to do it, and that'll give you six months to sweep her off her feet."*

I'd told her no way, that I wasn't about to be some plot point in one of her romance books, and tried to forget she ever mentioned it.

And damn if she hadn't gone and done it, even though I'd told her not to. That crazy, wonderful old woman. The hope that had started to unfurl now bloomed across my chest. Maybe I really *did* have a chance with Devon. "Did you have something to do with this?"

Chief gave me an innocent look. "With what?"

I snorted. I bet he did. Probably thought the whole idea was his first sure match in town.

"But now that she's here..." He gave me a look.

"Now that she's here, nothing." I wanted him to stay out of it.

"How would you know?"

"How would who know what?" Price asked, strolling into the kitchen and flipping open the box of muffins. "Mmm, banana nut. My favorite." He plucked it out of the box and looked expectantly at the two of us. "So?" He waved his hand and shoved half the muffin in his mouth.

"Your brother's crush is back in town," Chief said.

"Okay, enough." I held up my hand. "She is not my crush, and she has a name."

Price rubbed his hands together. "Ooh, is this the infamous Devon Rayne?" Crumbs flew out of his mouth as he spoke.

I nearly choked on my own saliva. "How the fu—?"

He cackled. "It is! Oh, this is good. I gotta tell Will." He wiped his hand on his shirt and pulled his phone out, and I felt the text vibrate in my pocket seconds later.

PRICE

Baby brother's crush is back in town

I bit back a curse. I was the youngest, but damn if they wouldn't ever stop calling me "baby brother."

Will's reply came almost instantly.

WILL

Devon's back?

Price laughed gleefully and kept typing. Meanwhile, I tried to make peace with the fact that apparently everyone who mattered to me knew about my thing for Devon and said nothing about it. I wanted nothing more than to dig a hole and bury myself in it for the entire time she was here.

But maybe I'd check on Devon tomorrow, because that really had been a major fall. Her knees had been bruising even as we stood there, and her chin didn't look so hot, either. It would be a professional visit. Strictly professional. Doing it would ease my conscience about Gigi's meddling from beyond, too, because I could see Devon, see if that look on her face meant anything, and move on with my life.

My phone kept buzzing with my brothers' texts, both of them giving me shit. I turned it off and left the kitchen, flipping Price off as he laughed behind me.

6

DEVON

5 MONTHS, 28 DAYS TO GO

I POURED MYSELF a coffee. In Gigi's kitchen. With a coffee maker I'd bought yesterday. Because I was *not* going back to the Daily Dose anytime soon.

I grinned in victory, then cursed at the pain in my jaw. I really, *really* didn't have time for this. Opening the bottle of ibuprofen I'd grabbed along with the coffee maker yesterday, I tossed back four and chased them with a swig of water. I'd keep icing like I did yesterday, because today was day one of...whatever it was I was supposed to be doing.

I took a sip and sighed contentedly. A good, strong cup of coffee could set a lot of things right in this world.

It could not, unfortunately, tell me what I was supposed to do next. The house needed so much done, and even if my plan was to give the place to Rick when my six months were up, I couldn't just sit around and look at it until then. Thankfully, Gigi had set aside some money for house repairs in her will, because my meager savings had no chance at covering the costs.

Should she have handled the repairs herself when she was alive? Um, yes. But she wasn't around for me to argue with, so I needed to get on with it. Besides, sitting around only led to thinking, and I didn't like to think. Especially about Aaron, who'd made a few appearances in my thoughts in the past twenty-four hours.

I'd spent yesterday walking through the rooms, an ice pack held to my face, wallowing in memories and simultaneously wondering at the accuracy of them. Because the house looked like it'd been heading toward a state of general disrepair for far longer than five years. Three floors of fading wallpaper, peeling paint, partially clogged drains, stale and dusty bedrooms, it went on. How had I not noticed in the years I was still here? Had it been like that even then? Had I been so wrapped up in myself that I'd simply looked right past it?

I took another sip of coffee, taking care to open my mouth only the amount I needed to, and looked out the kitchen window into the backyard. It needed mowing. I picked up my phone and shot my brother a text.

> Did you handle the mowing?

You think she'd let me near a mower?

I snorted. He was legendary for his inability to mow a straight line. The man was amazing, don't get me wrong—he could fix anything that needed fixing—but yard work? Not his thing.

Pretty sure she did it herself with the electric mower. Look in the shed in the back.

The doorbell rang, so I pocketed the phone and headed to the front.

An older man stood on the porch, pointing to the street. "I'm Mark Waters. Got the rental trash bin here."

I looked past him and saw the giant green metal container taking up the entire length of the front yard. "Back it in to the driveway." It was the one thing I'd managed to pull off before getting here. If I was going to be stuck here for six months, I at least needed to make it productive and get the house back in shape.

As the old man headed to his truck, I heard a woof. Trotting up the street and smiling at me like I was his long-lost owner was none other than Samson. The menace got a pat from Mr. Waters before turning and beelining to me, still grinning like a fool.

I shook my head. "You're going to be trouble, aren't you?" I leaned down to scratch his chin and ears while he wagged his tail. "Too bad you caused all this yesterday." I pointed at my knees and chin.

He licked my hand and sat, looking up at me expectantly. I had no idea what he wanted, but if it was food, he could forget about it. I didn't need a stray dog attaching himself to me. What would happen once I left? The devastated look on his little face, watching me leave after thinking he'd found his happily ever after…Nope. No thanks to that.

Besides, Samson was clearly being taken care of in the food department, even if his fur was a disaster. Maybe he wasn't a stray at all, come to think of it. I sat in one of the rocking chairs to drink my coffee while Mr. Waters worked. The porch needed more attention than I'd realized yesterday. The white paint peeled off the wooden slats and was totally gone in places, but it didn't matter because the wood itself probably needed replacing —something I couldn't do if I wanted it to actually look good. In between the two rockers stood a small, circular metal table with a glass top, still covered with a thick layer of yellow-green pollen from spring's emergence a couple months ago. And the welcome mat in front of the door needed a good shaking out, too, no doubt full of dirt in addition to the ubiquitous pollen situation.

After Mr. Waters got the bin dropped off and waved his goodbye, I stood and opened the door to go inside. Before I

could react, Samson darted inside with a grin and a wag like he
knew exactly what he was doing.

Well, hell.

"Better not pee or poop in here, Samson, or you're dead to
me." Little dog acted like he owned the place. I took a picture of
him and texted it to Rick.

> Gigi didn't adopt a scraggly dog in the last six
> months, right?

Nope. Especially not one that ugly.

> He's not ugly!

If you say so.

I chuckled and Samson cocked his head at me. I pointed a
finger at him. "Seriously. No peeing or pooping"

After pouring a second cup of coffee, which still felt like its
own sort of victory, I took a shower. By the time I was dressed in
my usual uniform of ratty t-shirt and shorts, my phone was
buzzing with texts.

CECI

I sure hope you planned on drinks this week
with me and Jodi, because they're happening.

JODI

Ooh, yes! Also, where are you this morning?

CECI

Fending off two three-year-olds and drinking
lackluster coffee from home.

JODI

I meant Devon.

CECI

Well, I love you, too.

JODI

Don't get your panties twisted. Where are you, Devon???

I rolled my neck to ease the tension in my shoulders. Between these two and Samson, you'd think I'd have been here for years, not days, and they sure weren't acting like I had an expiration date. I took a deep breath.

> I bought a coffee maker yesterday and am about to start working on the kitchen.

CECI

Wow, coming in hot with the purchase of her own coffee maker and a none-too-subtle reminder that she's not sticking around. Was Jodi's coffee that bad?

I grinned. At least Ceci was picking up what I was laying down.

JODI

BLASPHEMY

JODI

But really, I can keep you in better coffee. And pastries!!

> I appreciate it but I need to save the cash. So: $20 coffee maker.

CECI

Back to drinks. The whole reason I started this convo. Thursday?

JODI:

I'm in!

I considered it. How bad would it be if I didn't go? They'd never leave me alone about it, that's for sure.

> Send me the details.

JODI

YAY!!

JODI

Wait, does that mean you're coming? Or is this your version of a Southern no?

I chuckled and typed.

> I'm in. See y'all Thursday.

Almost immediately, Ceci forwarded a link to a burger place I'd never heard of. But that wasn't surprising, seeing as how I'd been gone so long. Then I looked closer. It was the old sports bar in the town square we'd frequented when I lived here. Just a new name. Guess some things didn't change *too* much.

I shoved the phone in my back pocket and opened up all the cabinets in the kitchen. Figured this was an easy place to start, because I didn't need much and I'd bet that Gigi had all sorts of things.

And...yeah, she did. I blinked rapidly, fighting the sudden tears that appeared at the sight of the dinner plates we'd used my entire life. Dammit, I missed her. I missed the talks we'd had in this very kitchen while she cooked, and damn her for making me do this.

Samson appeared in the kitchen doorway right as someone rang the bell. He hopped and danced in a circle, then headed right for the front.

I heaved a breath to pull myself together, then followed Samson to the door. This was beginning to feel like Grand Central Station.

"Can I help y—" The words died on my tongue as soon as I saw who it was. "Aaron." My belly clenched and my mouth went dry.

He smiled, crinkling the skin around his eyes. "Good morning." A sheen of sweat covered his face and neck, and he held a half-empty bottle of water in his hand. A sweet-looking brindle pit bull stood behind him, ears perked and tongue lolling.

Beside me, Samson jumped on his hind legs and pawed the screen door. Clearly the dog was a better host than I was, because while I stood there like a lump on a log, he managed to rattle the door enough that it opened.

"Sorry, hi, good morning." Did I really sound as flustered as I felt? It was like he'd put me into a trance the second I laid my eyes on him. I pushed the screen door the rest of the way open and the pit bull bolted straight inside for Samson.

Aaron gestured at the dogs. "I'd planned on coming by after my run, but Daisy here seemed to be on a mission to find this little guy. And there's really no catching a pittie when they're after something."

I laughed and tried to snap out of it, the image of Aaron running cartoon-like after his dog flashing through my head. "Guess she likes him."

He chuckled. "Something like that."

I stepped back. "Come in. You want some coffee? More water?" The words were out of my mouth before my head could catch up.

His grin widened. "That sounds good, thank you." He stepped over the threshold and squeezed past me, deftly stepping around the dogs and trailing a scent that had me wanting to bury my nose in his chest.

Which obviously I was not going to do.

But holy mackerel, the man smelled good. There was a hint of firehouse, which should have sent me running in the other direction, but somehow only beckoned me closer. Combine that with a magical mystery ocean-clean smell and I straight up wanted to huff him.

Get it together, Devon. I clenched my jaw, nearly died at the pain it caused, silently cursed a blue streak, and walked past Samson and Daisy as they played with each other. "Kitchen's this way."

What was going on? It wasn't possible that I was feeling something about him, no matter that it felt like I was magnetically drawn to him. It was too much. *He* was too much. I grabbed a cup, saw it was chipped, and grabbed another. I grabbed the coffee pot with shaky hands and clenched my jaw again. God*dammit* that hurt. "Coffee?"

"Please."

"Cream or sugar?"

"Black is good."

Not like Jason, who'd used coffee as a sugar delivery system. I squeezed my eyes shut as I pushed the pot back into place, dizzy from the roller coaster of emotions. Finally, I turned and handed it to him.

"Thanks." He tipped the cup at me and sipped.

We stared at each other, and it probably should have been awkward. I clocked his running shoes, shorts, and the half-marathon race tee he wore, trying and failing to keep from noticing how the shirt stretched perfectly across his chest. I forced my eyes up to his. Eyes that were much more gray than I realized. Then again, before yesterday I'd been careful to never get too close to him. And judging by the way my body was reacting, thank god I stayed away. "So. You run?"

He nodded and smiled sheepishly. "Try to, at least until Daisy decides otherwise. But yeah, I run. If it's something that'll keep me outside, I pretty much do it. You?"

I twisted my lips. "I only run if a bear is chasing me. But I love to hike, and no bears have chased me while I hike." I huffed out a laugh. I'd started hiking after Jason's death because I just needed to *move*, same as after my parents died, I guessed. But it quickly became something more than an escape. "Stretching my legs for miles, seeing the top of a mountain and knowing I can get there, then having the view as my reward…it's pretty amazing." I stopped. What was I doing? I didn't blab like this. "Sorry."

He grinned. "Nothing to apologize for. I like to hike, too."

I caught his eye. "You're not saying that to make me feel better, are you?"

Now he laughed. "No. Definitely not."

Oh. That laugh. It warmed my insides. Or maybe that was just the crap air conditioner. I clenched my jaw, then winced.

"May I?" He nodded at my jaw. Of course he'd noticed. He noticed everything.

"It's nothing." I waved it off. "Just sore."

He gave me a look that said he knew I was lying. "Devon. I think it might be more than sore."

God, the way he said my name, low and full. Until this moment, I hadn't thought it was a particularly sexy-sounding name.

I wanted to argue with him, but if he looked at my jaw, it meant I could smell him again.

Which of course was a bad idea.

The worst, actually.

But. "Okay."

He put his coffee on the counter and came toward me. His demeanor shifted as he walked, and his gaze sharpened as he focused on my jaw.

I tried to relax. He was being professional. This was professional.

"Can you turn your head to look at the window?" he asked, his voice low and soothing.

Honestly, I'd do whatever the man asked if I could keep breathing him in. It was a problem, and I knew it, but I couldn't quite make myself care the way I needed to. I did as he asked, taking in the white wisps of clouds in the blue sky before closing my eyes against the morning sun. Maybe my pulse would get under control if I wasn't looking at him.

"I'm going to touch you now," he murmured.

Jesus Christ.

I gripped the counter, needing something to clench that wasn't my jaw. Heat bloomed and pulsed deep inside of me as his fingers pushed my hair back. Then he cradled my head, his fingers not quite smooth but not calloused, either, and I barely kept from moaning. I shouldn't feel like this. *He* should not make me feel like this. I was in my grandmother's kitchen in the town where my husband had died.

"You're not very bruised." He ran his finger lightly over my jaw, then hummed, the sound of it low and sexy. Would he hum if I were draped on top of him, naked?

My eyes flew open. What was *wrong* with me?

Aaron flinched and pulled his hands away. "Did that hurt?"

I felt the blush stain my cheeks. "Um. No. Well, I don't know."

He studied me. "We need to go."

I blinked. "Go? Go where?"

"To the hospital. I think it's broken."

I gaped at him, then of course I winced because it freaking *hurt* to open my jaw that much. Dammit. "Seriously?"

He nodded. "Seriously."

"I don't have a car."

His gaze softened. "If I had a portable X-ray machine, I promise I wouldn't make you go. I'll run back home and then drive back over."

"You don't understand."

Aaron reached for my hand, and against my better judgment, I let him take it. His grip was warm. Comforting. When was the last time I'd been touched like that? "You can trust me, Devon." The gentle authority in his voice, the reassurance of it, was like a warm bath I wanted to immerse myself in. "I won't let anything bad happen. I'm going to get my car, and when I get back, we'll go. Okay?"

I nodded and fought the tears that threatened at his kindness. But what did I expect? This was his job. He was still in job mode. And that is precisely where he needed to stay, forever and ever, amen. "Okay."

His thumb traced my palm, which, okay, was decidedly not job-like, then he gave my hand a gentle squeeze before letting go. "Okay." He whistled for Daisy as he left the kitchen, and I tried to ignore his muscular legs and ridiculously tight ass in those running shorts.

I sagged against the kitchen counter and rubbed the bridge of my nose. There was so much about Aaron that brought up memories of Jason, but instead of making me want to run screaming in the opposite direction, it pushed me to him. And I didn't need or want that.

I didn't want anything this town offered, even if it did come in a six-foot-plus package of sinfully-built muscles with a mischievous smile and bright gray-blue eyes that seemed to pierce right through me. Which they'd always done. When I was married and Aaron was another co-worker of Jason's, it was easy —well, easy enough—to brush off the sensation of being *seen*. But now?

No way.

7

AARON

I RISKED A glance at her as I drove us to the hospital. She looked out the window so I couldn't see her expression, but her legs were crossed and she wiggled her top foot non-stop.

I was so fucked. Even like this, nervous and folded in on herself, she was gorgeous. Her short, dark blonde hair fell back from her make-up free face. She wore a faded concert tee of New Kids on the Block with at least one hole in it. Her jean shorts left almost nothing to the imagination, and my hand itched to touch her legs. It was clear she'd had no intention of seeing anyone this morning, and yet she had me on my knees.

Gigi was probably looking down and cackling with glee, rubbing her hands and imagining all the ways this could go. I swear, that woman had read more romance books than was healthy. I was certain it was why she'd come up with this insanity. Still, I couldn't help but be grateful for the chance she'd given me.

I gripped the wheel to keep from shaking my fist at the heavens. What would happen if Devon found out this was Gigi's plan all along? No way was I telling her, that's for certain. Whatever progress I was making—if any of this even counted as progress—would disappear in a flash.

We moved out of Gigi's tiny neighborhood and toward the square with the Daily Dose and firehouse, then got on the short highway to the hospital.

"Who does Samson belong to?" Devon asked, breaking the silence and pulling me out of my head.

Thank god. Here was a nice and safe topic I could get behind. "He's everyone's. He showed up near the firehouse about a year ago, looking even more scraggly than he does now, and Chief took a liking to him. We gave him some food and then he saw Daisy, and it's been impossible to get rid of him ever since."

"No one came looking for him?"

I shook my head. "No. He's a good little thing, but refuses to be tied down to any of us. I tried bringing him inside my house for the night once, and he wasn't having it. Woke me up out of a dead sleep, whining to get outside." I glanced at her. "You're the only other person I know of that he's gone inside with."

Her glossy lips parted in shock. "Seriously?" She laughed. "The way he came into Gigi's house, I half thought he might have been hers."

"Nah. She would have toted him around everywhere if he was."

"You knew her?"

My stomach squeezed. I needed to be careful here. I didn't want to lie to her, but I also wasn't sure it was time to reveal just how well we knew each other. "A town this small? Of course. I was the medic on scene when she broke her arm a couple years ago, and I kept up with her after that."

I felt Devon's gaze on me. "I bet she liked you," she mused.

I chuckled. "I'm easy to like."

A moment later, I turned into the hospital's Emergency parking lot and found us a spot.

"Am I really worth all this trouble?" Devon asked, her eyebrows raised.

Yes. "Sorry, force of habit. Look at it this way: with me bringing you in, we'll at least get you looked at quickly."

She nodded and got out of the truck, folding her arms protectively across her chest and frowning. I empathized with her; coming here couldn't be great seeing as how I'd wager the last time she was here was related to her husband, but that jaw needed looking at. And I had a feeling she was the kind of person who'd ignore her own pain until it had completely incapacitated her.

We walked into the doors and the admitting nurse smiled up at us. "Aaron Joseph. To what do we owe the pleasure of seeing you not in uniform?"

I nodded to Devon. "Hi, LaToya. This is Devon Rayne. She—"

"Aaron thinks something is wrong with my jaw, and I think it's just bruised. We're here to prove I'm right," Devon said, taking over the conversation.

LaToya looked at the two of us and grinned. "Devon Rayne? Shirley's granddaughter, right?"

Devon nodded, a small smile on her face. "Did you know Gigi?"

"Not well, but she was buddies with my grandmother. Played cards—"

"Every Wednesday night?" Devon interrupted.

LaToya laughed. "Exactly."

Devon's smile widened. "Gigi loved those nights."

"Sure was sorry to lose her." LaToya's voice was laced with sympathy.

"Thank you."

I stiffened, wondering if LaToya would mention Jason as well, but she didn't. Instead, she grabbed a clipboard with about an inch of admitting paperwork and handed it to Devon. "Fill this out and we'll get you back there."

An hour later, Dr. Osmond was pulling up the X-ray and pointing to it. "I'm afraid it's broken," he said grimly. "And we'll go ahead and do surgery today."

Devon's eyes popped. "What? No. No, I can't—"

"The longer we delay, the worse it's going to be," Dr. Osmond said, steamrolling over Devon's protests. "Unfortunately, we'll have to wire your jaw shut, so you'll be on a liquid diet."

"Stop!" Devon said loudly, holding her hands up and glaring at Dr. Osmond. "Stop. You're not even looking at me while you talk."

I took in Devon's flushed face and bit back a grin. I knew Dr. Osmond's pompous ass from rolling patients into the ER, but I never got to watch anyone call him out on it. Honestly, was it any wonder I thought the woman was incredible?

"So slow down, explain everything to me, and look me in the eye while you're doing it," she said.

Dr. Osmond stared at her for a beat, blinked, then used his pen to point to the X-ray. "See right here? That's your jaw. Except this dark shadow, near the back where it opens and closes? That shouldn't be there. You've definitely broken it."

Devon hissed out a quiet curse, then nodded. "Keep going."

Dr. Osmond adjusted his glasses. "The only way for a break of any kind to heal is to put it back in place and not let it move. For a jaw, that means we have to wire it shut, usually for six to eight weeks."

She exhaled loudly, collecting herself. "And you'll do that today?"

Dr. Osmond nodded. "Normally we'd schedule this for a few days from now, but I had some unexpected time free up, and the sooner we get it done, the better. It's not as bad as it sounds."

"Um, you're wiring my jaw shut. It's *exactly* as bad as it sounds," Devon shot back.

Dr. Osmond nodded. "Well, yes. But the process by which we do it isn't as involved as you might think."

As he was speaking, a nurse came in and nodded to all of us. "I'm Jessica. I'll explain everything and start getting you ready."

"I've got to see some more patients," Dr. Osmond said. "I'll see you in a bit."

He left, and before the nurse could continue, Devon's eyes flitted to me. "You don't have to stay here; I'll text Rick and Ceci."

I shook my head. "I got you into this. I'll see you through it."

She laughed softly. "Fair enough. But I really do need to let them know what's going on." She tapped at her phone and looked back at the nurse when she was done. "How does this even work?"

Jessica smiled. "Well, first of all, you'll be asleep for all of it."

"Thank god."

"Let's get an IV started, and I'll make sure to give all the aftercare information to your boyfriend here," she continued.

"Oh, she's not..." The back of my neck heated and I rubbed it, self-conscious. "I mean, I'm just..." Shit. I didn't know what I was. A nuisance by this point, more than likely.

"Sorry," she said. "I assumed..."

"It's okay." Devon grinned at me, and I couldn't help the stupidly happy smile that crossed my face in response.

I passed the hours in the waiting area. The room was empty of people, and in my line of work, I took that as a blessing. I stretched and ignored the growls coming from my stomach.

"There he is!" Chief waltzed into the room and smiled broadly. "Had some paperwork to do and thought I might find you here."

I groaned. If Chief Suarez knew where to find me, it was only a matter of time before my brothers were blowing up my phone. "Hey, Chief."

"Broken jaw, huh?" He stood with his feet apart and tucked his thumbs into his uniform belt.

"How did you know?"

He shrugged. "A man has his ways."

I raised an eyebrow. I'd bet my house that Ceci Rayne called him the second she found out Devon was here. "You mean a man has his gossip network. You're the nosiest person I have ever met. You make the old timers that sit in front of the Daily Dose look like amateurs. You know that, right?"

He pointed a finger at me. "Mark my words. It's only a matter of time before you two are an item."

I threw my hands up. "An 'item'? Is that what you and Ceci are calling it?"

His eyes shone. "I admit nothing."

My phone pinged and I pulled it out. And there it was.

PRICE

Broken jaw? Looks like no action for you for a while.

WILL

gif of Michael Jackson eating popcorn

Wow. Even Mr. No-Personality Will had gotten into the game. I showed the screen to Chief. "You're killing me."

Chief shrugged and grinned the grin of a very satisfied meddler. "The only one holding you back is you." He looked at his watch. "I gotta go. But Aaron."

"Chief?"

"You deserve to be happy. I know I rib you a little—"

"A lot."

"Okay, a lot. But it's because I love you. You're like a son to me."

I swallowed the emotion suddenly clogging my throat and

nodded tightly. My dad died of a heart attack when I was seventeen. Chief was already in our lives thanks to both my brothers heading straight into the department out of high school, and he'd been the one to keep me from falling apart when neither of my brothers knew how. It was Chief who made sure I ate and went to school. Chief who sat with me at the kitchen table as I filled out college applications, and Chief in the audience at my graduation four years later. "I know."

"Take the chance," he said softly. "What've you got to lose?"

The last bit of hope that at least one woman will find me worth sticking around for. The thought was like a neon sign in my head, unbidden and unwanted, but true.

Chief searched my eyes, nodded, and turned to go.

"Chief?"

He doubled back. "Yeah?"

I swallowed again. "Thank you. For...everything."

He nodded again, then left.

My phone pinged again, and my brothers had only ratcheted up their teasing.

> Don't you two have better things to do?

PRICE

> Just give Daddy Will what he wants and he'll leave you alone.

WILL

> Fuck off, Price.

I sighed.

> I'm waiting on her to get out of surgery. Nothing has happened and nothing is going to happen.

PRICE

> Keep telling yourself that.

"Aaron?"

I looked up. "Hey, LaToya. She out?"

She nodded. "None of her family here yet?"

"I saw her text her brother and his wife, but..." I shrugged.

"Well, you're close enough since you brought her here. I'll take you back there."

I pocketed my phone and followed her to the room.

Devon blinked slowly from the hospital bed, still not quite back to the land of the conscious.

Jessica smiled up from the electronic pad she was logging notes in. "She's just now coming out of anesthesia. She'll be a little loopy, of course. We'll need her to drink that." She indicated a bottle of apple juice. "But after that, you can help her get dressed and get her out of here."

I opened my mouth to object. I may have liked Devon—okay, *more* than liked her—but I had no business getting her dressed. Sure, I'd seen plenty of bodies in plenty of situations in my years as a paramedic, and I really could maintain my professionalism with Devon if it came down to it, but still.

"Um."

Jessica looked at me expectantly.

Ah, fuck. "Never mind," I said, resigned. It would be just my luck. Here, Aaron, get the woman of your dreams dressed. Pay no attention to how close you are to every bit of her. Ignore all details of her panties and bra.

Jessica finished up on her pad and left, and I turned my attention to Devon.

She blinked and squinted. "Can't focus," she said. "Oh. Words."

I chuckled and moved to sit in the chair next to her. She sounded drunk, and I wasn't sure how much was the anesthesia and how much was the wired jaw, but it was easy enough to understand her. "Hey."

She turned to me, still trying to focus. "You."

I smiled. "Yeah. Me. You're coming out of some serious drugs. Take your time. You want some juice?" I picked up the bottle and started to hand it to her.

"No. You."

I kept smiling. "Still me. And you have to drink this before we can bust you out of here. So. Juice?"

She hummed and took the bottle, then aimed the whole thing in the direction of her face.

Yikes. Professional or not, I wasn't ever around for this part. I leaned in. "Maybe I'll help, okay?" She nodded as I took the bottle back and held the straw to her lips. "Remember your jaw won't open," I say, right as she clearly tried to do just that.

"Owwww," she whined softly.

I bit back a laugh. Definitely not the time, and I'm certain it really hurt, but she was adorable. Finally, her lips closed around the straw and she drank. I wiped her mouth with a napkin, then met her eyes. They were hazy with drugs, but it didn't matter. They were still heart-stoppingly beautiful, an ice blue ringed with navy.

"Let me know when you want more," I said, leaning back in the chair.

She nodded and took a deep breath and let it out, then closed her eyes and relaxed against the mattress. "Long time ago."

I stilled. Where was this going?

"You saw me, didn't you? Like, *saw* me saw me."

I sent a prayer to the gods of anesthesia and nodded. "I did." I wet my lips. The way she'd connected with everyone around her, giving them her complete attention. How she'd laughed, full-bodied and loud. She'd been the center of every room she was in, but never seemed to notice. My heart pounded. "I still do. See you, I mean."

She lifted her head and met my eyes. They still weren't focused, and I wasn't sure how much, if any, she'd remember of this conversation later. "You scare me." She let her head fall back and stared at the ceiling. "I like you, and I shouldn't and that scares me."

Holy. Shit. I looked around, like someone else would be there to confirm what I'd heard, but it was just me and her. Wired or not, and coming out of drugs or not, she wasn't *that* hard to understand.

She...liked me?

"All this scares me," she repeated. "I'm talking so slow. Am I slurring my words? I think I'm slurrying. I mean slurring." She giggled. "I'm like Voldemort. Only not."

I beamed at her, taking all of it in. She was higher than a kite and so damn cute. And she *liked* me.

Then she focused on me again, or at least tried to. "Do you like me?"

"Yes." I couldn't answer fast enough.

She huffed and flailed her hand. "Not like a friend but like, do you *like* like me."

I grinned, my heart soaring with the wings it now had. "Yes, I *like* like you."

"Good." She smiled and I got a look at the impressive amount of metal holding her mouth shut. "Cause I like you. We'll be like Daisy and Samson." *Shamson.* She giggled again. "I'm Voldaisy. Daisemort. Voldaisemort!" She snorted and laughed.

I laughed again. If she remembered any of this, it would be a miracle. I'd been given this gift of knowing, but a kernel of doubt planted itself in the back of my head. She was interested, sure, but that didn't mean she'd stay. My own mother hadn't stayed and my record hadn't gotten any better since then. How in the world was I enough to keep a woman who barely knew me in town?

"Juice," Devon said. It came out like 'juish.'

I jerked back to the present and handed the bottle to her. "You got it this time?"

She nodded. "Think so." She sounded more coherent as she took it and drank. "Did the nurse say something about you getting me dressed?"

"Ah, she did. But I'll leave."

A voice sounded behind me. "Damn right you will." Rick walked into the room.

I stood and grinned at Rick, then shook his hand. "Good to see you. I was wondering when you'd get here."

"Ceci," he said, as if that explained everything. "She was supposed to be here but the twins apparently decided a mud fight was in order. So I got tagged in. But that doesn't explain your presence."

"Rick!" Devon said, smiling and oblivious to the way Rick was frowning thoughtfully at me. "My favorite. You're the *best*. Ow, hurts," she whimpered.

"You gonna sound like that the whole time, little sis?" Rick grinned at her. "Am I the *besht*?"

"I'll get going," I said.

Rick tipped his chin at me. "See you."

"Aaron?" Devon looked over at me, her eyes clearer than before. "When did you get here?"

My heart squeezed in disappointment. Guess there would be exactly no remembering the conversation on her part. It was for the best, I knew that, but it didn't stop my stomach from twisting. "I brought you. Been here the whole time. I'll be in touch?"

She nodded. "Sounds good."

She turned her attention to Rick as I left the room and shut the door behind me. Devon *liked* me. But would she admit it later? To me or even to herself? I didn't know. And it wouldn't matter anyway, because she didn't plan on staying. She'd never said it out loud, but of course she'd leave.

I certainly wasn't enough to make her stay. My history with

women proved that the second I started something remotely serious with them, it guaranteed they'd leave town.

Mom: left.

Leighton, the girl I dated in high school: went to college out of state and never came back.

Rebecca, who I dated for two years in college: left after graduation for her career.

Grace, a preschool teacher: got a job in another state.

Allison, an accountant who planned to run a national bank by the time she was forty: took a promotion in Birmingham and didn't look back.

Kristen, who lived in a neighboring town—see what I did there? Not local!—and ran the local library system: tapped for a job at the National Archives in D.C.

I wasn't mad they'd all left. This was a small town and I didn't begrudge them their careers. But when would I ever be enough?

If I were smart, I'd stop dating. But smart packed its bags the second I saw Devon at the coffee shop, blinking up at me with those baby blues.

I thought back to what Chief said, about taking the chance. Despite his meddling, he was right. There really was something there. It'd been around all those years ago, and I'd dutifully squashed it. So now, when I actually had a chance? I'd regret it if I didn't at least try.

8

DEVON

5 MONTHS, 21 DAYS TO GO

THERE'S A LOT to be said for being waited on hand and foot by people who love you. Some of those things are even nice. But after a week of being forced to stay at my brother's house, I was ready to crawl out of my skin.

The twins had proven their reputation as angels was more fantasy than truth, but I was willing to give them the benefit of the doubt. Especially when they were standing in front of me, water guns loaded and aimed, smiling maniacally.

"Hello, my sweet loves," I crooned, sounding ridiculous but unable to do anything about it. My 's' sounds came out like 'sh,' so *sweet* sounded like *shweet*.

"You thirsty?" Luke started.

"We brought water!" Eva finished with a flourish.

I took in their dual blond-haired, blue-eyed expressions of helpfulness and sighed. "When was the last time those things were properly rinsed out?"

"Never," Ceci said as she walked in. "Why in the world would you think three-year-olds are going to clean their water guns?" She turned to the kids. "Go outside and see if you can find Samson. I bet he'd like them."

"Yeah!" Eva squealed.

Luke took off with Eva right behind him. "Samson!"

I heard the kitchen door slam shut and smiled up at Ceci. "Thank you for saving me." I stood, happy that the movement no longer caused me brutal pain. For days, any movement that caused my blood to pump faster meant that my jaw would throb painfully. Getting a jaw wired shut was not for the weak. "And now, I'm going to beg that you drive me by the Piggly Wiggly to load up on baby food and smoothie mix, and take me home. Please. Because if I have to endure one more night of Rick's dad jokes, I might actually die."

Ceci laughed. "I told Rick he was being a little overbearing."

"A *little*? Ceci, it's been more than a little. I definitely needed to be here two or three days, but I've got this whole no-solid-foods thing down pat."

"How's the pain?"

"Other than an incessant need to put balm on these poor lips, I'm pain-free. Haven't popped one of those pain pills in two days."

Ceci nodded. "Okay. Let's get you out of here."

A few minutes later, my bag was packed and the kids were loaded into the back of the minivan. Samson sat on the driveway watching the proceedings, his grungy little face forlorn.

"I'm just changing venues, Samson," I said. Stupid dog wouldn't stop coming around, which of course had led to the twins begging their mom to keep him. I'm sure Samson would have had plenty to say about that if Ceci had relented, but she knew the dog's deal as well as anyone.

Samson cocked his head and perked his ears.

"See ya at the house, buddy."

He woofed as we backed down the driveway, then hopped up and took off to go who knew where, scraggly tail wagging.

It took well over an hour to make my way through the grocery store. And had it been because Ceci had decided to do her own shopping, that would have been one thing. But no. No, it was because the town gossip mill was on full alert the second I set foot into the store, and I got stopped in almost every aisle.

First, it was my English teacher from high school, asking if I still wrote poetry. (I don't.) Then it was a lady from Gigi's church, offering condolences about Gigi and pretending she didn't know I wasn't staying past the required six months. After that, there was an old classmate and an old neighbor. And all of them, every last one, looked at me with a mix of pity and curiosity, saying how sorry they'd been when Jason died, how happy they were to see me again. How were they still talking about Jason? It'd been five years.

I could practically hear Gigi taking me to task. *They wouldn't be if you'd stayed, but this is the first time they're seeing you. What did you expect?*

Which, fine. True. But even so, by the time I'd loaded up on baby food, smoothie mix, and protein powder, I was ready to empty the wine aisle of all its bottles. My chest was tight and I gripped the cart like a woman about to fall off a ledge.

As I turned the corner, I caught a glimpse of blue uniform. Aaron. My heart kicked into overdrive and I couldn't keep the smile off my face as the uniform came into full view.

And Chief Suarez grinned in response. "Well, if that isn't pretty enough to light up a room. Devon Rayne, as I live and breathe."

I kept the smile frozen in place and swallowed. Served me right for getting excited and thinking it was Aaron. "Chief. I guess it was only a matter of time before I ran into you. How are you?"

He gestured at my jaw and chuckled. "Better than you." He leaned in. "By the way, it was the cashier."

"Helen? I knew it," I said, fighting to keep my voice light

even though being accosted in the aisles had soured my mood. "Is there a group chat dedicated to me?"

He laughed and nodded. "Of course."

I tilted my head. "I actually believe you."

"You should." Then his eyes softened. "But really. How are you?"

I stiffened. The last time I'd seen him had been when he brought all of Jason's belongings from the firehouse to Gigi's a few days after the funeral. By the look on his face when he saw me, I knew he'd gone there because he'd thought I'd be at home. Taking them to Gigi's had been his attempt to make things easier on me.

He was a decent man who'd always looked out for his crew and their families, and that's what he was doing right now. I needed to remember that. "I could be better. But all in all, I'm good."

"Yeah?" He waited a beat, classic Suarez, but when I gave him nothing else, he continued. "That's good. You, ah, been to see him yet? Jason?"

My heart skipped two beats. I swallowed. "Um. No." I slid my eyes away. Visiting Jason's grave was something I'd only had the courage to do once.

"Right. Well," Chief said and cleared his throat. "I've kept up with you on social media, you know. Seems you've had quite the adventure these past five years. You look great, Devon. The hair's new."

I touched my shortened locks. "Yeah."

"I'm happy to see you."

"Just here to do what I have to do to keep Gigi's house—but I'm sure you know that."

He smiled. "Of course. Glad Aaron was around to take you to the hospital."

I bit back my surprise at the shift in his tone. I knew Chief used to fancy himself a matchmaker, but would never have figured he'd turn his sights my way.

At the same time, there was no mistaking the way butterfly wings fluttered against my stomach at the mention of Aaron, either. So there was that. Still, I wasn't giving Chief an inch. "Yep, guess so," I said, blatantly ignoring the smile that spread across his face and focusing instead on Ceci and the twins, who had appeared at the end of the aisle. "I should go."

"See you around," Chief said.

"I'm sure you will," I muttered under my breath. Then I plastered a smile I didn't feel onto my face for Luke and Eva, and we headed for the register.

"Ew, what's all that?" Luke said, pointing to the contents of my cart. The cart that did not, unfortunately, have any bottles of wine in it.

"I thought baby food was only for babies," Eva said.

I managed a semi-grown-up response to them, but I was not nearly as good when we rolled up to Helen. It was stink-eye central for her. "Helen," I said, drawing her name out and making it sound sickly sweet. Normally I'd keep my frustration to myself, but I was d-o-n-e done today. "How nice of you to alert half the town that I was here."

Her eyes widened and her mouth dropped open, and I kept going.

"Be sure to let everyone know that I'll have my jaw wired shut for at least a month, okay? And I've been staying at Ceci and my brother's, but now I'm heading back to Gigi's like the plan has been ever since I got to town." I leaned back. "By the way, is your husband still causing a ruckus at the bingo hall, or did you finally convince him to stop cheating?"

She stared at me, twin spots of color on her cheeks.

"What's my total?"

She sputtered out a reply and I paid, then left as quickly as possible. This town wasn't *that* small, but it was small enough for people like Helen to wreak havoc on me in the name of gossip.

At Gigi's, I couldn't get out of the minivan fast enough. I gathered my bags and gave Ceci a grateful smile. "Thank you. For everything."

"We're all here for you, Devon. You know that."

I nodded. "I'll see you soon." *But not too soon.* Because I loved them, but I needed some serious alone-time. A bath in a quiet house sounded like the most decadent thing I could possibly ask for.

With wine. A bath with wine. Because even though I'd failed in my attempt to get wine of my own, Gigi had been the buy-a-case-from-Costco kind of woman, and I knew exactly where she kept it. After I set down my purchases—for the record, baby food wasn't awful, but it wasn't awesome, either—I beelined for the dining room sideboard.

"Praise baby Jesus," I muttered, taking in the beautiful sight of no less than ten bottles of Costco's branded Merlot and Pinot Grigio. I grabbed one of each, put the Pinot in the fridge, opened the Merlot, and poured it into a coffee cup. Because I was classy like that. "Cheers, Gigi," I said, then raised the cup to the house and took a sip—through a straw, of course.

I raised my eyebrows. Not bad by Costco.

My phone beeped with a message. I pulled it out, and my belly swooped.

AARON

Heard you broke out of jail.

I grinned. I'd not really heard from him since I got to Rick and Ceci's. Just a few "how are you" texts that seemed more professional courtesy than anything. But this one felt different right off the bat.

I did. Who told you?

Chief.

Damn. Chief moved fast. I wasn't sure how I felt about it, to be honest. Another text appeared.

Care to stretch your legs with a hike tomorrow?

I shouldn't encourage him, but it'd been a long time since someone had given me actual butterflies. I took another sip of Merlot to fortify myself, then responded.

That sounds amazing.

Pick you up at 8?

I'll be ready.

I put my phone down and considered. If I was losing at least half a day to hiking tomorrow, I needed to work on the house.

Two coffee cups of wine later, I'd made exactly no progress. Unless "progress" consisted of opening a closet, realizing I had a shit-ton of work to do, wondering why I was bothering, closing the door, then reminding myself I loved this house and opening a different closet. I stood in front of yet another closet, contemplating a third cup of wine, when there was a knock on my door.

I opened it to find a woman of no more than five feet standing in front of me, wrinkled as the day was long and sporting a full head of curled-and-set hair that I knew she'd deliberately dyed baby pink.

She smiled. "Devon!"

I smiled back. "Miss Betty!"

She leaned in for a hug. "Oh, it's so good to see you, sweet girl."

"You, too." Betty Savage lived next door and had been one of

Gigi's best friends. "Sorry for the way I sound." I gestured at my face. "Jaw's wired shut. Want to come in?"

She waved a hand in the air. "Oh, no. And honey, we all know about the jaw. Whole town does. I was getting home from my card night with the church ladies and saw the lights on. Wanted to swing by and let you know I joined the historical society." She looked at me meaningfully.

I pretended to clutch my pearls. "You're not Team Mrs. Withers, are you?"

She grimaced. "Lord no. That woman is a boil on my butt."

I barked out a laugh, which of course hurt my jaw.

"I'm Team Shirley all the way. Already fighting for you and this house, Devon, don't you worry."

"Aw, thanks, Miss Betty. But I think we have it under control." What could Mrs. Withers possibly do at this point?

"Well, we'll see." She patted my arm. "So you're staying?" she said, changing subjects abruptly.

"Just the six months."

"Oh?" she asked, blinking up at me. "I figured you'd stay."

"Um." My stomach churned. I blamed the wine. "I, um, have plans." I had no plans. Obviously.

She smiled up at me and patted my arm again. "Of course you do, dear. I'll come by again soon and bring you some of my lemon squares."

As she turned to leave, I wondered which of my old East Coast gigs I could line back up. Maybe Coney Island? Too cold by the time I was done here. Or something in Florida? Maybe even California.

As long as it wasn't here.

9

DEVON

5 MONTHS, 20 DAYS TO GO

WERE EMOTIONAL HANGOVERS a thing? They should be. Or maybe it was the wine.

It was probably the wine.

Either way, I woke up with just enough time to wash my face, throw on clothes and brew some coffee before Aaron pulled up exactly at 8:00 on the dot.

And...wow. Did he get hotter in the past week? I watched as he got out of his truck in shorter-than-normal hiking shorts, revealing tanned thighs and calves that were clearly the product of never-missed leg days and running. He wore a thin blue t-shirt that clung to his chest, and I was beginning to think chest-clinging shirts were all he owned, and honestly? I was here for it.

He stepped onto the porch in well-worn hiking boots, then pushed up his mirrored sunglasses to give me a warm smile as I opened the screen door.

Cue the butterflies and racing heart, because good lord, the way he looked at me. Something had changed, and I couldn't quite pinpoint it, but my body's reaction to him was visceral. "Good morning," I squeaked and gestured for him to come in.

"Good morning." He stepped over the threshold and I inhaled. Yep, still smelled good as hell. Eyes sharp, he studied me. "How are you?"

Ah. Professional Aaron was making an appearance. I positioned my jaw for inspection. "Bruising is basically gone, the only pain is my ego's, and my only addiction is to cherry chapstick," I joked.

His gaze narrowed thoughtfully. "Mind if I take a look?"

And have him within inches of me? *Yes, please.*

I stilled as he closed in, taking sips of air as his deliciously rough-but-not-too-rough fingers skimmed the column of my neck and chin. It felt like maybe he lingered longer than he needed to, but eventually he stepped back.

"How did your follow-up go?"

Shrugging, I said, "Fine. Doctor was still an ass, and by the way, I'm saying ass like a donkey, not ash like the remains of a fire. I can tell I'm gonna be *really* over this by the time I'm free of it."

He smiled in understanding, then nodded at the travel cup in my hand. "I promised Jodi we'd swing by and get coffee, if that's okay. Pretty sure she's having withdrawals from not seeing you. You game?"

With a start, I realized that I missed her, too. It probably helped that she and Ceci were relentless texters and Jodi had quickly determined I was a sucker for baby farm animal videos. "Sure, let's go by there."

I gathered my things, and Samson appeared as I was locking up.

"You want to bring him with us?" Aaron asked as he scratched the dog's ears. "I have Daisy on the rear bench already."

Samson must have known we were talking about him, because he woofed and trotted in circles, a smile on his face.

I shook my head and fought a grin. "Might as well. He'll be the saddest pup in the world if we don't."

"That's true." He whistled for Samson to follow him, opening the back door of his truck to let him in.

He swung around to open my door next, and I caught another whiff of him as I climbed into the front. My pulse rocketed up. The man had no right being this fine *and* smelling this nice. Never mind his manners and the wolfish look I'd seen on his face when he thought I wasn't looking.

I settled myself into the seat as he walked around, then was hit with the vaguest of memories. I was in the hospital, fresh out of being turned into the wired terror of Alabama, and I said...something. What was it? The details were just out of my reach, but if I squinted...

Aaron climbed into the driver's seat and shut the door, then started the engine. "We're heading to the Talladega Forest. Have you ever hiked the Pinhoti Trail?"

"So, confession: I've never hiked anywhere in Alabama."

He glanced at me. "Really?"

"Never did anything really outdoorsy until—" I cleared my throat—"until Jason died and I left."

"Then it will be my greatest pleasure to show you the best trails in the state," he said, not missing a beat.

"Thanks," I said, my voice low. I allowed myself the luxury of studying his profile while he drove. He looked completely at ease, not at all thrown off by the ghost of Jason that I'd unceremoniously brought into the cab. I'd had flings with other men over the years, and every one of them had gotten spooked when they learned I was a widow.

But Aaron didn't seem to mind.

I shook off the ideas that were trying to take hold. I wasn't here to start anything. It didn't matter that I'd been aware of him when Jason was alive. Maybe that's why I needed to not let anything happen now. I needed to, I don't know, take shallow breaths when Aaron was around. Stop breathing him in, physically *and* metaphorically.

The line at Daily Dose wasn't short, but Jodi and another barista managed to clear it quickly.

"Hi, you two," Jodi said. "Good to see you out and about, Dev."

"Thanks. It's all the baby goat videos you sent me. They were absolutely healing."

"How could they not be?" she said and smiled, then took my travel mug. The mug with a straw, thank you very much, because that was how I was rolling these days. "Cold brew with one raw sugar?"

"Yes, please!"

"Aaron, your usual?"

He nodded.

"Coming right up." Jodi turned and started making the coffees.

Aaron looked at me. "I've got us a picnic packed. You need anything else?"

A picnic? This man was also thoughtful enough to pack a picnic? "Exactly what did you pack for me? Because, you know" —I pointed at my mouth—"Metal Mouth here can only do so much."

"Girl, please," Jodi butted in. "Knowing him, he's created his own special smoothie for you. You know he's an incredible cook. You should let him—"

"Jodi." Aaron cut her off, looking a little embarrassed. "Can I just pay, please?"

I snorted. At least I wasn't the only one Jodi was making heart-eyes at.

Jodi huffed good-naturedly and handed over our coffees. In the truck, Aaron looked at me sheepishly from the front seat. "Sorry about that. She's...well, you know how she is."

I laughed. "I do. I've known her a long time, and I promise, she's always been like that."

Aaron pulled onto the street. "Yeah, we grew up together. Went to the same school, anyway."

"That explains why I didn't know you until...."

"Until we saw each other at the station?" he finished. "Yeah. You and Rick went to the fancy private school, right?"

I nodded, grateful he'd taken over. It was bad enough I'd alluded to Jason once already. "So did you and Jodi ever...?"

"Date? God, no. She's younger than me, and we are not each other's types. At all. Besides," he started, then stopped. "Never mind."

I perked up. "Oh, no. you can't stop. Besides *what*?"

"I've never been the Joseph brother she's had the hots for."

"Wait—really?" I said. "You've got two brothers, right? Price and Will. Which one is it?"

He shook his head. "No way. I've said too much as it is."

I rubbed my hands like a villain. "I'm not letting this go. Is it Will? I can see how she'd like the whole stern daddy thing he's got going on."

Aaron coughed. "Did you just describe my brother as a 'stern daddy?'"

"Don't avoid the question. Is it Will?"

"No comment," he said, shaking his head and laughing.

I tapped my chin. "Hmm. I admit, I've not been around a lot in the past five years, but I've traded a lot of texts with Jodi this last week and I'm thinking...Price."

Aaron's mouth twitched.

I pointed at him. "Yes! It's Price!"

"I admit nothing," he said.

We laughed and fell into an easy silence, the dogs content behind us. As I took another sip of my cold brew, it hit me: I'd not been sad about Jason the whole time we were in that shop, and even talking about how long I'd known Jodi, I'd not felt any twinge of sadness.

10

DEVON

5 MONTHS, 20 DAYS TO GO

TURNS OUT THAT Samson wasn't the biggest fan of being on a leash…shocking exactly no one. But since the trail seemed to be empty, we let them off-leash. Daisy was exceptionally trained, and Samson would follow Daisy to the ends of the earth.

Tall, lush trees loomed overhead, shading us from the summer sun. The trail was worn but narrow, shiny tree roots laying like speed bumps across the light brown dirt. Dotted here and there were clumps of what I assumed were native flowers blooming along the forest floor, pops of yellow and white staking their claim in the greenery.

It was nothing like the starkness of Arizona, where I'd spent the last few months as a hiking guide. "You know," I mused, "I basically grew up in this state, but I know exactly nothing about Alabama's native plants and trees."

"I'd venture to say most people don't," Aaron said from ahead of me.

"Yeah, but now that I'm out here, it feels kind of, I don't know, disrespectful. Like, I've spent a lot of the past five years giving tours, mostly outside, and I had to know a lot about my surroundings. Now I'm on this gorgeous mountain and I don't know if that snake ahead on the path is venomous or not."

"What?" He stopped and his voice went up an octave.

I laughed. "Kidding. There are no snakes."

He raised his sunglasses and glared playfully at me. "Keep it up and I'll leave you out here to fend for yourself."

Before long, we were scrambling up and down paths that weren't nearly as well-worn but that Aaron seemed familiar with. I took the lead, needing to feel the stretch in my legs that only a hike could do.

"Is this a race or something?"

I turned but kept walking. "Can't keep up?" I teased.

"I'm too busy enjoying the view," he said, raising an eyebrow.

I flushed, completely surprised at how forward the comment was. "Um."

He laughed as he caught up with me. "Come on. We're almost at the top." He held his hand out, and after a millisecond of considering it, I took it.

The zing was immediate. Of course it was. Because my body was a betrayer of the highest order.

So, fine. This could be purely physical. I was attracted to him, and he was attracted to me. We were adults. No one said I couldn't have something physical with him, right? Right. Which meant I could totally enjoy the sensation of his hand around mine, strong and sure, and I could enjoy anything else we might eventually end up doing, and it didn't have to mean anything.

Except, it didn't feel like that. Every look he gave me felt like it meant *something*.

Samson raced to us, his nose leading him, and I tripped as he bolted through my legs. I yelped and flailed, certain I was going down, but Aaron moved quickly, pulling me flush against him. Our bodies pressed together as his arms wrapped around my waist, trapping my hands against his chest.

Well. This didn't suck. I could feel every glorious muscle he had, from the pecs beneath my palms to the stomach muscles pressed against my body.

"Are you okay?" His voice was low.

I swallowed and looked into his eyes. This close, I could see the flecks of blue dotted among the gray. The way he looked at me—intimate, all-seeing—was going to be my undoing. "Um. Yeah," I croaked. I blinked. "Yes."

He let me go, but stayed close. "I'm beginning to think Samson is a liability for you."

I stepped back, needing to put space between us. I was an idiot if I thought I could have anything as simple as a fling with this man. "He is most definitely a liability for me," I said. *And Aaron was even more of one.* "I'd say I'd race you to the top, but I think Samson would find a way to kill me."

Aaron laughed, a deep, throaty sound that seemed to come from what I now knew was his incredibly taut stomach. And I liked how it sounded. Too much. "Let's go," he said.

He held his hand out again, and even though I knew I shouldn't, I grabbed it.

We reached the summit, still holding hands, and I exhaled. Mountains rose up all around us, flush with summer green, and the sky was cloudless and marble-blue. A red-tailed hawk circled in the distance, looking for its next meal. As a breeze blew the tendrils of my hair away from my face, I spoke. "This is why I hike. Right here. The view is absolutely incredible."

"It is," Aaron said. He looked directly at me.

My cheeks heated. "You know what we need?"

"A magic portal to take us back down?"

I laughed. "No. A picture. Come on, turn around." I pulled him close and turned him. He circled an arm around me, tucking me beneath his chin. *Safe.* It was disconcerting how instant it was. How I wanted to close my eyes and burrow into his chest, wrap myself in him and feel his arms curl protectively around me.

No. Absolutely not. Aaron was as far from safe as it got. So I shoved all thoughts of burrowing out of my head and moved my cheek near his, positioning the lens to get the mountains behind us. "Say cheese!"

I took the shot and we inspected it. "That might be the best selfie I've ever been a part of," Aaron said.

It really was a good picture, even with my metal mouth on full display. We looked good together, like it was the most natural thing in the world. But that was just the angle. Had to be. I clicked the phone off and tucked it in my back pocket.

"You seem to take a lot of pictures," he said. "On Instagram, I mean."

I tried not to flush with pleasure at the thought of him scrolling through my page. I had plenty of followers, but I bet if I looked, I'd find that he'd liked a lot of my posts. "Social media's been a big part of the gigs I've had. I've definitely learned a thing or two. What about you?"

"Me?" He stopped unpacking lunch and quirked a smile. "Social media is definitely *not* a big part of my gig."

"Har har," I said. "You're a paramedic now, right?"

He straightened and handed me the water bottle he'd carried. "Yes. When we first met, I was an EMT. I kept going to school to get the paramedic license."

I nodded. "But you're not," I swallowed, "you're not a fire-fighter, right?" *Please say you're not. I can't take it if you are.*

He shook his head. "No."

I breathed out.

"But," he said, his eyes on mine, "I've thought about it. Chief has encouraged me; I've probably got half the training in my head already for as long as I've been at the station, but, Devon." He put a finger under my chin, forcing me to look at him. "I haven't committed to anything." His eyes searched mine, looking for answers to a question he hadn't asked.

I swallowed and stepped back. "You should do what you want."

"Don't do that," he said, his voice low. He closed the distance between us again. "Don't throw a wall up, Devon. I've got you."

I made myself hold his gaze, unable to stop the buzzing in my head. My breathing was shallow, and I squeezed my hands to keep them from shaking. *This was insane.*

"I haven't committed to anything," he repeated.

I forced a breath into my lungs and nodded. "Okay."

He studied me. "Devon. I'm serious."

I kept nodding, pulling myself out of the abyss I'd almost fallen into. "I believe you." And I did. So help me, I believed the man would do whatever I asked him to. And it was terrifying.

"You ready to eat?" He gestured to the backpack he'd emptied on the flat rock behind us, clearly trying to change the subject. "Processed food awaits."

I took the out he offered and looked at the impressive array of packs of squeezable yogurts, smoothie-like packets, and fruit-and-apple sauces. I faked a swoon as I surveyed the spread. "You really know how to pack the perfect wired-jaw picnic."

His face cleared, and he leaned down to grab one. "You jest, but this? This right here?" He brandished the pack. "This is quality apple sauce in a handy, wired-jaw-approved delivery system. I checked. Just unscrew the lid and you're in business. Classy. Only the best for you, Devon."

I laughed and held out my hand. "Let me have this quality apple sauce. Plus, ooh, the protein smoothie pack. And the strawberry-banana yogurt, too. Those are mine."

He smiled affectionately and handed them over, his fingers brushing mine. We settled onto the ground for the picnic, and all my unease faded away. We talked like we'd been around each other for years. And as much as I didn't want to admit it, I really, *really* enjoyed his company. He was funny, and intelligent, and with everything he said, every move, he made it clear what he wanted.

And what he wanted, was me.

It was heady, this feeling. But I couldn't let it get too far.

After we finished and the dogs had some water, we packed up and got ready to head back down.

Aaron held his hand out. "For safety," he grinned.

Like the utterly confused woman I was, I took it.

A couple of hours later, we pulled up to Gigi's house.

On the porch, he said, "I had a good time, Devon." His eyes seared into me.

Damn those things. Could they see how I warred between wanting his lips on mine and running as far away as possible? "Me, too."

He reached for my hands, the now-familiar strength of them wrapping around mine. I wanted to know what they would feel like cupped around my breasts. I hitched a breath.

He closed the distance between us. I felt the heat of him, mere inches from me, and it nearly incinerated me. My heart pounded. He spoke, his voice low and husky. "Devon."

I swallowed. I could do it. All I had to do was tilt my chin, and I'd learn what his lips felt like, wired jaw or not.

A car honked, and I yelped as we jumped apart. Aaron smiled, his cheeks pink. The moment was lost as Jodi's car pulled to a stop in front of the house.

"Devon!" she called from her open window. "I brought you a smoothie!"

Aaron chuckled as I groaned. "I'll check in on you later," he said tenderly.

"See you soon?" The words came out before I could stop them.

He smiled brightly as he walked backwards down the steps.

"Absolutely."

"Hi, Aaron," Jodi sing-songed as they passed each other. She turned her attention to me, giving me a silent thumbs-up as she waggled her eyebrows suggestively.

I rolled my eyes.

Jodi practically tackled me once she got to the porch, and I stumbled back at the impact.

"I have been waiting for *days* to come see you and that mean old brother of yours wasn't having any of it," she whined into my neck.

"You saw me this morning," I said.

She let me go. "Doesn't count. But now that you're back at Gigi's, I can bring you my specialty smoothie whenever I want."

I accepted the smoothie she held out. It was green, and didn't smell great. "Um. Thanks."

"It's a spinach-lime smoothie with bananas and blueberries, along with a scoop of protein powder. I promise it tastes better than it looks."

I took a tentative sip. "Oh wow," I said. "It's actually good."

She rolled her eyes and smiled, and for a moment, she looked so much like her brother it made my brain stutter. "Yes, it *actually* is."

I sat on the porch swing and patted the empty space next to me. "Sorry. But it *is* a pretty impressive shade of green."

She settled beside me and we began to move back and forth. "Videos of baby goats aside, I've missed you."

I winced. She was diving straight in.

She continued. "And if you're really only staying the six months, fine, but you need to know how I feel." She took a deep breath and I braced myself. "When you left, it was like I lost a brother *and* a sister."

My stomach clenched. I'd truly had enough of the deep emotions today, but we needed to have this conversation.

I faced her. "Losing your brother...I couldn't stay here, Jodi, surrounded by memories that were everywhere I turned. He was my life. He *was* this town. And once I left, it was all I could do to stay in touch with Gigi and Rick and Ceci. Mainly because I knew they'd send a search party out for me if I didn't."

Jodi reached for my hand and squeezed. "I might have stalked Ceci to keep up with you."

"I believe it. But being back here," I swallowed, "it's a lot. It's," I sighed, unable to put the past week and a half into words. And now? With Aaron? What the hell was I doing? "Just, a lot."

Jodi gave me an understanding look. "You don't have to feel guilty, Devon."

I felt guilty, all right. Only it wasn't just about not keeping in touch with her.

"But we couldn't really...grieve without you here. You know? We needed you. It's OK that you couldn't do it, no one blamed you. But that doesn't mean we didn't *need* you."

"I'm so sorry," I whispered. "I was an asshole."

She gave a watery laugh. "Yeah. You were." She wiped her eyes and stood. "Could you stop?"

"Being an asshole? I'll try," I quipped.

She looked at me thoughtfully. "I should go. I'll check on you later?"

I nodded, still sitting on the swing.

She hesitated, then closed the distance to wrap her arms around me in a quick hug. "Okay. Um. Bye." She bounded down the steps.

I stared after her. What was I supposed to do with all these feelings blowing through me? I'd never known. I guess that was part of the problem. Losing Jason had nearly flattened me, and I swore to myself that I'd never go through that again.

The only way to do that was to get the hell out of this town as soon as the six months were up.

And stay away from Aaron.

11

AARON

BREAKFAST SHOULDN'T BE this hard. But when you're cooking it for a bunch of ungrateful guys in a firehouse, it is definitely a pain in the ass. I slapped Price's hand as he reached for the bacon.

"Owww," he whined, cradling his hand against his chest. "The hell, man?"

"Wait till everything's on the table," I shot back.

"I was just going to see if it was crispy enough. You never make it crispy enough."

I rolled my eyes. "Ten years I've been making you breakfast and this is the first time you say anything about me not making the bacon crispy enough? Fuck off." I shooed him away with a laugh.

My only comfort was that the kitchen was big and bright. The windows were huge, the dishes were mismatched, the right front eye of the gas stove always needed a little extra love, and the appliances were new in the nineties, but the square footage was phenomenal. I'd take what I could get.

Chief pulled condiments out of the once-white fridge. "Price, set the table."

Price grumbled and leaned over to pet Daisy, who waited patiently for the bacon she hoped she'd get if she behaved.

Will walked in next, looking his usual dour self. It'd probably kill him to smile before seven a.m. He grunted and walked like a zombie toward the platter of pancakes.

I held the spatula up like a weapon and stopped him in his tracks. "Do. Not. Even. Think. About it."

"I think he's hungry," Price stage-whispered to Will.

"Nah," Will grunted. "Horny."

I poured another circle of batter and prayed for patience.

"Look, he's not even going to look at us," Price crowed. "How long's it been, man?"

I set a finished pancake on the mountain I'd made and saw all three of them, Chief included, staring at me. "None of your business." No way would I tell them it'd been almost a year. I was a long-term kind of guy, and the women kept turning out not to be.

I turned the eye off, flipped the gingham kitchen towel over my shoulder, and carried the platter to the oversized dining room table.

My brothers laughed and followed me, taking their seats on opposite sides of Mike, who'd smartly stayed out of the kitchen. Chief brought up the rear. I took my seat and looked around. Guess it was me and the let's-never-leave-Aaron-alone crew. Great.

Chief held his hand up, once again stopping Price from grabbing a piece of bacon. "Let's say grace."

"Good food, good meat, good God, let's eat," Price said.

I smirked as Chief glared at him. "Hands in your lap. Have some courtesy." After he was satisfied that everyone was sufficiently quiet, he said a quick, but much more mature, prayer. "Amen," he finished.

Price dove for a piece of bacon and shoved it in his mouth.

"So good," he mumbled as he chewed and rolled his eyes to the back of his head.

I laughed. "I *knew* I made it crispy enough, you bastard."

"You seeing Devon after your shift?" Mike asked after a few minutes of blissful silence.

Damn. Just when I thought they'd leave me alone, Mike comes in and does this.

"What?" he said at my glare. "I'm making conversation."

"Did Chief put you up to this?"

"No, but it's polite to answer a question when someone asks you," Chief said.

I looked around. Price was shoveling pancakes in his maw as fast as he possibly could, and Will was quietly eating his scrambled eggs. Chief's eyes danced mischievously and Mike stared square at me, with no trace of an agenda.

I sighed. "Yes, I'm going to see her. Happy now?"

The table exploded into laughter and I shook my head. "I hate all of you."

12

AARON

I'M JUST HERE *to help her with Gigi's house.* That's what I kept telling myself, even as she opened the door and her eyes widened in surprise.

"Hi."

She smiled and wrapped her arms around her stomach, as though she was holding herself in check. A far cry from last week, when she nearly let me kiss her. I'd replayed that moment over and over in my head. She'd been scared. I knew that. But there was something else there, a tentative trust, and that trust was what I was hanging onto.

"Hi," she said.

On instinct, I leaned in for a hug, catching her vanilla scent. It was distinctly her, no matter the time of day, no matter if she was sweaty from a hike or not. Basically, her body was trying to seduce me, and it was torture.

The embrace was stiff. "I didn't know you were off shift today," she said.

I thought about pointing out how she'd have known if she'd bothered answering my texts these past couple of days, but held back. We were definitely not on the same wavelength as we'd been last time, so I needed to tread carefully. Then I noticed what she wore.

Damn.

Those were the tiniest running shorts I'd ever seen. They showed off Devon's curves, framing the decadent swell of her hips and ass in a perfect shade of blue-green that emphasized the light tan of her skin. The shorts were popular with college girls, but I'd never paid any attention to them, because that was creepy. But on Devon? That was something different altogether.

I forced my eyes back up to hers and answered the question she'd asked. "Daisy and I thought you might need some help around the house."

She smiled, a crack in the wall. "I'll take it. Especially if it means getting Samson out of here."

As if on cue, the scruffy monster barked, his tail wagging ninety miles an hour. I leaned down to pet him, which got me eye level with Devon's legs. They were toned and more than a handful, and I wanted them wrapped around my waist immediately. Clearly I'd not appreciated them enough on the hike.

After petting Samson much longer than necessary, we put the dogs in the backyard and I followed Devon up the stairs to the second floor. I might have stared at her legs the whole time I followed her. I might have also gotten a healthy dose of her ass. I groaned, grateful for the creaking stairs that covered the noise.

"You okay?" Devon looked over her shoulder at me. Maybe the stairs didn't cover it as well as I thought.

But also, I wasn't okay. My head and my dick were on opposite paths. I wanted to throw her onto a bed *and* get her to open back up to me. To learn every bit about her body *and* soul.

"Yeah. Fine," I said. I needed work to do. Heavy work. Manual labor. Especially given how chilly she was acting. "Anything I can carry to the bin outside?"

"Yes." She pointed to the stack of black garbage bags that lined the hall. "These are all ready to go."

Thank Christ. I nodded and set to it, grateful for the distraction. I needed to get myself under control.

After five trips to the dumpster, I felt better. Sort of. Enough to remind my dick that Devon was actually a person and not a pair of spectacular legs connected to an even more spectacular ass, and to remind my head that Devon wasn't some box I could just force open at will.

She looked at me, her lips quirked in a half-smile. "What's with you today?"

I wanted to ask her the same. "Nothing," I lied. "What's next?"

She hummed, still assessing me, and said, "Attic. Seems like you need it."

I raised my eyebrows. Whether she wanted to admit it or not, she seemed to know me as well as I understood her.

Or at least, as well as I *thought* I did. Right now, I barely knew my own name for as much as my head was running in circles.

She moved past me, her arm brushing mine, and my skin felt electric. I followed her up to the third floor of the Victorian, keeping my eyes on the faded, rose-print wallpaper even though it was a Herculean task, and then we stopped in front of a half-size door.

I repeat: a door, only it was half the size it should have been.

"Um, what's that?" I asked. "The murder room?"

She laughed. "That's the door to the attic. Only half this floor is non-attic."

"So you're going to send me through that tiny door and lock me in there?"

"Nah," she said, her eyes dancing. "Not today."

"Have you been in here yet?" I opened the door and bent to peer inside.

"Not this go-around." She shook her head as I straightened. "But if it's anything like it was when I was a kid, it's filled with a bunch of junk. I don't know why it was easier for her to carry things up here instead of putting them on the street, but I'm pretty sure we'll need these." She held up the box of heavy-duty trash bags. "And you'll need this." She held up a blue bandana in her other hand. "Sweat, dust, whatever."

I nodded and took it, then shoved it in my back pocket. "After you." I gestured to the door. "I'm not going into the murder room first."

She huffed a laugh and clicked on the flashlight she produced from somewhere, angling a glittery smile back at me. She bent over, god *damn* that ass, walked in, and I followed. I would follow it anywhere.

I shook my head. I was a mess today. I blamed Price, Will, Chief, and even Mike. They were the four horsemen of my personal apocalypse.

I stood to my full height once we got inside and looked around. "Wait a minute. I thought the murder room was going to stay tiny?"

It was filled to the rafters, literally, with dusty furniture parts, boxes, trunks, and rolled-up carpets. It was entirely possible we could kit out a two-bedroom house with the stuff up here if we were creative enough.

"Not at first. It slopes." Devon pointed the flashlight at the back of the room, then she pulled on a string, bringing an ancient bulb to life that barely provided any light. "You ready for this?"

I was ready, all right. Just not for what she was talking about. *Focus on her heart, asshole.* "As I'll ever be."

Two hours later, my muscles were screaming at me and I was officially done. I held the bandana up and waved it after tossing a carpet into the dumpster. "Mercy," I begged, then used the massacred cloth to wipe my face.

Devon threw a contender for the world's ugliest lamp into the dumpster, then turned and flashed me another wired but still devastating smile. Turns out, she had a dimple in her right cheek and it only came out when she was torturing me. "Had enough?"

I held up the bandana once more, happy she'd warmed up over the past two hours. "I could fill a glass with the sweat from this."

"Hmm. Tempting. But I prefer tea." She waved me back inside. "Come on."

I followed her shorts—*her*, I meant *her*, I swear I had mostly good intentions—to the kitchen. While she busied herself preparing what she called 'the perfect iced tea,' I washed my hands and took a wet paper towel to my face and neck. Finally cooled off, I threw it away and came face to face with Devon.

"Well, hello there."

She grinned, the shiny hardware of her mouth on full display. "Hello yourself."

I smiled like an idiot, ready to cheer at the way she held my gaze. It seemed she was back.

"Sooo," she said. "I need the trash can." She winked as she swung a desiccated lemon between her fingers.

"Ah." I scooted over, and she opened the door under the sink to throw the lemon away. I'd like to say I didn't notice how her tank top fell open to reveal a little more of her breasts. I'd like to. But I'd be lying.

"Pretty sure it's cooler outside," she said as she grabbed the glasses. "Besides, it doesn't get any more Southern than drinking tea on your front porch, so we're going all in."

The dogs raised their heads from their spots in the shade on the porch when we appeared, then laid them back down with twin sighs. I chuckled. "So much for them staying in the back yard."

Devon hummed in agreement, then dropped into a rocking chair as I did the same. I accepted the tea she handed me, raised it to her in a salute, and took a sip. "Whoa."

She smiled. "Told you."

"I don't really even like tea that much, but this is"—I took another sip—"okay, this is really good."

She preened. "You're welcome. One of the tricks I picked up from Gigi over the years."

"It's better than Gigi's," I said.

She tilted her head. "What?"

I hesitated. This was the perfect opportunity to tell her I knew Gigi better than I'd let on. That Gigi wanted the two of us to meet, and I was fairly certain she'd brought Devon home for precisely that reason. But I couldn't do it. I was scared Devon would clam up, and I wanted her to open up to me. It already felt like I was too far gone to bring it up now.

"I mean, it's the best iced tea I've ever had. I don't see how hers could've been better."

She looked at me skeptically, clearly not buying it.

I doubled down. "I am the world's foremost authority on iced tea and I hereby declare this is the best."

She laughed. "You just said you don't even like tea that much."

I tilted my head at her. "Precisely why you should believe me."

Her forehead smoothed out. "I don't know about that, but I do make a good iced tea."

I held the glass up to the sun to inspect the contents and collect myself. It was a pretty presentation. The glass itself was clear with yellow bands around it, filled with a good ice-to-tea ratio and a generous lemon round perched on the rim. I shrugged and took another drink, then another, then downed it. "Yes. Yes you do."

She held her hand out for the glass, but I shook my head and stood. "Hand me yours."

After a moment's hesitation, she gave it to me. I returned to the kitchen, filled the glasses with a second round, and met her back on the porch, the screen door thwacking shut as I handed her the tea.

She regarded me with a curious expression. "Thank you."

"You're welcome." I lowered myself into the rocker gingerly, eyeing the rusted nails on the arm rests and making a note to bring my toolbox the next time I visited.

She got quiet, studying the street.

"Did I miss something?"

She huffed a soft laugh. "No. Sorry. It's been a long time since…since anyone's done that for me."

"Gotten you a drink?"

"No," she answered. "And yes." She looked away and waved it off. "It's not a big deal."

"But it is."

She took a sip through her straw and I got quiet, thumbing the flaking paint off the rocking chair's arm. Eventually I said, "My dad died when I was seventeen."

She faced me.

I focused on the paint flecks. "My mom left six years before that. No explanation. Just, gone. While I was at school. I guess…I wasn't enough for her to stay."

"Aaron," she said softly.

"What I'm saying is, I've lost people, too." I finally met her gaze. "And it's not the same. I get that. But it hurts. Hurts like hell." I glanced away. "At least the people you loved actually loved you back."

She put her hand on mine, stilling it, and waited for me to look at her before speaking. "I'm sorry. We all process grief differently, I guess."

I threaded my fingers through hers.

"It's hard to explain," she continued. "Jason…he was the love of my life. Before coming back, I could forget about him for days, sometimes even a week. But being home…" She met my eyes. "I thought being here was going to be the worst thing that'd I'd experienced since he died. Broken jaw aside," she said, smiling wryly, "it turns out, maybe I've been wrong. But to be honest?"

I held her gaze, stomach tight. This was when she'd tell me that even though she liked me, she didn't plan on staying. Exactly like my mom, and like every other woman I'd dated. "Honesty is good," I said.

"I'm confused."

I breathed out. "Is that good or bad?"

She gave me a half-smile and shrugged, unthreading our hands. "I don't know." She gestured between us and continued. "What are we doing?"

I sat back in the chair, my heart doing flip-flops in my chest. "Taking it one step at a time?"

She nodded thoughtfully.

It seemed we were both terrified, just for different reasons. I was half in love with her already, and I had no idea what she was going to do after the six months were up. "No matter what happens, I'm glad to have had time with you. And I hope you keep letting me have it." My voice was soft as I held her gaze, wanting her to read everything I felt.

She swallowed. Did she know how expressive her eyes were? Every feeling, every hesitation and wonder, every impulse or shot of self-control...her eyes gave her away each time. And right now, they gave me hope.

"You know what we need?" she asked.

I raised my eyebrows. "What?"

"A picture. We should be documenting all the work we're doing!"

Well, that was one way to climb out of the serious conversation we'd been in. I nodded, wanting to give her whatever she needed.

Decision made, she stood and grabbed her phone, then

surveyed the scene. "Stay there,"she commanded, moving to the back of my rocking chair.

Samson lifted his head and regarded us with interest. I pointed a finger at him. "Samson, stay."

He tilted his head and perked his ears, but stayed in place.

Devon crouched beside me and held up the phone. "Say 'Devon's tea is awesome'!"

I grinned for the picture and noted how she'd managed to get the tea and porch into the frame as well.

She snapped the photo and stood. Right as she moved, Samson bolted toward us. Devon moved to avoid him, but instead of behaving like a normal dog that wasn't trying to constantly harm people, Samson tangled himself in her legs.

"Ah!" Devon screeched and started to fall.

I grabbed her arm to steady her, but the move ended up pulling her into my lap.

"Oof," she said as she landed full-throttle against me.

I cradled her in my arms. For one brief moment, it was just her deliciously soft body pressed against mine, and it was glorious.

She pulled herself upright almost immediately, but Samson woofed and pawed at the two of us, keeping her on my lap.

Thank you, you magnificent dog. Such a good boy. The *best* boy.

"I'm so sorry," she said, attempting to stand up. "I swear he's trying to kill me."

He was doing something, all right, and I was beginning to think he was as much of a meddler as Chief. I grinned and tightened my arms around her, hoping she'd take the hint. "It's okay."

She stilled, and Samson gave one final woof before joining Daisy back in the patch of sunlight on the porch.

I owed that dog a steak dinner.

Devon relaxed, but stayed upright on my lap. Our eyes met.

Wordlessly, I trailed my fingers up her arm, from the soft underside of her wrist up to her shoulder and back, and she steadily melted. After a few minutes, she lay against me, her head against my shoulder, her body perfectly curled into mine.

"Aaron." Her voice cracked.

"Devon," I whispered, and kept tracing her skin.

She twisted so that she was looking at me, one arm holding herself upright while the other snaked around my neck. Her eyes were the blue of the sky right before sunset, and her cheeks were pink. Her lips parted.

"You are gorgeous," I said, my voice low, reverent.

She flushed even more, her eyes resting on my lips before meeting my gaze again. "This won't be the best."

"What won't be?"

"This kiss."

I tightened my grip on her waist as I wet my lips. Her eyes followed the movement. When they met mine again, they were dark with want. My heart pounded and I moved my hand down to her legs, finally giving in to the urgent need to touch them, and pulled her closer. "How about you let me be the judge of that?"

She hesitated a fraction of a second, and I leaned up to meet her. All I wanted was to feel her lips on mine. "Is this okay?" Even though she'd started it, I needed to be certain.

Devon nodded, closing the inch left between us, and finally, her lips were on mine. My brain stuttered to a halt, and my entire world zeroed in to the way her lips felt, lush, soft, and pliant. I gripped her tighter, and she shifted on my lap. She pulled away for a breath, and I pulled her back, immediately pressing her mouth to mine again. She tasted of sweat and cherry chapstick. I licked at the seam of her lips, teasing them open even though I couldn't go any farther because of the wire, then fusing our lips together again.

I moved her so that she faced me as much as possible, not

caring that she could definitely tell how excited I was, and wrapped my arms around her. She moaned and rocked against me, all shyness banished now that she was in my arms. She felt incredible, all luscious curves and softness, her skin silky beneath my hands, the shorts practically non-existent in this position.

I gripped her velvety thighs and sipped at her lips, unable to get my fill of the tiny sighs and sounds she made. I would stay on this porch forever. I would wait however long it took, and I would battle whatever demons needed battling. If Devon was the prize, I would endure anything.

I swallowed her groan. "Aaron," she whispered. She rested her forehead against mine and pushed her hand through my hair, exhaling a soft swear. "Never have I hated having my jaw wired shut more than right at this moment," she said, her voice low.

I met her eyes, dark blue now, as her fingers traced down the side of my face to my chest. "Agree. That was still a great kiss, though."

She giggled, and her cheeks flushed. "It wasn't bad."

"Not bad?" I feigned hurt. "It needs to be the best."

Her eyes glittered. "Guess we need more practice."

"Come here," I growled, and gathered her to me once more.

13

DEVON

5 MONTHS, 12 DAYS TO GO

I FLIPPED THE switch, then watched as the overhead light blew out. "Great," I muttered. With this final bedroom, the entire upstairs was officially in the dark. Every room's light had blown this morning, and I knew it wasn't the bulbs. This was definitely a wiring issue, and wasn't that awesome.

At least it was daytime. I crossed the room to open the curtains, and dust flew out at me. I sneezed, then wiped my watery eyes.

Undeterred, I grabbed the cord to yank the blinds up, but they didn't budge. I bit back a groan. Of course. Why would they move? That would be far too easy. I tried again, really putting some muscle into it and looking up at the top of the window at the same time. Instantly they came off, popping out of their casing and flying out to land with impressive precision on my head, then flopping down to my arms and landing in a dusty heap of cheap plastic on the floor.

Super.

Gigi was probably laughing, absolutely ecstatic at the mess I'd found myself in. And maybe later—much, *much* later—I'd think this was funny. As it was, exactly none of this was delightful.

I kicked the blinds off the vent they'd fallen onto, then stood over it to let the cool air shoot up at me. Although calling the air "cool" was a stretch. The house needed a new HVAC system as well, but replacing it was dead last on the to-do list, and that was only if the money Gigi left managed to last that long.

"You're doing so good," I said, hoping the praise to the HVAC was enough to keep it going.

I sighed, then turned to open the closet door. It flew open, and I'm not gonna lie: I flinched. Between falling blinds and a dog that seemed hell-bent on killing me, I was a little gun-shy.

But nothing fell out on me, so that was positive. The closet was stuffed to within an inch of its life with boxes and bags of who knows what. I shook my head. Like every other room, it was filled to the brim with *things*.

I reached for my sippy cup, as I called the giant Tervis tumbler that had a permanent place by my side, and took a long drink from the straw, considering.

Had she always been like this, collecting and keeping and storing away with no rhyme or reason? With the amount of stuff in the house, she must have been. But how had I never noticed? And why hadn't she ever asked for help, if she even wanted it?

But I guess she had, in her own way. In every call and with every short visit I made, she'd made no secret of wanting me to move back to Talladega from the minute I left. What she never understood was how every street, every place in this town, was filled with memories of Jason.

Only now, I was making new memories. Like the hike I'd taken with Aaron. And yesterday's searing-hot make-out session.

My belly swooped and my whole body warmed at the thought of it. I touched my lips, amazed they weren't still swollen like they'd been for hours after he left. The way he'd looked at me, held me as though I was something precious…it'd felt right. Like I could lay my grief down and just *be*.

It was terrifying. Because if I fell for him, and then lost him? It would destroy me.

I regarded the closet. Nothing to do but get on with it, I supposed. I pulled the first bag out, threw it on the bed, and opened it. Clothes. That one was easy: it would go in the donation pile. Speaking of which, I needed to sort out a place that would come and pick up the donations that were steadily piling up in the front living room. I bet Miss Betty knew of an organization. I made a note to myself to ask her, because she was certain to come by. She'd made a point of it every day, not even trying to hide that she was trying to get me to stay, and today would be no exception.

After pulling out a few more bags of clothes and getting them downstairs, I hauled another box out of the closet. I opened it, then laughed at the contents. "Never took you for this level of sentimental, Gigi," I murmured.

It seemed as if all the cards my brother and I had ever made or sent her, whether birthday or thank you or otherwise, were in the box. Along with some truly bad artwork by me and Rick, too. I laughed, then sat down to flip through the box's contents. It was all destined for the trash, sure, but not before I looked through it.

The next two boxes were more of the same: sweet little keepsakes that surely meant a lot to Gigi, but that I could easily toss or give away. Then I found a photo album. I pulled it out, my chest tight, and ran my fingers over the embossed, cracking leather.

'Our Wedding,' the letters read. The album was old, and probably very expensive when she bought it. I'd never seen it before. Maybe it was hers? Come to think of it, I'd never seen her wedding album. But why would she have kept it in a box instead of with the other family albums that were on a downstairs bookshelf?

I should have started at the beginning, but I picked a spot at the end, the glue cracking against the leather and sending a whiff of old paper toward me as I did so. The second my eyes landed on the picture, I inhaled sharply and slammed the book shut.

I squeezed my eyes tight, as though that alone could block the memory. Why was that photo in this old album? It was of me and Jason as we left the church, lines of friends and family blowing bubbles on both sides. I'd jumped onto his back for an impromptu piggy-back ride, and my arms were wrapped around his chest while his were holding me up behind him. The smiles on both our faces were full of promise.

Shit. This was why I'd avoided coming back home to live. I couldn't handle this. Didn't *want* to handle it. And I didn't have to. I'd sworn I would never grieve the way I did after my parents died, and I didn't. For as much as I loved Jason, he never got all of me. I couldn't let him.

We'd fought that morning. He'd yelled that he was tired of me keeping him at a distance, of never letting him all the way in, and like an asshole, I'd told him to deal with it or leave.

He left.

And I didn't chase him, because I knew we could make up later.

Only there was no later.

So the last memory I had of him wasn't of me telling him I loved him, or of hugging and kissing him goodbye. No, it was telling him to leave.

I wiped the lone tear away and stood, then took the album in one hand and a bag of trash in another. I walked outside to the dumpster and heaved the bag into the bin, and readied to throw the album in after.

No.

I stopped myself just as the sound of nails scratching on street pavement brought me back to reality. I turned, my hands shaking, as Samson smiled and woofed as he ran to me.

I swallowed the tears that threatened and leaned down to pet his dingy yellow head. *Focus on the good. Focus on the now.* I could do this.

Samson licked my hand as I kneeled in front of him, then went up on his legs to lick my face, snuffling as he did so.

"You really do know how to make an entrance, don't you?"

After a moment, he backed up and woofed again.

I nodded, tightening my grip on the album. "I know. Keep it, right?"

He headed to the house, and it was as good of an answer as I could expect. I opened the door and he trotted in. Inside, I put the album on the coffee table in the living room, unable to do anything but get it out of my hands.

14

DEVON

5 MONTHS, 11 DAYS TO GO

A S I OPENED the door to the Daily Dose, the smell of delicious coffee wafted over me. I closed my eyes, wishing the aroma alone could fix all that ailed me. But it wouldn't. I was here to meet up with Ceci, because as much as I loved my brother, I needed to gripe and gnash my teeth and shake my fist at the heavens. Ceci was perfect for that. Saint Rick, on the other hand, would silently listen to me rant and then offer something ridiculous like a logical solution.

I loved the guy. I really did. But sometimes, a girl wanted to vent.

"You're blocking the door."

My eyes opened, only to narrow as I saw who it was.

Mrs. Withers.

The woman stood in front of me in hot pink polyester pants and a trippy pink, red, and white blouse that she'd probably had since the seventies. On anyone else, the shirt might have worked. On her, it was nauseating.

"A pleasure to see you, Mrs. Withers." My voice dripped with sarcasm but again, after this morning, I had zero fucks left to give.

"I talked to my nephew about you," she said.

I raised my eyebrows and said nothing.

"He's on the Town Council. Said you couldn't run. You'd have to be a resident for at least two years, *and* file a notice of intent. It just so happens that the deadline has passed." She glared at me and sniffed, pleased as punch with herself.

"Honestly, Mrs. Withers, it's flattering you checked on that for me. I appreciate you doing that. Saved me the effort of figuring it out." I made to move out of her way, but she stepped with me.

"I don't know what games you're playing at, missy, but you should be aware that you've picked the wrong woman to go up against." She glared up at me. "Everyone sides with me. Always has. Your grandmother never had this town's best interests at heart, you see. Just looked out for herself and that house."

I bristled. "'That house,' as you so eloquently put it, has been in my family since it was built."

"God willing, that'll change soon enough," she shot back.

"That's not happening."

She looked at me, a cat who'd eaten the canary. "You don't know about the vote that's up at the next meeting, do you?"

I stilled. "What are you talking about?"

Behind me, the shop door opened and Ceci came in. "Devon, hi! Mrs. Withers, hello."

Mrs. Withers harrumphed, hoisted her purse up beneath her arm, and walked around me.

Ceci watched her go. "What's got her so riled up?"

"Do you know anything about a vote at the next Town Council meeting?"

She raised a perfectly arched brow at me. "Devon. Between the twins, my father, and your brother—who I love dearly but who is still, bless him, a man—it takes every moment of every day for me to hang on to the tiny shred of sanity that I still possess. What makes you think I pay any attention to *Town Council* votes?"

I pursed my lips. "Good point. It's probably nothing, and Mrs. Withers is just mad to be mad. Let's order."

We ordered from Jodi, and I put the old woman and her antics behind me for the moment as we settled into the over-stuffed chairs in the corner.

Ceci unwrapped the blueberry muffin on her plate. "Smell this. Grace Thomas makes them, and don't tell her I said so, but they're the best damn muffins I've had in my life. Irritates the shit out of me."

I leaned in for a sniff. "It's mouth-watering and I hate you for making me smell something I can't eat."

She shrugged. "Can't help it if you're clumsy."

My eyes widened. "Wow, that's low."

She grinned as Jodi walked up with our drinks. "Spinach-kale-pineapple smoothie for you," she said, handing the cup to me, "and lavender latte for you." She set Ceci's down with a flourish, her hair framed by a bandana that matched the matte red of her lips. "Drink up!"

I thanked her and took a sip through the straw. "Delicious. And way better than what I'm coming up with at Gigi's, so thank you."

She grinned. "You're welcome."

"But if spinach is in the wires after I'm finished, I'm going to kill you."

"Forget about the smoothie," Ceci said, waving her hands in the air. "And tell us all about him."

"Give me, like, thirty seconds," Jodi said. "I need a coffee for this." She ran behind the counter, poured herself a cold brew, and bolted back, skittering into the chair Ceci pulled up for her.

"Okay, spill," she said, propping her hands on her chin and batting her eyes at me. "Preferably in the next sixty seconds before something else happens back there and I fire Darius, and since he is the only other person who works here, I will regret it immediately."

I laughed, unable to resist the two of them when they were looking at me like this. "Well, he followed me here."

Jodi's eyes lit up and she looked around. "Where is he?"

"Outside."

She and Ceci kept looking. "I don't see him," Ceci said.

"Four legs, scruffy yellow hair, ugly cute?" I prompted.

Ceci huffed and scowled. "You know good and well we didn't mean Samson."

I grinned evilly. "He keeps coming into the house, but I still refuse to feed him. Can't have him depending on me." Which was true. I didn't need him on my conscience, no matter how cute he was.

Ceci held up a hand. "Quit avoiding my real question, which is, how are things going with Aaron?"

"Because we know you went for a hike with him," Jodi said.

"*And* we know you two were on the porch all cuddled up a few days ago," Ceci finished.

I nearly spit my smoothie out. "Who told you that?"

"Please. You think your neighbor is blind?" Jodi asked.

I blanched. "Miss Betty?"

"Of *course* Miss Betty," Ceci rolled her eyes. "Saw you two drinking tea on the porch and was good enough to close her curtains. Which, for the record, I would not have done. Now come on. Spill." She gestured in a *get on with it* motion.

"You know, I'm not sure you two even deserve details."

"Did. You. Kiss. Him?" Ceci demanded in a growl. "For God's sake, I am living vicariously through you and right now, I am wound up tighter than a bra around the arm in a washing machine."

"That's...oddly specific."

"Now, woman!" She banged the chair cushion and glowered at me.

I laughed and held my hands up. "Okay, okay. Yes, I kissed him."

Both of them erupted in a hailstorm of squeals and claps that had the entire shop looking at us.

"Could you two not?" I hissed.

"Tongue?" Ceci asked.

"Really?" I said, baring my very much un-openable teeth and pointing to them. But his hands, on the other hand, the heat of them against my skin, and the possessive way he'd pulled me to him, it had set me ablaze, not to mention the package he was clearly working with...

Jodi's eyebrows hit her perfectly curled bangs. "You're squirming in your seat."

Shit.

Ceci opened her mouth to say something when the bell above the door jingled. She glanced up, and her expression changed to pure delight. "Well, well, well, look who's here."

Double shit. Because it definitely had to be Aaron. No other person would have that expression appearing on my sister-in-law's face.

I turned in my seat, and Aaron strode purposefully toward us, eyes locked on me, clad in his dark blue uniform. I swallowed. Christ almighty the man was *hot*. I managed to drag my gaze off his chest and up to his face, and he smiled like he'd won the lottery.

"Devon," he said, his voice a little lower and scratchier than usual. Was this his morning voice? Wait. It wasn't morning. Imagine what it'd sound like if I heard it first thing as he rolled on top of me, wrapping me in those arms as he settled between my legs, the length of him pushing—

"Devon?" he asked.

I shook my head and pulled myself together. "Aaron, hi!" My voice was a full octave higher. Jodi and Ceci giggled behind me and I mentally flipped them off. "Hello." I jumped up and led him to the counter, grabbing his arm and trying not to gawk at the steel I found in place of a bicep. Clearly I'd not felt the man up nearly enough on my porch. "Let me buy you a coffee."

He grinned, his eyes glinting in the light. "You don't need to do that."

"Maybe not, but I *do* need to get away from Bippo and Boppo," I said, jerking my head back at the table.

His smile widened in delight. "Then you'll be sad to know that Jodi, who I'm going to guess is Bippo, is about to appear in front of us in three, two…"

"Your usual, Aaron?" Jodi asked, winking at me.

I groaned. Was it possible to get away with murder?

"Yes, please." He dropped some bills on the counter and turned his attention to me. His eyes softened, turning into liquid pools of almost silvery-blue. "Is it okay if I tell you I missed you?"

I warmed under his gaze. "Of course."

He ran a hand down my arm, causing goosebumps to raise in its wake. "Good. Because I did."

It'd not even been forty-eight hours, but I felt the same way. I nearly said it, too, but caught myself. I needed to keep this under control. This couldn't get deep.

"Coffee," Jodi said, pushing the to-go cup across the counter with a smirk.

Aaron took it and guided us away from the register. "I'm starting a two-day shift, but maybe I can come over when it's done?" His tone was hopeful as his thumb traced circles on the inside of my wrist.

My entire being centered on his thumb and I blinked slowly. I didn't want him to stop touching me or looking at me with such tenderness. I also needed him to quit immediately. A universe of pent-up emotions clawed at the door to be let out. I had no idea what I was doing.

I nodded.

He smiled again, sending my stomach tipping. "I have to go." He leaned down and kissed the side of my cheek, enveloping me in his scent, then straightened. "I'll see you soon."

I watched him leave, marveling at the sheer perfection of his butt in those uniform pants. As the door shut behind him, I slid my gaze over to Ceci, who watched me with a satisfied smile. I walked to my chair, sat down, and sighed. "I don't know, Ceci."

Jodi reappeared and took her seat. "Don't know what? Because wow, the sparks between you two!" She fanned herself.

"Anything. Everything. I'm so...and he's so..." I lifted my hand and let it drop. I didn't know what. Or maybe I did. My world was tilting on its axis, and I was flailing to stay upright.

"Perfect for you?" Ceci finished. "The best thing to happen to you since Jason?"

I flinched.

"I'm right," she pressed. Her voice lowered and she leaned forward. "Honey, I can't imagine what it's like to lose someone I love. And to lose more than just one person is unfathomable. So I would never tell you to get over it or move on, because that timeline is something that only you know."

My throat tightened and I blinked rapidly to fight the tears that threatened. That had to be it. Because I'd been fine until I got back here. I'd faced my grief and moved on. At least, I thought I had. But the guilt. The look of hurt and disappointment on his face as he left our home the last morning he was alive. When would I be able to lay *that* down?

Jodi grabbed my hand and squeezed it tight. "I miss my brother, Devon. I do. But he is gone. He's been gone for five years. We are entirely different people now. You deserve to be happy. And if Aaron makes you happy, then why not let him?"

Because I will not survive losing another person. I swallowed the lump in my throat. "I don't think I know how."

Ceci let out a low, throaty laugh and leered at me. "Oh, I'm sure Aaron would be happy to remind you. Over and over and *over* again."

They laughed, and I forced a smile. "It's not that simple."

"Oh but honey, it *can* be," Ceci said.

Jodi nodded in agreement. "No one's saying you gotta marry the guy."

"Look," Ceci said, "Where's the harm in seeing where things go?"

"Because...what happens when I leave?" It wasn't just me I was worried about.

"What if you don't?" Ceci's voice was soft.

I put my head in my hands and groaned.

"Okay, okay, let's not worry about that part. One day at a time. Remind me: when do you get all that mess off?" Jodi gestured at my jaw.

"So the kisses can turn into other things." Ceci leered again.

"You two are the worst," I said, grateful for the shift. "Not soon enough for the two of you, apparently."

I took a sip of my smoothie and felt my chest loosen a smidge. Could I do what they were suggesting and take it one day at a time? Aaron didn't take unnecessary risks. He wore his seatbelt. He was healthy. Wasn't a firefighter...at least not yet. Aaron was tailor-made for me to take a chance on.

15

AARON

I IGNORED THE pitiful look that Daisy gave me as her tail thumped the floor. "You'll be fine here at the station, girl. You're surrounded by all your favorite guys, and about a million kid hands will be here later to pet you."

Chief took in the scene as he walked up behind me, then bent to give Daisy a scratch. "She staying with us?"

"Yeah. Daisy's always a hit with kids, and since students from the Montessori school down the street are coming, she's yours for the day."

He grunted, a knowing look in his eyes. "You love it when those kids come. You got other plans? Maybe some that involve a certain blonde?"

I shook my head. "Wouldn't you like to know."

He smiled. "That means yes."

I gave him a pointed look. "I'd appreciate it if you didn't blab to the entire station about it."

He held his hands up innocently. "I would never."

I snorted. "You're itching to text my brothers." But even Chief's nosy, meddling ways couldn't put me in a bad mood. I gave Daisy one last scratch behind her ears, then headed out, my steps light. Devon had invited me over, and in my book, that was definitely a step in the right direction.

The sun shone bright and the humidity was thick, a combination that felt like Mother Nature insisting that even though the calendar had flipped to September, we were nowhere near being let up on heat-wise. I didn't mind it; never had. I rolled the windows down in my truck as I drove the short distance between the station and Devon's house, waving at the runners and dog walkers as I went.

I considered stopping at Daily Dose but decided against it. I didn't feel like going a round with Jodi, and based on the scene there the other day with Devon, I had a feeling I'd get the third degree from her. So I grabbed smoothies from another spot instead.

It was ten o'clock by the time I rolled to a stop in Devon's driveway. My phone buzzed with texts and I pulled it out.

WILL

I went by your house. Where are you?

PRICE

He's going to Devon's. You gonna show her your muscles?

WILL

Pfft. What muscles?

I rolled my eyes. Of course Chief blabbed. It's precisely what I asked him not to do, which in hindsight was a bad idea.

I'm here to help a friend. Which you two would know nothing about.

WILL

Is that what you're calling her?

PRICE

Wait, are you there already? Why are you texting us?

Since when do you care about how I'm behaving?

PRICE:

Since you took the blame for the Great Goat Escape of Fall Festival 2010, bro.

Not by choice. I was an innocent child and you two ganged up on me. Mrs. Singer still gives me the evil eye whenever I see her.

WILL

Time to let it go, Aaron.

I didn't start it!

PRICE

Get out of your car, Muscles McGee.

I startled and looked around.

Are you stalking me?

PRICE

No. I'm just that good.

I sent them a middle finger emoji and got out with the smoothies. It would be a miracle if my brothers ever left me alone.

Devon opened the door as I walked up the flaking porch steps, a warm smile on her face. I nearly tripped at the way she looked, luminous in the morning light. Her blue eyes shone and her hair was held back in a way that showed off the graceful curve of her neck. She wore her near daily outfit of well-worn t-shirt and denim shorts, and I thanked the heavens for it.

"Good morning," she said. "Where's Daisy? But more importantly, what's in your hands?"

I smiled. "Daisy's at the station. And I brought smoothies. Since I can't ply you with pastry yet." I stepped closer to her, figuring she'd step back and let me inside. Instead, she leaned up and kissed my cheek.

She blushed prettily when she lowered down. "For the smoothie."

Before she could step away, I cupped her jaw with my free hand and stroked her soft skin with my thumb. "Devon." Her eyes darkened, giving me all the permission I needed. I leaned down and met her lips with mine. They yielded to me without hesitation, velvet and sweet. She brought her hands to my waist and tugged me closer. She tasted like mint and coffee, and I wanted more of her. So much more.

She whined and pulled away, pressing her lips together. "I hate this damn jaw," she said, her voice low and breathy.

"Three and a half weeks left," I growled.

"Don't I know it." She cleared her throat and stepped to the side to let me in. "Come in." As she walked ahead of me, she called over her shoulder, "And bring those smoothies."

Yes, ma'am.

I followed her to the living room and took a seat on the couch, a plush, cream sectional, complete with recliners on both ends. It was entirely out of place with the rest of the room, which was filled with delicate pieces that matched the lace curtains and gold-framed paintings. I had to give it to Gigi, though: this couch was outstanding. The naps I could take on it would be epic. Then my eyes landed on a cabinet across from the couch. "Let me guess," I said, nodding at it. "Television?"

Devon sipped the smoothie and nodded. "Oh, yeah. Gigi didn't care what matched and didn't match. She liked what she liked, and this couch was her pride and joy. When I lived here, she'd curl up in it and watch 'her stories' every weekday."

Devon's eyes took on a faraway look as she spoke. After a moment, she turned to me. "So what convinced you to hang out with me on your day off? You gonna let me put you to work?"

I nodded. "My body is yours."

Her eyes widened and she blushed again at the double meaning, then she smiled. "Good to know. I don't suppose you're an electrician?"

I looked at her quizzically.

She sighed and pointed up. "The entire upstairs is shot. No electricity. Even Rick can't fix it."

"Did you check the breaker?"

She leveled me with a dark look. "Really?"

I held up my hands in defense. "Easy there, killer. It's a question I would have asked anyone." She huffed and rolled her eyes, but I refused to take the bait. "I know a guy, but he might be booked." I pulled my phone out and texted his contact info to her.

Her phone pinged. "Thanks. Now I only have five million other things to do."

"What's this?" I leaned up to look closer at the leather-bound book on the coffee table.

Devon shot forward and pulled the book onto her lap. "Nothing."

I squinted, recognizing it now. "Is it a wedding album?"

She stood abruptly, her eyes sliding away. "Yep. Just old family weddings. Boring stuff. You, um, ready to help?"

I studied her. I knew that album; Gigi had showed it to me once. I wasn't worried about seeing the photo of her and Jason, but regardless, she'd thrown up that familiar wall that I was just starting to knock down. I put my smoothie down and stood up. "Hey," I said softly, then reached for the album. "I told you I had you, remember? It's fine. Show me when you're ready." I set it on the coffee table.

Devon followed my movements, only relaxing when the

book was out of my hands and I'd straightened. She shut her eyes, seeming to need to collect herself. A moment later, she opened them and let out a deep breath. "I'm sorry."

"It's okay. I promise." I pulled her to me for a hug, gripping her tightly and waiting for her to relax in my arms. She finally did, and I held her a bit longer, selfishly enjoying the feel of her pressed against me.

"Thank you," she said, tipping her head up. "For being...you, I guess," she laughed softly.

My chest warmed at her words. "Anytime. You want to get out of here? Forget the house today. Let's go for a hike."

"Yeah?"

I kept my arms wrapped around her. "Just you and me. No dogs."

She smiled brightly. "That sounds amazing."

An hour later, we were surrounded by trees, the sun dappling through the canopy above us. Birds called to one another across the lush, late-summer trees, and our feet moved steadily against the worn dirt path. The only hint that fall might consider gracing us with its presence was in the yellowing of a weed I couldn't name, growing in clumps along the forest floor.

We barely spoke, but it didn't matter. Because ahead of me, Devon seemed to relax with every step, her shoulders lowering and her gait loosening as we moved along the trail. And that was exactly what I'd hoped for.

Two miles in, the trail split. "Left is where most hikers go," I said. "But right is better. There's a hidden waterfall that you really have to work to get to, but it's worth it."

She nodded and smiled, her face flushed from the heat and the hike's exertion. "Then let's head to the right."

I stepped past her to take the lead, grabbing and squeezing her hand as I did so. She gave me another smile, this one so full and genuine that it made me stop in my tracks. "There you are."

"Been here the whole time," she said.

I faced her. "You're back out of your head," I clarified. "Fully present."

She frowned and looked down. "I'm sorry."

"Oh no you don't," I said, tipping her chin up and capturing her gaze with mine. "You don't need to apologize for having to work through things. In fact, I'm pretty sure that's why hiking was invented," I joked, relieved to see a corner of her lips curve up.

She went up on her toes and gave me a quick kiss, then smiled again, her eyes clear. "Did anyone ever tell you how amazing you are?"

I laughed. "Definitely not."

"Well, you are. *Definitely*." She held my gaze, finally breaking it when a chipmunk tore across the trail at lightning speed. "Ready?"

I nodded, then turned and led us to the waterfall.

She gasped when it came into view. "Oh, wow! It's not at all what I expected."

I took her hand as we walked closer. The water fell from fifteen stories up and was only about ten feet wide. But it caught the sun perfectly, shooting off rainbows as it plummeted down to the river below. Best of all, you could hike behind it.

"No one's here," she said, looking around as we made our way across the rocks to get behind the waterfall.

"I know. It's amazing."

She laughed. "I thought you liked people."

I held out my hand to steady her up a slick rock and looked her in the eyes. "I like you better."

She smiled, showing her dimple. "Is that so?"

I was dead serious. "Absolutely."

She looked away, but the smile stayed on her face. Another win.

We picked our way slowly up and over the wet rocks until we were perfectly behind the waterfall, which began about five stories up from where we stood. It was almost like a cave, made up of nothing but rocks and carved out of the mountain over centuries. It was cooler back here, and windy. Tendrils of hair swept across Devon's face and goosebumps erupted on her arms and legs from the temperature drop.

"This is amazing." She pulled out her phone and snapped pictures. "I can't believe no one is here."

I smiled, grateful to see her so light and free. A far cry from the woman holding the wedding album a couple of hours ago.

"Come this way when you're done," I said, then rounded an almost hidden corner to my favorite spot, a massive chunk of shale that lay flat and dry against the very back of the mountain and was shielded from view by another upright piece of shale. The waterfall was still visible, but no one could see you back here.

Eventually Devon appeared, her expression brightening even more at the scene. She shrugged off her backpack and set it next to mine, then came and sat on the thin blanket I'd laid out beside me. "Perfect make-out spot," she said playfully.

I raised an eyebrow. "Here I was thinking we were just going to relax."

She leaned over, eyes sparkling. "Kiss me, Aaron."

I wanted nothing more in the world. I met her lips, and tasted the sweet cherry of her lip balm. She whimpered and pushed her fingers through my hair, making me groan in return. "This jaw," I said, my voice thick and my forehead resting against hers.

"You have no idea." She shifted and straddled me, surrounding me with every luscious curve she had.

Oh, I was pretty sure I did. I pulled her even closer, my hands skimming the backs of her legs to squeeze her perfect ass as I rained kisses down her neck.

She tilted her chin to give me better access as her hands went up my shirt, flattening against my pecs and then moving to my stomach. She cursed. "You're killing me," she groaned. "Who actually feels like this, especially sitting down?"

I laughed against her jaw, grateful for all those hours in the gym, and continued worshipping her. I listened for every gasp, every moan, to tell me what she liked best. She arched against me and I held her tight, content to follow her lead. As she relaxed, I breathed her in and ran my hands over her, tracing her curves through her shirt.

I couldn't believe she was letting me do this. But rather than think about it, I focused on her. She rocked against me, hissing as I pushed my hands up her shirt. Her skin was hot, silky. Addictive. I licked the hollow of her neck, then bit it, tracing her nipples over her sports bra. "Please," she murmured, taking my hands and positioning them at the base of the bra.

I looked at her. "Are you sure?"

She nodded, her eyes unfocused.

Good enough for me. Together we pushed her sports bra up, revealing breasts that were as exquisitely generous as the rest of her body, dotted here and there with freckles that I desperately needed to trace with my tongue. So I did, making her squirm and gasp as she gripped my shoulders. I took a nipple into my mouth and squeezed the other, pulling her tight against me. Every intake of breath, every sigh, told me she needed to be held hard, as if I was tethering her to the earth. In response, her rhythm increased as she rode my length, her whimpers audible over the waterfall.

Fuck. This woman.

I'd worn my loosest pants, but they were still restrictive. I leaned back quickly to adjust myself, and she popped her eyes open. They were hazy with need, deep pools of turquoise. "Hang on, sweetheart," I soothed. "I know."

She nodded wordlessly, moving her hands between us and unbuttoning her shorts. "Aaron." Her voice was low, urgent.

I shifted us, laying her back onto the blanket and covering

her body with mine. She whimpered. I pushed a hand into her panties, cupping her center roughly as she arched into me. "*Aaron.*"

Fuck. She was on fire, and she was absolutely gorgeous. I nipped at her shoulder, desperate for her skin, pushing one finger into her, then two. She threw her head back and gasped as I licked her neck, her entire body quivering against me. Her cries mixed in with the sound of the waterfall, and I lost myself to her. She was exquisite, flushed and keening.

I moved lower, kissing her stomach and shoving her shorts and panties down and off one leg. I took her in hungrily, the softness of her abdomen, the tautness of her legs, and sent up a prayer of thanks. Pushing her legs apart, I took her center into my mouth, licking and sucking.

"Oh, fuck. Ohmygod."

I pushed my tongue into her, moaning as she bucked against me. She was as sweet as I'd imagined. Then I focused on her clit, pushing my fingers back into her. She moaned and gripped my hair.

"Harder," she gasped.

I gave her what she wanted, and it wasn't long before her legs stiffened. "Aaron, oh fuck, fuck, *fuck*," she chanted as she came.

Her cries grew unintelligible as she pulsed against me, and I took her through the orgasm until she relaxed, languid against the blanket.

I held her to me, pressing light kisses on her stomach. It was as silky and soft as the rest of her. Perfect. I looked up, taking in the flushed skin of her chest and neck, the constellation of freckles across her breasts, and I was undone. If I'd liked her before now, then I'd just taken a leap off the tallest mountain in the world.

"I can't believe…" she started.

I pressed more kisses on her stomach, then began to pull her panties and shorts up. "Believe what?" I murmured against her neck.

She didn't answer. Instead, she planted a sweet kiss on my forehead, then pulled her sports bra and shirt back into place. She relaxed and held me against her, running her hands over my arms, back, and chest. I closed my eyes and lost myself to the pleasure of her touch and the way it felt to be the absolute center of her attention. I wasn't going to move a muscle until she stopped.

She moved to unsnap my shorts and I stilled them. "Not yet," I murmured. "This isn't about me."

She trailed hot kisses up my neck. "Promise I won't bite," she whispered into my ear. Then she pulled back and chuckled, her eyes twinkling. "I literally can't right now."

I caressed her cheek and pulled her up to me for a kiss. "I'm in no rush, sweetheart. We've got all the time in the world."

A shadow crossed her face, but she replaced it with a saucy grin. "I don't want to give you a huge ego or anything, but I have never come that fast, or that intensely, in my life."

I tried and failed to squash the warmth that bloomed in my chest. "You're welcome," I joked. I gave her another kiss.

She laughed against my lips. "I also can't believe that we did that in a place where anyone could see us." She blushed. "It was hot."

I smiled broadly. "Yes, you are."

She pursed her lips. "Even with this metal mouth?"

I nuzzled her neck and found another spot that made her gasp. I ran my fingers through her short hair, greedily drinking her in as her eyes closed and a smile played across her lips. God, she was spectacular. "Devon, there is literally nothing you could do that would make me think you were anything other than the most stunning woman on the planet. You are perfection."

Her eyes opened in surprise and she focused on me, deep

ocean blues I could live inside forever. So expressive. I could see the walls she still had up, but I didn't care. I could wait.

"I'm far from perfect."

I hummed. "Guess we'll have to disagree on that."

She lay back and I shifted us again, so that my back was on the blanket and she was nestled against me. I squeezed her tightly.

"See, that right there," she said, her breath almost tickling my shoulder. "How do you know that?"

I chuckled. "As much as I'd love to be a mind-reader, because it would be so handy as a paramedic, I don't know what you're talking about."

"The pressure."

"Ah." Everything clicked into place. "The way I hold you so tightly?"

"And…other things," she said.

I smiled. "Well, you *did* say harder."

She swatted my arm. "You knew it before that. How?"

"It's something I picked up on pretty quickly."

She shook her head. "But how?" she repeated. "I have never told anyone because until you, I never realized how much I needed it. Craved it."

I shrugged, the cave floor hard beneath my shoulder blades. "I pay attention to you, Devon. I always have."

Her eyes flared and shuttered as a range of emotions played across her face. She shifted and tensed, before seeming to try and force herself to relax again.

I cradled her face with my hands. "I'm sorry. I shouldn't have said that. Take your time, Devon. I'm here. I'm not going anywhere."

She cupped my hand with hers and huffed out a dry laugh. "You might be the most emotionally mature man I've ever known, Aaron Joseph."

I grinned, desperate to keep her here, with me, and out of her head. "Thanks?"

She rolled over and stood, then held her hand out for mine. I took it and hauled myself up. She pulled her hair into place and nodded to the waterfall. "We should get back."

I leaned to kiss her, unwilling to let her shut down and knowing that touch was the way to do it. "Lead on."

16

DEVON

4 MONTHS, 28 DAYS TO GO

I launched the text to my brother without a second thought.

> We need to talk.

Worst phrase in the history of mankind.

> I thought that was 'I'm pregnant with twins'?

I'm currently watching those twins play in the bathtub since you're hanging out with my wife this evening.

> This house is a money pit.

So are my twins.

> You're a mechanic.

Last time I checked.

> What's your HVAC knowledge?

Fair to middling.

> I'll take that. When can you swing by?

This weekend?

> Sounds good. As thanks, I'll be sure to get your wife totally wasted tonight.

That's not how this works.

> That's exactly how this works.

I grinned and clicked my phone off, looking forward to this evening.

I felt...lighter. I couldn't explain it and if I looked too hard, things got fuzzy. Even though I'd been here just over a month and hadn't heard from any of the out-of-town jobs I'd applied for, I wasn't as worried as usual. No plan to speak of still made me itchy, but there were so many things to do at Gigi's that I couldn't honestly see myself leaving anytime soon. The air conditioner wasn't cooling the house below seventy-nine, the electrician hadn't managed to fix the issue upstairs, and now I had to deal with mold in the basement. And no way could I think about trying to redecorate the place or anything—everywhere I turned it was manufacturing delays and supply chain issues. There was no easy, or fast, way out of this.

But maybe it wouldn't be so bad if everything took more than six months. And even though it seemed impossible, because I fought the guilty memories of Jason near-daily since getting here, I was beginning to think that maybe I was okay with staying longer. Maybe it really was okay that I didn't have a job lined up.

Wait. Did I mean that? I patted my legs and arms, confirming I was indeed still here and I hadn't spontaneously combusted or something. This kind of thinking was very new. I felt my forehead: no fever.

Huh. If I told Ceci and Jodi, they'd know exactly who to blame: a certain hot paramedic who wasn't letting me focus nearly as much as I needed to.

I busied myself around the kitchen, needing to put the introspection aside. Because right now, it led me to thinking about the things Aaron did with his tongue, and the news I'd gotten at my check-up today. Which did not, unfortunately, bode well for *my* tongue. Or my jaw.

That whole "unwiring in two weeks" thing had become "we'll see you back in two weeks and don't plan on getting unwired" thing. I eyed the tequila and seriously considered a pre-game shot.

Beside me, Samson woofed and perked his ears.

"Hellooo," Jodi's voice called from the front. "Your two favorite women are here!"

Unable to help myself, I grinned and hollered back. "Then get into the kitchen and let's have some margaritas!"

Ceci came in first, clad in black yoga pants and t-shirt, her jean jacket in one hand and a bottle of tequila in another. Jodi was next, wearing a blue, polka-dotted A-line skirt and a white button down rolled at the sleeves. Her red lipstick was flawless as ever. She wrapped me in a hug, enveloping me in her coffee-and-pastry scent.

"Thanks for having us," Jodi said as she pulled away. "I needed this like you couldn't believe. Hey, Samson." She leaned down to pet him.

Ceci nodded and set the tequila down. "Same. I love your brother, Devon, but sometimes." She shook her head and hugged me.

I laughed as she released me and gestured to the blender. "I have a fix for that. Who wants a frozen margarita?"

"Bless your soul. And is that chips and salsa from Los Amigos?" Ceci asked.

I nodded. "Obviously. Just because I can't enjoy them doesn't mean you shouldn't. And tacos are warming in the oven."

Jodi blinked rapidly. "I might marry you."

"Oh good. I was on the market," I joked. I peered at her. "But...are you okay?"

She sniffed and waved her hand to fan away the tears that glistened. "I'm fine. Really. Let's have some margaritas first."

I looked at Ceci, who shrugged. I pointed at Jodi, my voice stern. "You're not fine. But let's get some food and drink in you, and then you're talking."

Jodi nodded and gave a watery grin, and we got to work pulling everything together. Within minutes we had a pitcher of frozen margaritas ready to roll, and they'd made their plates while I loaded up on a delightful spread of baby food. Sweet potatoes, green beans and bananas for the win. Yay. Feel the enthusiasm.

I led us to the dining room off the kitchen, which looked more than a little desolate now that I'd pulled all the 1980s-era flower pot paintings down. The walls were dark magenta, and the grain of the walnut sideboard, table, and chairs were also stained a deep color.

"This room is depressing," I commented, suddenly seeing it through their eyes. "Definitely should have left the paintings up."

Ceci looked around. "I guess you're right. We've spent so much time here that it never occurred to me how dark Gigi kept everything."

I nodded, thinking about the deep blue walls in the living room and the dingy tan flowered wallpaper in the kitchen. Only the bedrooms upstairs had anything close to redeeming value, with their brightly painted bedrooms and bathroom. Not that it mattered, since you couldn't see anything up there right now. I couldn't hold back my groan. "It's endless, the list of things to do. I swear this house is sabotaging me at every turn. And Miss

Betty next door, she keeps insisting I should turn this place into a bed-and-breakfast." I made a face and poured our margaritas. "She swears it won't go against the will *and* the historical society would be good with it. Well, all but Mrs. Withers."

Ceci looked at me thoughtfully.

I tilted my head and narrowed my eyes at her. "Don't do that."

Her eyes widened. "Do what?"

"That," I said, waving at her face. Whenever she got that look on her face, it meant she was scheming. I knew that she'd hold on to whatever idea it was like a dog with a bone. "Whatever *that* is, stop it."

She grinned. "Never."

I needed to change tactics. "Any word on finding a home for Samson?"

At the sound of his name, Samson appeared and jumped up onto a chair, his little scraggly body shaking with excitement as he surveyed our tacos.

I laughed and shooed him down. "Seriously. I'm still not feeding him."

"I saw water bowls," Jodi said. "Plural. One outside, and one inside. He's getting to you."

"He's not the only one," Ceci sing-songed.

"Shut it. We're talking about Samson." How was this going off-track so quickly? I took a gulp of my margarita.

"Give it up, girl. Samson has treated no one, and I mean *no one*, the way he treats you. He's yours, whether you want to admit it or not."

"I could say the same about someone else," Ceci said out of the side of her mouth.

I swatted her.

"People literally laugh when they see your pathetic sign at the coffee shop," Jodi continued. "I took it down today."

My eyes bugged. "What?" I'd put up a "Found" flyer at Daily

Dose two weeks ago, certain that someone would claim him. "I'm bringing a fresh one tomorrow."

Jodi laughed. "I'm just going to take it down. He's been here longer than you, and when you showed up, it was love at first sight."

Ceci coughed. "Again, I could say—ow!" she said, rubbing her arm from the punch I'd given her.

"We are not talking about Aaron," I said. "We're going to talk about Jodi, because we have consumed tacos and alcohol. So," I turned in the uncomfortable chair and gestured at Jodi. "Spill."

She sighed, then tilted her glass up to polish off her drink. I stood to pour her another, and she sipped it before beginning. "It's nothing."

I raised my eyebrows. "Clearly, based on the way you're taking down those margs."

"I'm losing my mom."

My stomach dropped through the floor. "Oh no, is she okay?" I should have visited her. She was literally ten minutes away. I was a terrible person.

"Oh my gosh, yes," Jodi said in a rush, putting her hands on mine. "She's not sick or anything. I'm so sorry."

I slumped with relief. "Oh, thank god."

Jodi continued. "But she's leaving. Moving to South Carolina to live with Nana, who's not doing so well."

A rush of memories flooded back. Driving with Jason and Jodi, the rest of their family in a separate car, to visit Jason's grandparents in Charleston every July and taking them to Isle of Palms for the fireworks, which they said were the best in the area. Going back for his grandfather's funeral, listening to his mom complain about Nana not wanting to move back here. I squeezed Jodi's hand. "I'm so sorry."

Jodi wiped at her eyes. "Thank you. It's just been me and

Mom for so long. Dad's…well, you know how Dad took off after Jason died."

I winced and reached across to squeeze a hand while Ceci grabbed the other. "I'm so sorry." I'd heard about his leaving from Gigi. The story was he'd wanted a divorce for years but never done anything about it. After Jason, he'd simply packed up and moved to Florida. They still weren't divorced.

"And forget about Miss Perfect Jess." A trace of venom lined her words.

I looked at Ceci, who widened her eyes. I sat back in my chair. "I thought we were good with Jess?"

"Well, we aren't," Jodi said. "She's the worst little sister anyone's ever had. She's a total mess but makes it seem she's got her shit together."

"Oh, goodie, a little sister worse than me," I joked.

Jodi waved my comment away. "You're nothing like Jess. She's a self-centered jerk who can't see beyond her nose to notice the rest of the world around her. Especially if that world includes her big sister."

Whether she meant it or not, Jodi's comment hit home. Over the past few weeks, I'd come to accept that my years of running had clouded my ability to notice Gigi's clear need for help with this house. Thing was, I hadn't taken into account how my leaving might have affected more people than just Gigi. I was looking at two of them right now.

"The point is, when Mom leaves, I won't have any family left here."

"Aw, babe, you've still got us," Ceci said.

My chest squeezed. I wanted to agree with Ceci and tell Jodi that I'd be here, but I didn't know if that was true. I didn't know if it *wasn't* true, but we weren't talking about me right now.

"She's already sold the house," Jodi continued.

I gasped. "What?"

She laughed sadly. "She didn't tell me anything. Wanted to wait until everything was finalized, she said, because she didn't want to upset me. Well, surprise!" she grit out. "I'm upset!" She took another big drink. "It gets better."

Wordlessly, I topped off her drink, then refilled mine and Ceci's. This room was getting darker and darker.

"I'd actually gone to her to talk about a loan. Apparently I was an idiot when I bought the shop because I didn't realize my payments were jumping. Like, by a lot. I can almost pull it off, but..."

"Um, your mom sold the house," Ceci said.

Jodi cut her eyes at Ceci. "I know."

"So, she has the money to help you with the payments," Ceci said, a look of exasperation on her face.

"Ha," Jodi said.

"What do you mean, 'ha'?" I asked, scooting forward. "Ceci's right. This is fixable."

"Not when your mom was so terrible with finances that the reason she sold the house was to get out from under it," she said, her voice cold. "There's no money. None. Zip. Zilch." She laughed bitterly. "At least I know who I get my financial wizardry from."

I looked at Ceci and grimaced. She shook her head.

"No," I said. "I refuse to think this isn't fixable. We can *do* something."

Jodi held up her hand. "Dev, I love you. I do. You're like a big sister to me. But right now, I'm not looking for your help to find a solution. I just want to drink and complain about it."

"Okay, but—"

"Uh-uh," she stopped me. "No buts."

"Fine," I said. "*And*—"

"Devon!" she said, exasperated. "I'll figure it out. Something always comes through. It has to, right?"

She sounded so hopeful and sad that all I could do was nod and smile. "Right." I raised my glass to hers and we drank.

"On that note," Ceci said, "I vote we clean up our tacos and take our drinks to the porch."

"Seconded," Jodi said. "This room really *is* depressing."

I stood. "So moved. Let's get out of here."

17

DEVON

4 MONTHS, 28 DAYS TO GO

O UTSIDE, THE SKY was darkening and the wind was cool in the early September evening. We settled onto the porch, me on the rocker and Ceci and Jodi on the swing. Samson considered his options, then jumped into my lap.

"Don't say it," I warned the other two as Samson made himself at home. I scratched his ears as he gave my other hand a lick.

"Don't say that he's definitely your dog?" Jodi said.

"And that there's a sale on dog food at the Piggly Wiggly?" Ceci chimed in.

I rolled my eyes. "Exactly. None of that." I looked down at Samson. "He *is* a good boy."

"The very best," Jodi said.

"Can we *please* talk about Aaron now?" Ceci said.

"Why do you immediately jump to Aaron every time we're talking about Samson?" I asked. "It's kind of weird."

"Oh please. Anyone can see that Samson's a metaphor for Aaron. Did you not read *any* of Gigi's romance books growing up? I've seen the collection she had."

I tipped my glass at her. "Fair. Fine. What do you want to know?"

Ceci squealed and Jodi perked up.

"Wait," I said, the alcohol loosening my tongue. Too bad it couldn't do the same for the wires. Ha. "Bad news first."

"You're not leaving," Jodi said.

My stomach clenched. "What? No." *Not at the moment, anyway.*

Ceci raised her glass. "Good. Then whatever it is, it can't be that bad." She chugged the drink.

I raised my eyebrows. "Depends on your version of what can't be that bad. Because my jaw doesn't get unwired in two weeks like I thought."

"Ha!" Ceci said.

"Oh, see, now that's just mean," I said.

"Sorry. You're right. I'm sorry."

I twisted my lips at her. "You're not sorry, you twisted woman." When she shrugged, basically admitting I was right, I continued. "Turns out the bone is taking longer to heal than they thought it would. No reason, either. Just 'wait and see.'"

Jodi grimaced. "That does stink."

"It does." Untold amounts of protein shakes stretched out in front of me.

"So back to Aaron," Ceci said.

"Are you sure you want to hear this?" I asked Jodi.

Jodi stopped the swing and gripped the seat with both hands, leaning forward to make her point. "Devon. I don't know how to be any clearer. I loved Jason. You loved Jason. Jason is dead."

I flinched.

"Sorry," she said, her voice softening. "But he is. I'm not saying you have to move on. But damn, woman. You have really got to think about moving on."

I swallowed. "What if I'm not ready?"

"It's been five years. We've been through this. It's no one's job to tell you when you're ready or not, but shit, Devon. *Five. Years.*" She shook her head. "Hell, my own mother seems to be moving on; she sold my childhood home. Never mind that she and Dad can't bother with a divorce. But still. If she can find a way to move on, then maybe you can do the same."

I polished off the drink and leaned over to pour another, grateful I'd refilled the pitcher before we came outside. Samson shifted and glanced at me, as if to chastise me for disturbing him.

"You're scared," Ceci declared.

"Fuck you," I shot back, then widened my eyes. "Holy shit. Did I say that? I'm sorry."

Ceci laughed and waved it away. "It's okay. Between laughing at you for being wired longer than you thought and this, it seems I hit a nerve."

I heaved a sigh. "Maybe."

"Um, *definitely*," Jodi said.

"Okay, so let's talk about Aaron!" I said, "Because I am nothing if not confused, and I don't want to talk about the Jason part."

Jodi and Ceci exchanged a look. "Are you following this?" Ceci asked her.

"Nope," Jodi said. "But I am not even close to being sober, so maybe that's why?"

Ceci scrunched her face, considering. "Yeah. Same." She launched their swing back into action and tipped her glass in my direction. "Spill," she commanded. "Your words. Not your drink."

I clapped my hands, pleasantly buzzed and happy to let it take me wherever it wanted to. "Yay! So, Aaron." I leaned forward, squishing Samson. "Have you *seen* that man in his uniform?"

Ceci laughed and clapped. "*Now* we're talking!"

"Every day he's on shift, yeah," Jodi said, a grin spreading across her face. "The better question is: you been underneath him yet?"

I nodded. "Yup." They squealed, and I continued as the alcohol warmed me in the cool night air. "The man has a six-pack. At least, that's what it felt like. I haven't actually seen it yet."

Ceci lurched the swing forward. "Continue. I need this information in my life, seeing as how my dear husband is getting perilously close to rocking a dad bod. Not that he doesn't know what to do with that bod, but still."

I waved my hands. "Stop. I can't hear about you and my brother. Not from him, and not from you."

She raised an eyebrow. "He talking about me?"

I laughed. "*No*. And we're keeping it like that."

She harrumphed.

I continued. "You ever hiked Noccalula Falls? Gone to the waterfall?"

"I've heard it's beautiful, but no," Jodi said as Ceci shook her head.

"So he took me there a week ago. There's a secluded spot right behind it and, um," I stalled, taking a drink. How much did I want to tell them?

They leaned forward, drinks in hand. "You can't stop there," Ceci said.

So I told them, crossing my legs and shifting in my chair as my body relived the moment.

"Outside?" Jodi said, her mouth still agog. "He... you...*outside?*"

I laughed. "I assure you I stopped thinking about where I was pretty damn fast."

Jodi cackled and gave me a high five as they swung close. "I *knew* he looked happier these past few days. Also, I'm super jealous. I could use a boyfriend to get my mind off things." She grinned wickedly.

I grinned back, my whole body warm with the memory of Aaron's tongue between my legs, the attention he'd lavished on me.

Wait. Did she say...? "He's, um, we're not...he's not my boyfriend."

"Relax, Dev," Jodi said. "I didn't say he was. I said I needed a boyfriend. I totally want you to stay in town, but I'm not labeling your life."

I swallowed. "Thanks." Then I remembered what Aaron had said. I leaned forward. "Speaking of hot Joseph men, is there maybe a brother you've got your eyes on?"

Jodi blushed and looked away. "Nope."

I pointed at her. "Ha! Not true! Look at your face!"

Ceci peered at her. "Is it Will? He's so...*stern.*"

I laughed. "You like a good stern daddy, Ceese? Wait. Don't answer that."

She waggled her eyebrows. "You know, your brother is *very* —"

"La la la, I can't hear you," I sang and plugged my ears with my fingers.

"Fine, fine, back to Jodi."

Jodi avoided both our gazes.

"It's Price," I said.

At his name, Jodi blushed even harder. "Shut it, you two. He doesn't know I exist, and that's fine."

I shook my head. "We need to do something about this."

"No! No no no," she said, her eyes wide and pleading. "Please no. Drop it."

Ceci and I shared a look. "It's nice not to be the center of everyone's romantic attention for once," I said. "But we'll let it go. For now."

Darkness fell and I lit some candles, the three of us drinking and talking for hours. Eventually, my brother pulled the minivan into the driveway and he got out. "Ladies," he said, tipping his baseball cap as he stepped onto the porch.

"Husband!" Ceci slurred, launching herself off the swing and into his arms. "Why are you here? Where are the kids? Oh gosh," she hiccuped, "what time is it?"

Rick chuckled. "Sounds like y'all have had yourself a fine time of it."

I smiled and tipped my nearly empty glass at him. "We have indeed." Although I hadn't had nearly as much as the other two, seeing as how I was basically on a liquid diet and wasn't interested in a tequila-infused hangover.

"I called our neighbor over to man the house while I came and got you two home," he said. "No way are you driving."

Ceci went on her tiptoes, still wrapped around Rick, and whispered something in his ear. Even in the dim candlelight, he turned beet red.

Jodi and I giggled as she stood up and wobbled. "Seems we need to get a move-on," she said, then bent down to pick up her shoes.

As we said our goodbyes, Aaron's truck pulled up in front of the house.

Ceci, still being held up by Rick, squealed and pointed. "Lookie! Dev, it's Aaron!"

Rick laughed and it was my turn to blush a vegetable shade of red. "Oh my god, please take her home."

"Let's go, love of my life," Rick said, pulling Ceci down the stairs and to the car. He waved at me and turned to Jodi. "You, too. Come on."

"Got it," she said, taking the steps a hair too fast. She was definitely more sober than Ceci, but at this point, that wasn't saying much.

Aaron got out of the truck and Samson bolted to him, eager for a new pair of hands to pet him. Aaron leaned to give him a scratch, then straightened, his eyes immediately landing on mine. His lips tilted in a smile meant only for me, and it sent a zing right through my core.

"Aaron, you're a *beast*," Ceci yelled.

Oh god. I was going to kill her, and then die myself. "Ceci!" I called. "Shut *up!*"

"What?" she said. "Am I wrong?"

Dying. I was dying. Mortified, I covered my face with my hands, then peeked through them as Jodi pin-balled into Aaron. He helped her into the minivan as Rick corralled Ceci into the front.

Finally, Rick reversed the car out of my driveway and Aaron turned to me, his eyes twinkling. "A beast, huh? Exactly what did you tell those two?"

"What gets said on this porch stays on this porch," I answered playfully. "So I'm not at liberty to say."

"Is that so?" he said, his voice dropping low.

I nodded, my mouth going dry as he stalked to me, his eyes darkening with every step. Without a word, he crowded me, walking me backwards, until my back pressed against the screen door. My body heated as he caged me with his arms, getting so close I had to tilt my head up to look at him. His irises were a storm, dark blue mixing in with the gray. He dipped his head and I breathed him in, dizzy with want.

"Did you tell them how I made you come, Devon?" he asked, his voice husky and deep. His mouth hovered above mine. "Where my hands were? What my tongue did?"

Jesus *Christ*. I closed my eyes and groaned.

His lips captured mine, insistent and greedy. He wrapped his hands around my waist and pulled me to him, and I melted against his body. We matched like puzzle pieces, fitting into each other, hard against soft, silently giving and taking. He tilted my head as I pushed a hand into his hair, which was just long enough for me to grip it. He growled.

I wrenched away and gasped. "The things I'm going to do to you when my mouth can open," I grit out.

His tightened his hands around my waist and closed his eyes, clenching his jaw and seeming to try to get control of himself. After a moment, he let go. "You're going to kill me before then."

I grinned naughtily. "Same." I stepped away from him and blew out the candles, then grabbed the empty glasses. "Come inside?"

He nodded, then opened the screen and front doors for me.

Naturally, I stumbled on my way in. He stepped forward and grabbed my arm to steady me. "Just how drunk are you?"

I leaned into him to feel his warmth and hummed. "A teensy little bit," I admitted.

"Let's get you upstairs." He took the glasses from me and set them on the coffee table. "I'll clean up."

"What? No," I said, attempting to move around him and failing miserably.

He laughed softly. "Come on. I'll just tidy things, not scrub your kitchen sink. Okay?"

I'd like to think that it was drunkenness that caused me to sway lightly as I stared at his gorgeous face. But. It was probably the offer to clean.

Also, was it the tequila that had me this flushed, or was it him?

I grinned.

He laughed louder, a deep belly-laugh that sent shivers up and down my spine. "You're a mess. Come on, sweetheart. Up you go."

I grabbed the battery-powered lantern at the foot of the stairs with a flourish and turned it on, then let him lead me upstairs and to my bedroom.

"Also, super-bad news," I said. "Wires are on indefinitely."

He grinned wolfishly. "Doesn't mean we can't have fun other ways."

My body flushed and I stumbled over a step. He caught me, his laugh a low rumble, and pulled me closer.

Once we got to my room, I sat the lantern inside the doorway.

"Um, Devon?"

I hummed.

"Did Barbie decorate this room?"

I swept the room, taking in the deep pink comforter and light pink walls, the white dresser and bed frame. Honestly, at this point, it was the only room not a complete shit show. "I liked pink growing up," I sniffed. "And Gigi never did anything halfway."

"You're adorable." He turned me to him.

"And *you're* smoking hot." It was late, I was maybe a little drunker than I was going to admit, and I was tired of being careful. Careful not to let anyone get too close. Careful not to let *myself* get too close. Careful to keep the memory of my dead husband wrapped around me like a security blanket.

What if I tried it? Tried letting myself live for more than just the moment, and opened myself up to actually *feel* something?

Aaron pulled me to him. "Smoking hot, huh?" he repeated, his eyes dancing.

I nodded like a bobblehead. "Yep. And...."

He tilted his head and studied me. "And?"

"And I think maybe I like you."

He smiled broadly. "You finally admitting that?"

I kept bobbing my head. "Yep." I ran my hands over his t-shirt, feeling the taut muscles of his chest and abs beneath it.

"That's good, because I like you, too."

"Question."

"Answer."

"Did I tell you that when I was coming out of anesthesia?"

His eyes danced in the dim light. "You did."

"Why didn't you say anything?"

"Because no one should be held accountable for the things they say when they're not completely in charge of their minds."

His hands were hot on my waist. I wanted them in several other places. I gripped his shirt. "You should take this off."

He let out a soft groan. "I would like nothing more than to give you whatever you want, but—"

"No buts," I interrupted, then reached around to cup the back of his jeans. "Unless we're talking about this butt. In which case." I waggled my eyebrows.

He laughed. "*But* you're not sober. I can't take advantage of that. As much as I'd love to," he planted a soft kiss on my forehead, "it's bedtime for you."

I pushed my lips into a pout even as I let him guide me to sit down on the bed. "Bedtime is stupid."

He kneeled to pull off my shoes and socks, and my center throbbed from the nearness of his mouth. I felt his breath on my knee, and wanted it higher.

He looked up at me, his gaze heated. "Bedtime is necessary."

"Ugh," I said, flopping back into the softness of the comforter.

He straightened, taking my ankles in his hand and pulling me gently into sleeping position. Then he leaned over so I was between his arms as his fists pushed the bed down on either side of me. I was surrounded by him, breathing in his oceany scent and drowning in the deep gray of his eyes. He bent down and kissed me, soft and sweet, before straightening his arms once more. "I'd love to help you get ready for bed, but I don't have that level of self-control."

I blinked slowly, lulled into quiet by this beautifully thoughtful man. Still surrounded by him and holding his gaze, I cradled his jaw and felt the blond stubble that barely showed. "Thank you," I said softly.

"For what?"

"Just. Thank you." I couldn't say more. My throat tightened.

He bent down and feathered kisses on me, tracing a path across my cheeks, nose, forehead, and eyes, forcing them closed, before lifting off the bed.

I kept my eyes closed as I heard him back away and pick up the lantern. Then the room clicked into darkness. From the doorway, he spoke, his voice low, scraping across my heart.

"Whatever you want, Devon, I'm yours. However, whenever, wherever."

I opened my lips to speak, but nothing came out.

He turned and left.

18

AARON

I ROLLED OVER and came face to face with Daisy's brindle face, mouth open, tongue out, breathing some major morning dog breath in my face.

Pretty much the opposite of the dream I'd been having, which involved a naked Devon, with no wired jaw, in my bed, and a night stretching out in front of me.

Daisy leaned forward and licked my cheek, snuffling as she did so.

"I know, I know." I sat up and got out of the bed. "Good morning and where's your breakfast."

Daisy circled and jumped, knowing what came next.

I headed to the kitchen and let her out the back door, then drank a glass of water. Memories of last night warmed my chest. Had all of that really happened? Jaw wired shut or not, she'd been wide open for me. She'd also been drunk, so was it the tequila talking or was she really ready to dive into something?

Through the window above the sink, I watched Daisy race back to the door. I let her in, then fed and watered her.

I wanted this to be different. I wanted Devon to be different. And I was an absolute idiot for it.

I'd planned to spend the day as far away from the firehouse as possible, but that would have entailed me planning ahead and ensuring I had basic necessities like coffee and food at my house. So I got ready, and Daisy and I hopped in my truck, Daisy's body wiggling with excitement, and we headed to the Daily Dose.

The bell over the door chimed as I walked into a packed shop. I took my place in line, Daisy safely outside accepting pets from passersby, and nodded at the person in front of me. Our little town wasn't as little as it used to be, but I still recognized most folks. Some of that was the paramedic gig, but most of that was a fact of growing up here.

Jodi smiled brightly at me as I approached. "Fun seeing you last night at Devon's house."

My chest warmed at the memory. "You, too. How are you feeling?"

She winked. "I'm young. I'm still friends with tequila."

I chuckled, remembering Ceci. "Wonder how Ceci's feeling this morning."

She snorted. "Probably regretted it the second she and Rick had to wake up to handle the twins. Makes me glad I don't have any. Your usual?"

I nodded. "And a bag of beans to go, please."

She rang me up and turned to pull everything together. Before she handed it to me, she leaned forward and lowered her voice. "Hey."

"Yeah?"

She cast her eyes down and paused, then looked back up. "It's great to see you so happy. You know? You deserve it."

I blinked, taken aback. "Thanks, Jodi." We'd known each other for literal decades, but this was the first time she'd ever been so serious, so frank with me. So I countered. "Are you okay?"

Instantly her eyes watered and she straightened, pushing my

coffee and beans to me on the counter. "I'll be fine," she said, throwing her smile back on and blinking furiously. "Have a good day!"

I grunted and studied her as I grabbed my cup. What was going on with her?

The bell chimed and announced another customer. It was Devon. She looked radiant, the early morning sun catching her crystal-blue eyes as they scanned the shop. Her wavy hair framed her face, and I wanted to run my lips along the curve of her bare neck. She wore an Aerosmith t-shirt and black leggings, and as I checked out her legs I decided that leggings were one of the greatest inventions of all time.

She broke into a smile as her eyes landed on me, and I swear it felt like I grew a foot in height. "Aaron."

I swept her into a hug. She tightened her grip on me, and I could have died a happy man right there in the coffee shop.

"Good morning," I said, warmth infusing my words.

She tipped up and sealed her mouth over mine in a kiss that was probably too long for a coffee shop, but damned if I was going to stop it. Her lips were so soft, and she smelled so good. I was in heaven. I pulled her tighter with my free hand, feeling her round curves against me.

She broke the kiss and beamed, her eyes diamond bright. "I didn't think I'd see you this morning, but I was out with Samson and he saw Daisy, so I figured..." she shrugged and gave me another smile.

It was official. I'd died and gone to heaven. I squeezed her hip. "I'm glad you stopped."

"I wish you hadn't last night," she murmured. Then her eyes widened and her cheeks reddened. "I can't believe I said that out loud."

I chuckled. "I can."

She leaned into me, butting her head against my chest before looking back up. "My mouth is developing a habit of saying things before my brain catches up."

I pushed a tendril of hair away from her face. "I'm not mad about it."

She smiled. "Well. At least we know where we stand."

I started running emergency protocols through my head to take my mind off the searing-hot scenarios that immediately sprang to mind, all of them involving a Devon with no clothes, and squeezed my eyes shut. "We do," I choked out.

She laughed. "What are you up to today? Don't you have the day off?"

I noticed she didn't move back. We still stood close, her chest to mine, my hand on her hip. The shop may as well not have existed. "I do."

"You want to come over later? I promise I'll behave," she said, even as a mischievous smile grew. "Mostly."

I kept running those scenarios. "Definitely. I'll text you?"

She nodded. "You will."

I tilted her face to mine and studied it, lost in the possibility of where this might be going. Was this really happening?

"Knock it off!" Jodi called out. "This is a family place."

I turned and she grinned. "You two are kind of sickening. Obviously I've already texted Chief."

I stepped away from Devon and rolled my eyes. "Of course you did." Because I couldn't do anything without Chief or my brothers knowing, including saying hello to my...Wait. Was I about to call her my girlfriend? Is that what we were?

I wasn't asking. I knew enough to not push this. I took another step back. "I'll see you later."

As I walked outside, the bell dinging above me, my phone buzzed. My chest warmed. Was she texting me already? I held off checking, stopping instead to give Samson a pet and then get myself and Daisy situated in the truck. I took a healthy sip of my coffee and pulled my phone out, but the grin died as soon as I read it.

> UNKNOWN
>
> I'm coming into town soon. Planning a dinner at Will's place.

My stomach turned and a sour taste formed in my mouth, my high of seconds ago now dead and buried under the weight of the words I read over and over.

It was like this every time. I never knew when I'd see her. Her number changed constantly because she couldn't hold a job long enough to pay for a plan, so she just rotated burner phones. Price and Will seemed to trace her movements better than me, but only marginally. I didn't know why they bothered. She sure as hell didn't care. When was the last time she'd reached out for a holiday? I'd be shocked if she even remembered my birthday.

I could practically see Will frowning and telling me I needed to give her a chance.

Well, Will could fuck right off.

> Who is this?

The dots started, then stopped. She was going to have to say it.

Beside me, Daisy whined and pawed at my leg. I reached over and petted her. At least I had one constant woman in my life, even if she was four-legged.

My phone buzzed.

> UNKNOWN
>
> Mom.

I clenched my jaw. She didn't deserve the title. Not after she'd left and didn't look back. No note, no nothing. Gone. I'd gotten myself up and ready for school like always, knowing Dad was on shift at the station and she'd be passed out in their bedroom, because she was drinking a lot and only behaved when Dad was home to monitor her. Will and Price were already gone, both of them picked up for early-morning middle school football practice. I didn't play football, plus I was only in fifth grade, so Dad had made sure I knew the bike route to take to school and considered the job handled.

It's funny, how even now I can still feel the weight of the house, how it always felt like I was moments away from being crushed.

I'd left for school, locking the door to a silent house. And even though I didn't see Mom's car in the driveway, I figured she was somewhere else: a bar, maybe, or a friend's, sleeping it off. It wasn't until I'd come home and found my brothers waiting on me, dual expressions of sympathy and resignation in their eyes, that I understood.

I'd been the last one standing, and it hadn't mattered. *I* hadn't mattered.

I tossed the phone into the cup holder, started the car and headed home, trying desperately to remember the feeling I'd had when Devon wrapped her arms around me.

19

AARON

I LOOKED AROUND my living room, assessing it. Devon was coming over and I'd spent the morning cleaning, much to Daisy's confusion.

She sat on her haunches in front of me now, her sweet brindle face turned up at me, eyes big and pleading.

"I know, girl. You want a treat for being so helpful, don't you?"

Ears perking at the word, she yipped and headed for the kitchen.

I followed to give her the treat I'd promised, then took a shower and headed to get Devon. I'd practically had to extract a blood oath from the woman to let me pick her up instead of Wanda, the town's only regular Uber driver. She cherished her independence like nothing else.

Thanks to my work schedule, I'd not seen Devon at all this past week. Chief had us doing some annual training, and I'd had to cover for another guy when he got sick. Devon seemed intent on punishing me for "leaving her hanging" on girls' night, as she put it, and had taken to sending me increasingly sexual texts that had me about crawling out of my skin.

She met me at her door, stepping out in a dark yellow, figure-hugging t-shirt dress. At least, I thought that's what it was. I was too busy letting my eyes drive around her curves.

"Damn, lady. Get over here." I pulled her into my arms as I growled, then nuzzled below her ear, delighting in the giggles it produced.

"You like?" She crossed her wrists behind my neck and preened.

"I like," I said, dropping a kiss on her lips. "Ready to come see my place?"

It was a weekend, so I drove through the square. Our firehouse, and Jodi's coffeeshop, were on one side, and across the way was a local bookstore, the only barber shop worth going to, and some kind of lady boutique that I didn't understand. There were other shops dotting the square, but too many empty ones for my taste, as well.

But today, the square bustled. The grass in the center was thick and lush, welcoming the families and dogs that were on it. I counted at least five people with coffee from Jodi's and waved at that many more.

"You love this, don't you?" Devon teased.

I chuckled and gestured at the sun glinting off the wires in her mouth. "You're one to talk, you know."

She faked a pout, then recovered. "I just mean the way everyone seems to know you. How small this place still is."

"It's my home," I said simply. As we came to a stop, I wove my fingers through hers.

Her answering squeeze was enough.

A few minutes later, I pulled into my driveway and tried to see the house from her eyes. It was one story, white with crimson shutters—crimson specifically, as my one nod to my alma mater. Spindly rose bushes dotted the front, their tight pink buds wishing for water. A giant oak tree towered over the left corner of the yard and shaded the street, and a crimson door winked out from a small porch nestled in the center of the house.

She grinned at me. "Is now when I tell you I'm secretly an Auburn fan?"

"You wouldn't dare," I deadpanned.

Winking, she got out of the cab. "You're right. Orange isn't a good look on me. Your house is cute from the outside; now show me the inside."

I waved her in front of me, my gaze snagging on her ass, the way she sauntered up the steps and cocked her hip.

Evil woman. She smirked, knowing exactly what she was doing.

Forcing myself to keep my hands off her body, I opened the door, immediately making way for Daisy's full-bodied greeting of wiggles. Devon gave her the requisite pets, then straightened and took in her surroundings.

"This is my living room."

"Looks like a bachelor lives here," she said.

"I haven't spent a lot of time on it," I admitted. It was bright and roomy, and sparsely furnished: couch, flat-screen mounted on the wall, coffee table, area rug. So far, I'd let the walls remain white and the furniture bring the color. "I don't want to buy things just to fill the space. I want pieces that mean something. Pieces with history and permanence."

She looked at me thoughtfully. "Of course you do."

I grabbed her hand and rubbed her wrist with my thumb. "Come on. There's more to see."

The kitchen was next, sitting off a small dining room beside the living area.

"This is huge," she said.

I leered at her. "That's what she said."

She rolled her eyes, and they were filled with mirth. "Really?"

I grinned. "Made you laugh."

But the kitchen really *was* big. Lots of counter space, a spot for an island that I hadn't committed to yet, and a breakfast nook that I couldn't find the perfect table and chairs for. But I had plans. Plans of cooking for lots of people. I wanted the big family events with friends and neighbors, backyard barbecues for no reason, other peoples' kids running around, all of it. After the comment about history and permanence, though, I kept that part to myself. "I like to cook. You know that."

She reached for my cheek, palming it as she tipped onto her toes to kiss me. Her eyes sparkled. "I do. You owe me a meal, in fact. But for now, show me the rest."

Off the kitchen was the deck and backyard, which were the reasons I'd bought the house. I watched Devon's expression as she took it in. The property was half an acre of grass, wide open and ready for games of tag and catch, nights spent counting the stars, or huddled in tents. Beyond it was a forest, tiny for the most part, but perfect and safe for kids to get lost in them for hours.

But the deck was the real star. It was a sprawling extension of the house, stretching and tapering into the yard, but I'd seen far more potential. I'd added a fire pit and a bench to surround it, designated a place for an outdoor kitchen that wasn't there yet, but I'd already thrown sail shades over the area. One smaller section, off the master bedroom, was screened in and boasted a high-powered ceiling fan and more succulents than one man should own. I'd lined the whole of it with tiny lights that gave off a warm glow.

When I knew what I wanted, it was easy enough to make it happen. At least, when it came to *things*. People—Devon—were a whole other story.

"Holy shit, Aaron—you've been holding out on me," she said now, her voice full of wonder.

I grinned and mimicked her question of earlier. "You like it?"

She swatted my arm and let me pull her into my arms. "It's beautiful."

"Not as beautiful as you," I said, stealing another kiss.

I made to pull away, but she held me tighter. What I wouldn't give to sink my tongue into her mouth, to taste her, to finally feel what it was like to have all of her. My dick stirred, and Devon gave a low laugh.

"Something going on down there?" she murmured, running her hand down my stomach.

I caught her hand before it reached its destination. "I promised you a tour of the house," I said.

Her lips tilted into a smile. "Show me the bedroom, then."

"You're incorrigible."

"Ooh, big word from a big guy," she purred, then giggled again as I led her back into the house.

I glanced at her, taking in her bright eyes, her slightly-flushed cheeks. I loved her. I was a fool for it, I knew it, but I loved her.

Down the hall we went, and I pointed out the bathroom and guest rooms. I stepped back as we got to the master, letting her go in first and take it all in. It was basic, same as the living room in that it had only the essentials. For me, that meant an area rug to sink my toes into, navy blackout curtains, a king-size bed, and an antique dresser.

She waggled her eyebrows. "This where the magic happens?"

I swallowed. "No."

She stopped, tilting her head. "No?"

My neck burned and I rubbed it. "I've never brought anyone here, Devon. Only you." My voice was rough.

Her eyes softened as she closed the distance to me. "That means…"

I held her gaze.

"Was that a master bath I saw?"

I narrowed my eyes in confusion. "Yes, but—"

Wordlessly, she pulled her dress off, the fabric slipping up and away from her skin. She wore a black cotton bra and black panties, and my mouth watered at the sight of them against her tan skin.

"Let's take a shower."

20

DEVON

4 MONTHS, 21 DAYS TO GO

 ARON'S CHEST HEAVED as he looked at me, his eyes heating my skin as it traveled over every inch. This man.

This beautiful, sweet, incredibly sexy man was going to ruin me, and I planned on fighting it until the bitter end.

"Get undressed," I commanded softly, then headed for the bathroom, knowing he'd follow.

I turned the shower on, and when he appeared, he wore only underwear. I sucked in a breath as I took in the expanse of light golden skin, happy for a moment that my jaw was wired shut because otherwise it'd have hit the floor. "Jesus, Aaron. Did you just come from a firehouse photo shoot or something?"

He hummed a small laugh, standing still for my inspection. My god, he was a sight to behold. His shoulders were beautifully broad, the muscles rippling with each small movement he made. His chest was smattered with blond hair, and tapered down to an honest to god six-pack. His muscles had settled into themselves in a way that only came with age, lean and sinewy and compact. Black briefs hung low on his hips, giving me a clear view of the divots leading to his cock, which strained against the fabric. My tongue hit the back of my teeth, desperate for escape. Heat pooled between my legs.

"Shower," I said, my voice brooking no dissent. "Now." I pulled my hair into the elastic I'd had on my wrist and started to shuck my panties.

His eyes darkened as he moved to still my hands. "I'll be the one issuing commands, Devon." His voice was low as he nipped at the sensitive skin beneath my ear. "And I'll be the one to undress you the rest of the way."

My pulse spiked as his tongue laved at my neck and he crowded me against the sink, his skin hot on mine as the cold of the porcelain counter bit into my lower back. He was everywhere, filling my senses, his arms caging me, his mouth on my chest. I gasped as he thrust his leg between mine, giving me the pressure I so desperately needed.

He knew. He knew exactly what I needed and I almost hated him for it. Almost.

Pleasure overrode my brain, and I pushed his briefs down, feeling his cock spring free and press against my belly. He unhooked my bra and took it off, and as his hands wrapped around my breasts and squeezed, I managed to shove my panties off. Instantly his leg was back between my thighs, and I ground shamelessly on him, my need for release the only thing I knew.

His hand moved down and he hissed as his fingers found my slit. "Already so wet for me, Devon?"

I nodded, focused only on the pleasure he was giving me.

He picked me up as if I weighed nothing, setting me on top of the cold counter and sinking to his knees. "Spread for me, baby."

I obeyed. "This isn't why I brought you in here," I managed to say.

He grinned as though he'd gotten away with something.

"Too bad." With his eyes on mine, he licked my folds, then immediately went to my clit.

"Oh, fuck." My head fell back and I closed my eyes, unable to hold the intensity of his gaze with his mouth on me at the same time.

His tongue was magic, licking and swirling around every part of my pussy. My hips moved of their own volition, meeting his mouth again and again, and his answering praise only pushed me higher. He pulled my legs onto his back and my heels dug in as I gripped the counter.

His hands wrapped around my legs and squeezed right as his teeth grazed my clit, and I bucked. "Holy *shit*." He hummed as he licked and sucked, sending threads of electric pleasure through me. Even my head tingled, it was so good. My nipples peaked in the steam billowing from the shower. I felt the orgasm building, the threads gathering together, centering into one tight ball of delicious pressure.

"Aaron, I'm going to—"

My whole body shook as I came, streaks of bliss coursing through me as I pulsed on his tongue.

Aaron hummed and whispered softly against me, easing me down from the climax. After a moment, as I heaved a soft *"fuck,"* he rose and gathered me to him.

I peppered kisses along his chest and willed strength to return to my legs while he squeezed me tight. "That might have just altered my brain chemistry," I said against his skin.

He laughed, the sound low and rumbly against my lips.

Strength restored, I slid off the counter, running my hands over his chest and abs, then around to his ass. "Now it's time for the shower," I said, stepping in and pulling him with me.

He closed the shower door behind him and I took a moment to appreciate what was going on in here. It was a walk-in, but it was as though there were two of them combined together: two shower heads, and two built-in seats. Only one was going, so I stepped under it and pulled Aaron with me.

Water sluiced down our bodies as we held each other. I tipped my head back to wet my hair, then rotated us so that Aaron stood beneath the stream. With a wicked smirk of my lips, I sank to my knees.

"Devon—"

"My turn," I said, cutting him off. It wouldn't be a standard blow job, of course, but if I was careful, I could have some fun.

His dick was heavy as I took it in my hands, thick and twitching with anticipation. I rubbed my lips along its length as Aaron hissed above me. I fisted the base of him with one hand, pumping lightly as I wound my lips to the tip.

"Fuck, baby," he moaned above me.

I adjusted my position on the tile, but before I could do more, his hands pulled me up.

"But no." The word was a growl, even as his thumb caressed my jaw. "I'll wait until those wires are off. You can do something else for me instead."

I raised my eyebrows in silent inquiry as he angled the shower head toward one of the seats, then he sat me down and regarded me, his body blocking the spray. His gaze slid to my breasts, then back up to my eyes.

Wordlessly, I grabbed the soap and lathered up, watching his eyes darken as my hands wound around my breasts, squeezing and pinching my nipples. I sat up straight and grabbed his cock, swollen and heavy, and used it to tug him closer.

"You want to fuck my tits, Aaron?"

He groaned, his eyes shutting tight before focusing again on me. "Absofuckinglutely, baby."

I pulled him close and wrapped my tits around him, thankful they were big enough to make this work. As he began, I held my breasts tight, getting off on the feel of him slicking between them, velvet and hot.

He watched me, his eyes hooded, his mouth set in a hard line. One hand braced on the tile behind me as water ran down his heaving chest, and his abs were clenched.

"Fuck, Devon. *Fuck*." He was breathless.

God, I wanted more. The inability to take his dick into my mouth, to feel him hit the back of my throat, to hold him there as he came, was infuriating.

I squirmed on the seat, needing a release of my own. Aaron stopped, stepping away from me and hauling me up.

"Do you need me as bad as I need you?" he said, his forehead against mine, his voice rough.

I nodded, desperate, empty. "Condom," I bit out.

He cursed and nodded. We rinsed and stepped out of the shower and he took my hand, guiding us wet and dripping to the bed.

I scrambled onto the navy comforter, fully expecting him to follow, but he paused, running his hand over his face as he looked at me.

"Aaron," I breathed.

He crawled on the bed, and I lay down as he trailed hot kisses up my calf to my thigh, stomach, breast, and finally to my neck and mouth. He paused, his lips inches from mine. "Do you have any idea how stunning you are? These curves. Christ, Devon, they have haunted me."

My heart pinched. I ignored it. "Touch me," I begged. All rational thought had flown out of my head. I only wanted him.

His eyes finally left mine, dropping to my breasts as his hands came up to cup them. I let out a sigh of relief, then moaned as he pulled my nipples between his fingers and squeezed, hard.

"You like that, don't you?" he murmured, leaning back to hover his lips over mine.

"I like everything," I whimpered. "You *know* that. I need…"

He caught my mouth with his, swallowing my groan as he

hauled me flush against him, his cock against my stomach. Wrenching his mouth from mine, he angled up and toward the bedside table. In seconds he was rolling a condom on.

As he lowered his body onto mine, I exhaled in pleasure. The weight of him on me, the solidness of him, nearly sent me over the edge. I'd not done this with another man in years, literal years, not once I understood it never chased the loneliness away, and the reality of what we were about to do made my breath quicken.

"Devon?" He braced himself on his forearms, his expression soft but concerned. "Are you okay?"

I'd gone still beneath him. *Was* I okay? With a start, I realized I was. I was better than okay. I nodded, a smile blooming across my face. "Yeah."

His brow smoothed. "Are you sure? Because we—"

I stopped him with a kiss. "I'm sure." Then I grinned saucily, needing to change the mood. "What happened to the man issuing commands?"

His eyes darkened and his jaw ticked. "You want that?"

I didn't answer.

Taking my silence as a yes, Aaron grabbed my wrists and yanked them above my head, holding them in one strong hand while his other moved to my breast and squeezed. He leaned to it, pulling the nipple deep into his mouth and sending me into orbit.

I squirmed, wiggling my hips in a needy attempt to line him up at my entrance.

He smacked my hip with a light pop, surprising me enough that I stopped. My eyes went wide as I beheld him.

"You want to be commanded?" he asked, his voice gruff.

I swallowed, my pulse ratcheting up even as I grew wetter.

"Answer me."

"Yes." My voice was a whisper.

"Spread for me. Wide."

I obeyed.

He grunted his approval and bent back to my breast, his hand staying tight on my wrists. Streaks of pleasure bolted through me as he again pulled my nipple into his mouth, and I fought to stay still. But I wanted this. Wanted him. The safety of him, the certainty. The solid weight of him as his hips thrust against mine, still not giving me what I craved.

"I need you," I whispered.

"You'll wait."

The emptiness inside of me was an ache, pulsing with desire. My eyes rolled back into my head as he took his free hand and moved it down to my center. "Please."

He palmed me and squeezed, and I moaned.

"Fuck, Devon," he said above me. "You are spectacular. Look at you." He released my wrists and I moved my hands to his muscular ass. He squeezed between my thighs again and teased my entrance with a finger. "So needy. You want something?" He pressed the finger in just a little more.

"Your cock," I gasped. *"Please."*

"I like you begging," he growled, laving my breasts and licking a trail up my neck. "When that mouth gets opened..." he trailed off.

Without warning, he moved his hand and thrust into me, burying himself to the hilt in one smooth motion.

"Aaron!" I yelled.

He groaned and stilled as my walls fluttered around him. He squeezed his eyes shut, his head lowering. "Fuck."

"Finally." Finally I was full. I kissed his shoulder as he pulled out and pushed in again.

"Devon, my god."

"More. I need more."

He fucked me slow and deep, rolling his hips, exploring and feeling. I moaned with the pleasure of it, the bliss of him pushing into me over and over. He whispered sweet words to me as he moved above me, and I was nearly out of my head not being able to kiss him. It was torture. I couldn't take it anymore.

I dug my nails into his ass and caught his gaze. "Fast. I need you fast and hard."

His eyes flared and he pushed in hard. "Like that?"

I nodded against the pillow. "More."

He gave me exactly what I needed, fucking me how I asked, how I desperately needed, and almost immediately the heat coiled inside me.

"Baby, I can't—" Sweat beaded on his forehead.

"I'm almost there," I answered on a gulp of air. "Don'tstop-pleasedon'tstop."

"Never." He grunted and thrust harder, rhythm lost, until I tipped over, falling into the sweetness of the abyss and calling out his name as I went.

He pushed into me and held, grunting out a curse as his dick twitched inside me, his own orgasm ripping through him. "Oh my god." He dropped his forehead onto mine, his voice hoarse.

I wrapped my arms around him, squeezing him tight, and he kissed my cheek, nose, other cheek, and finally my lips.

"Those goddamn wires," he murmured.

"Worst things ever," I answered. Then I patted his ass. "That sex though."

He chuckled, still inside of me. "Good?"

I threaded my legs through his. "Excellent start."

We spent the rest of the day in bed, getting up only to scrounge for food in the kitchen and tend to Daisy.

21

DEVON

4 MONTHS, 14 DAYS TO GO

"JUST...ONE...MORE...there!"

"Did you really fix it?" I swear, if this man had finally fixed the kitchen faucet, I was going to drop to my knees in front of him. Six weeks of near-constant dripping might actually be at an end.

"Turn it on and let's see," he said, making his way out from underneath the sink. Beads of sweat dotted his forehead and streaks of who knew what lined his t-shirt, but he looked sexy as hell. He wiped his hands with a towel, his forearm muscles flexing with the effort. Ugh. What was it about competence with things around this house that turned me on so much?

"Devon?" he asked, his eyes dancing. "You in there?"

I quirked a smile at him. "Just thinking how I'm going to pay you for fixing my sink."

He raised an eyebrow. "Keep thoughts of your mouth to yourself. Those wires aren't getting anywhere near me."

I pouted. "The list of things I plan to do to you when these are off just gets longer."

He laughed. "I'm okay with that. Let's do the honors together." He positioned himself behind my back, and I felt the length of him, half hard against me. I pushed against him, my pulse spiking at his sharp intake of breath.

"Devon," he warned.

"Ooh," I teased. "What happens if I keep doing it?" I wiggled my butt against him and he growled.

"Just turn the faucet on, woman," he said, his voice strained.

I turned it on, and the water came out. But that hadn't been the problem. So I turned it off and held my breath, waiting for the inevitable *drip drip drip* that had been the stuff of my nightmares for months.

No water came out.

I squealed and clapped. "And now, I show you my appreciation. No wires, I promise." Grabbing his hand, I led him to the other side of the island, then pushed him against it. "Don't move."

"I wouldn't dream of it." He leaned back on his elbows, his eyes dark pools of mercury as they swept up my body.

I flushed under the heat of his gaze. I'd never get used to the way he looked at me, as though I were his most precious possession. I'd seen hints of it all those years ago, and ignored it. Of course I did. But now? He was slowly eroding my ability to fight it. To fight him.

I unbuttoned my shirt and let it fall off my shoulders, leaving only a peach lace bralette.

His eyes widened. "Did you wear that for me?"

I nodded, and his lips tugged up in a smile. I slid his t-shirt off, and he wrapped his arms around me, pulling me tight against him. This, too, I wouldn't tire of. I was safe here. Known.

He tunneled his hand into the hair at the nape of my neck, gripping and tugging it exactly how I liked him to. He tilted my neck and bit it, sending goosebumps of pleasure down my spine. Then he brought his lips to my ear and whispered, "It's my favorite color on you."

I undid his jeans and pushed them down. He toed off his shoes and stepped out of everything, leaving him only in boxer briefs. I cupped him and felt the heat of his cock through the fabric.

Aaron cradled my head and stared into my eyes. "Devon," he said. "You are everything to me."

I met his gaze, my heart racing with the intimacy of what I saw there, forcing myself not to look away.

He smiled softly, then guided my lips to his and kissed me gently, reverently. I melted into him, wishing I could kiss him deeper, allowing my body to give him what I couldn't manage to say. Because I probably did, but I couldn't even think those three words without panicking. So I tightened my arms around him like my life depended on it, because maybe it did.

He made a noise in the back of his throat and slid his hands down my side, squeezing me tight in return. Heat flared through my body and I whimpered, the pressure of his hold making me pulse with need.

"Aaron."

He looked down at me, his eyes glinting. "Turn around."

He bent over to get a condom out of his jeans and tossed it onto the island. "*Now*, Devon," he commanded, his voice low.

Oh. I guess sweet Aaron was gone. "Yes sir," I said as I obeyed.

He bit down on my shoulder and I hissed in pleasure, arching my back. He pushed his hands down my jean shorts and growled against me. "No panties?"

"No," I breathed, still caught between his teeth.

He pushed a finger through my folds as he released my shoulder, kissing and soothing the skin. Then he circled his tongue across my shoulder as his fingers played with my clit.

I moaned, pleasure swirling through me as I held myself up against the Formica.

He pulled his hand away and I whimpered at the loss of it as he undid my shorts and shoved them down. He put his hand back on me, his rough fingers once again rubbing against my sensitive bud. His other hand trailed across my stomach to my breast, cupping and squeezing it before pushing the bralette up. My breasts fell out, full and heavy, and I moaned as his fingers worked me.

"Spread your legs, sweetheart," he said in my ear. "I need that pussy."

I did and felt him position himself.

"I want to be gentle with you. But it's not what you want, is it?"

I shook my head and rasped, "No."

"You need it rough."

I nodded, whimpering in anticipation of what was to come.

"Then hang on, sweet girl." He thrust into me and I shouted, instantly filled up with him.

"So good," I moaned and circled my hips. He was heaven inside of me. He knew exactly what I needed.

His hands tightened on me and he pulled out and pushed again, deeper this time. My god.

"On your toes, Devon," he said, his voice like gravel.

I obeyed, and he thrust again, harder, deeper, again and again, and it was like nothing I'd ever felt in my entire life. He understood me better than anyone before him. My orgasm gathered, quicker than ever, getting closer with every push and grunt he gave.

"Fuck, Aaron," I gasped. "I'm going to—"

Abruptly, he stopped and pulled out.

"Oh, fuck you," I said.

"*That's* for teasing me earlier," he said, his voice low in my ear.

I whined, pushing my hips back against him.

He pushed me down against the counter, holding me with

one hand, and without warning, I felt his other pop against my ass.

I gasped and clenched my palms. "Did you just—"

Whack.

One to match the other side.

My pulse ratcheted up and I grew even wetter as his free hand soothed the spots he'd spanked. Holy *shit*.

He leaned over me and I felt the cotton of his shirt against my back as his cock nestled between my legs. His voice was gravel. "Tell me you like that."

My answer was swift. "I liked it."

He pulled off me and did it again, the sound reverberating through the kitchen.

"You going to tease me again?"

"If this is the punishment I get, then yes."

He growled and plunged into me.

I shouted, flattening my palms against the counter as his fingers dug into my hips. He lifted me up as he kept pushing into me, faster, harder, exactly how he knew I needed it.

My walls clamped down around him as I shattered, the climax ripping through me all the way to my fingers and toes. Aaron pushed and held against me, shouting as his own orgasm hit.

"Oh my god," I gasped, the aftershocks pulsing through me, gripping and releasing him as we came down together.

Aaron's arms were wrapped tight around me, the two of us still connected. We breathed hard as my thoughts swirled. He'd read me like an open book, naming what I needed before I even realized it, and giving it to me. He'd done it all week, since the first day we'd had sex at his house.

"If that's gonna happen every time I help you with the house," Aaron said, "then please make a long, long list of things that need to be done."

I laughed softly, then tilted my head to allow him access to my neck. He kissed it and sent shivers down my body. "Believe me, I can," I said.

His lips were soft and his scruff deliciously scratchy against my skin. He ran his hands up to squeeze my breasts. "These are the most spectacular things in the world," he said against my ear. "Except maybe this." He grabbed my ass.

After a few more minutes, we cleaned up and got dressed. Aaron's phone dinged, and I caught the confusion on his face as he read the text.

"What is it?"

He looked up. "Is Chief supposed to come by or something?"

I checked the time. "Is he here?"

Aaron nodded. "He's outside in his truck, giving me shit about being here and wondering if it's safe to knock on the door."

I laughed. "He's early. By an hour. He's here to inspect the wiring," I explained.

He pulled me to him and buried his face in my neck. "Glad he wasn't even earlier," he said, capturing my earlobe and wrapping his strong arms around me.

I sighed contentedly. "Would've served him right."

He chuckled. "Maybe, but I would never hear the end of it."

He let me go, and I turned to him. "How do I look?"

"Gorgeous." He grinned mischievously. "And freshly fucked."

I swatted at him and went to the front door. I waved Chief in from where he sat in his truck, windows down to let in the cooling-but-not-cool early fall air. He waved back and climbed out of the cab, making his way to me with a clipboard in his hand.

"Better to be early than late, right?" he said, then pet the dogs. "Seems like Samson's claimed you as his."

I smiled back at him. "Afraid so. I finally broke down and started feeding him, too." On a sigh, I leaned down to give him a scratch and he licked my hand and looked up at me, his little brown eyes piercing straight through my heart. *Damn dog.*

"I know." He straightened and grinned, hooking his thumbs through his uniform belt. "There was a whole thread on the community Facebook page."

I rolled my eyes. "Of course there was."

He stepped into the house and nodded at Aaron, who said, "You know there's a thread about us, too—at least, I'm assuming there is."

I felt my cheeks burn. "Seriously?"

Chief shrugged noncommittally and hitched his thumb toward the upstairs. "Should I get started on the wiring?"

"Sure."

I felt Aaron's hand on my shoulder. "I'll get Chief started. Stay here?" At my nod, he turned to follow Chief up the steps.

Stay here. That's exactly what I was doing. Right? I sighed. I still wasn't sure.

The wedding album caught my eye, taunting me from where it lay on the coffee table. This past week, it'd felt like I was moving forward, the loss of Jason and the guilt I felt finally easing into something bearable with every day that I spent with Aaron, and also with Rick, Ceci and Jodi.

How, exactly, I planned on making it all work was still something I hadn't figured out.

But wasn't I happy here?

Aaron appeared, a glass of water in his hand and a broad smile on his face.

I was happy. I was.

I drank the water and sat the glass next to the wedding album. Aaron gathered me into a hug, and I leaned against his chest and closed my eyes. His heartbeat was steady, solid. Just like him. I knew he wanted answers as much as I wanted to give them, but I also knew he'd wait. His patience was infinite and he was approaching Rick-like levels of sainthood.

Come to think of it, he might actually be approaching *all*

levels of Rick. Had I finally found the man who could hurdle the bar Rick set?

After a while, Chief made his way back downstairs and came into the living room. I stood and Aaron joined me.

"So what's the diagnosis?" I asked.

"Your guy was right. You need a complete re-do," he said. "This isn't as simple as re-wiring the upstairs. It's the whole house. Frankly, I'm not sure how the wiring survived as long as it has. Last time it was touched was in the forties, judging by how old it is."

I slumped. "Great."

"Only good news is that it's not a fire hazard. Yet." He was stern. "But you need it fixed, and fixed soon."

Aaron put his hand on my lower back, and I wanted to curl into the warm comfort of it.

"So who can do it? Unless they're all on Mrs. Withers' payroll and none of them will come near me without fear of retribution," I added dryly.

Chief chuckled. "It's not as bad as all that. I'll send you a couple of names when I get to the station." He paused. "By the way, I heard of a teaching position that's opening up."

I stiffened.

He continued, even though he had to have seen how the blood had drained from my face. "Over at the middle school you worked at. I'm sure they'd love to have you back. Not too many young teachers flocking to the town these days."

"I, no," I choked. "Where Jason died? *No*."

"Chief," Aaron said, a warning in his voice.

"Understood," Chief said softly, holding his hands up.

That was it. I was done. Today was done.

I tried to steady my breathing, feeling as though I was clawing to the side of a mountain. This was too fast. All of it was, and I needed everything to stop.

I needed time to think.

"I'm tired."

The men turned to me with twin questioning looks, and I repeated myself. "Thank you, Chief, for everything, and Aaron, I'll call you later, but right now, I need...I don't know, a nap or something. Please." I walked them both to the door, waving off Chief's apologies.

After Chief left, Aaron paused in the doorway. "Devon," he said softly. He brought his hands to my face and tilted it up, forcing me to look at him. They were sweet and understanding, but there was something else in there. Fear.

My gut twisted. I'd put that there. I leaned into his hand, closing my eyes and taking a minute to breathe.

"I'm sorry," I said, meeting his gaze. "This isn't you, I promise it's not you. I will be okay. We're okay."

His lips twitched up in the barest of smiles. "Okay."

I gripped his waist. "I'm here."

"You are," he said, but he sounded uncertain.

"I am," I repeated firmly. I didn't know if I meant for now, or for a while, or forever. I also wasn't sure who I meant the statement for most: me or him. "I just need some time. We've been all up in each other all week, except for your shifts, and I think I need...time. To think."

He nodded. "Okay."

I went up on my tiptoes to kiss him, and he wrapped his arms tightly around me. I lost myself to the embrace, putting everything into it that I didn't have the words for. That I cared so much for him. That I thought I loved him. That the idea of a job—a permanent job—apparently scared the crap out of me.

That I had no idea how to do this.

22

AARON

A BIRTHDAY PARTY for four-year-old twins is not for the faint of heart. I stood in the backyard of Rick and Ceci's house, a koozied beer in hand, and tried to remember my own birthday parties. They were pretty standard: some friends, some cake, maybe some games of one kind or another.

They did not consist of a blow-up water slide, a bounce house, a make-your-own cupcake station, and face painting with upwards of fifteen over-sugared kids running around. Which is exactly what I found myself gawking at. Rick sidled up to where I stood at the edge of the madness, and I clinked my beer to his. "Best of luck, man."

He laughed, a good-natured grimace on his face. "I know. If this is four, please sedate me for ages thirteen and up."

"Seriously, how do you do it?"

He glanced at me, his eyes remarkably cheery under his baseball cap. "Aw, I love those little hellions. Wouldn't trade them for the world. And Ceese makes it all worth it. Every day of the week."

I followed his love-stricken glance over to where Ceci stood with a bunch of parents from the pre-school the twins attended. "Fair enough."

"You want kids?" he asked.

"You making conversation or you asking as Devon's brother?"

He chuckled and took a sip of beer. "Friendly conversation. I know better than to try and get in Devon's business."

I arched an eyebrow at him. "You're a smart man."

He tipped his beer at me in response.

I answered. "Honestly? Kids are great, as long as they're someone else's."

Now it was his turn to arch an eyebrow. "Does Devon know that?"

I looked at him. "I thought you were staying out of her business."

He shrugged and grinned. "I lied."

I chuckled. I could see why Devon thought so highly of him. He made it clear he loved his family with everything he had. And that occasionally meant giving me shit like any big brother would.

Devon walked up in tight-fitting jeans and a short-sleeve dark green shirt. She gestured at the two of us. "This looks more dangerous than that kid with the plastic sword in the bounce house."

Rick blanched. "That's not really happening, is it?"

"It was, but not anymore," Devon said and curtsied. "Auntie D took care of it." Then she pointed at me. "Remind me never to have kids."

This time, I raised both my eyebrows at Rick. *Take that!* I nodded at Devon and smiled. "It would be my absolute pleasure."

"Guess I'll go see about this sword-wielding kid you mentioned." Rick shuffled off.

Devon watched him go, then wrapped an arm around my

waist and leaned into me. I pulled her close and inhaled her scent. "What *is* that, anyway?"

She tilted her face to mine, holding my gaze. "What's what?"

I couldn't help myself. I kissed her nose and said, "The vanilla smell."

She laughed. "We've spent the past six weeks hanging out. How do you not know?"

"I've been far more interested in other things." I growled and nuzzled her neck.

She giggled and hummed contentedly.

"Shampoo? Body wash?" I guessed.

"It's an oil," she said. "You know me: I travel light, and a body oil is easy to pack."

I ignored the way my stomach stress-flopped at the mere suggestion of her leaving and went instead with the smile. "Well, I love it."

"Thanks." She squinted at someone across the yard.

"Have you thought more about…" I started, then I stopped.

"Have I what?"

I was an idiot. She'd rebounded quickly after Chief's visit, and we'd spent the past week feasting on each other at every available turn. Clearly, it had mushed my brain. "Nothing." I hoped she'd drop it.

"Aaron," she cajoled.

I sighed. I deserved whatever I got after this. "I was going to ask if you'd thought more about," I cleared my throat, "about staying."

She hesitated.

I held my hands up. "I know. I'm sorry. Forget it."

"It's not that," she said. "I just—I don't know. But I don't know that I'm *not* staying. I'm working through a lot. Can you be okay with that?"

Hope flared within me, and I struggled to keep it in check. I gathered her into another hug and held her tight. "I can." I could be okay with damn near anything, if it means she would stay.

She squinted across the yard. "Is that Miss Betty?"

I looked. "It is."

Devon looked at me. "Do you know Miss Betty?"

I flailed. How did I do this without making it also sound like I'd been lying about how well I knew Gigi this whole time? *This is why I should have said something at the beginning. I wouldn't be so paranoid.*

"Oh, we all know Miss Betty," I said. Which was true. I needed to chill. "Small town, remember? In fact, I need to ask her about a lemon bar promise she made Chief." I ignored the questioning look on Devon's face. "Be right back," I said, then aimed for the pink-haired busy-body.

Miss Betty beamed as I stepped around some kids and approached her. "Aaron! Seems Shirley's plan is working."

I widened my eyes at her. "Could you keep it down?" I asked, my voice low.

She looked at me knowingly. "You've not told her?"

"I had nothing to do with it!" I sputtered.

She looked like she didn't believe me.

I pressed on. "Besides, what am I supposed to say? 'I'm pretty sure your beloved grandmother schemed to get you to come back home—hence the six-month thing—just so you could fall in love with me'?"

She nodded. "Why not?"

I groaned in frustration. "Because I am not yet at the age of giving no shits, as you clearly are!"

She grinned and reached up to pat my shoulder. "Calm down, dear. It's no good for your digestion to be so upset."

I hung my head in defeat. I knew when I was beaten: all those nights of playing cards with Betty and Gigi taught me that once they had an idea in their heads, it was impossible to let go.

I half wondered if Gigi purposely tampered with things in her house so they'd need fixing while Devon was here.

Seriously. That was the level Gigi played at. I wasn't sure Devon truly appreciated her grandmother's genius.

"Could you please not mention it until I have a chance to?"

Miss Betty waved her hand impatiently. "As if I'd tell her something like that. We have far bigger fish to fry. Devon, so good to see you!"

I turned to see that Devon had joined us. "Miss Betty! To what do we owe the pleasure of seeing you at my niece and nephew's birthday party?"

"I've known those two since before they were born," Miss Betty said. "I'm an honorary grandmother. I've been meaning to tell you what I learned about the Town Council, but I haven't seen you in a few days."

Devon stilled. "What did you learn?"

Miss Betty looked at her steadily. "They passed a residency requirement."

"Residency requirement?" Devon blinked at her in confusion. "What are you talking about?"

"That old biddy Withers is behind it, I'm sure of it."

"But what is it?" Devon pressed.

"Houses that are on the official historical registry, like yours—"

"Like *Gigi's*—" Devon corrected.

My throat grew tight while Miss Betty gave an assenting nod. "Like your Gigi's must be continuously occupied by their owners or it'll be donated to the historical society."

I drew closer to Devon as she went quiet. "So you're saying…"

"The only way Devon keeps the house is if she lives in it," Miss Betty finished.

"Permanently?" Devon asked. "Forever?"

The flare of hope I'd had just moments ago vanished as I

watched Devon shrink in on herself. I wrapped an arm around her and led her a few steps to a folding chair in the shade of the house. Miss Betty followed.

"What about family? Can it be family?" Devon asked. She was clutching at straws, and my stomach turned in on itself.

"I don't know yet. But it went into effect on the fifteenth, so it's done," Miss Betty said.

"What?" I said, my tone a little sharper than I intended. "Shouldn't they have been a bit more proactive about letting the public know and allowing a comment period? Isn't that normal?"

"Not with Mrs. Withers at the helm," Devon said bitterly.

"Get up," Miss Betty said. "Let's walk. You'll feel better."

Devon stood and let herself be guided away, and I watched gloomily.

I don't know what I expected, honestly. She'd come here expecting to stay the six months her grandmother's will required, and walked straight into a disaster of a house where one thing after another was breaking down. And now the Town Council had cooked this up. Part of me wanted to ask why the residency requirement was such a bad thing in the first place: if she didn't want to stay, then why was the Council taking it over a bad thing? But the other part was blindly cheering for Team Devon, so whatever needed to happen, is what needed to happen.

I drank the rest of my beer and felt a buzz in my back pocket. I pulled my phone out to read the text.

UNKNOWN:

Sorry to do this, boys, but I can't come next week. Something's come up, you know how it is.

I stared at the words. I wanted Will or Price to ask her for a reason, but she wouldn't give one. She never did. I'd been a teenager the one and only time I'd pushed her for a reason. She'd looked at me, her eyes dulled, and said, *"I don't owe you anything."*

Cured me from asking that again.

I looked back at the screen. God, what an idiot I'd been. To think that for a second this past week, the absolute tiniest of seconds as I'd lain in bed with Devon in my arms, I'd actually allowed myself to wonder what it might be like to have dinner with her and my brothers. The four of us around a dinner table, sharing stories. Telling her about Devon. Feeling what it might be like to have my mother smile at me.

Making the bet with my brothers that she wouldn't show up was never something I wanted to be right about, but here we were. Again. Was it terrible to feel good that she was breaking her promise in a group text? So at least I knew it wasn't just me she was avoiding.

Another text came in, this time on the Brothers Only group chat.

WILL

I don't want to hear it from you, Aaron.

I looked at his message, considering my words. Finally, I answered.

There's nothing to say.

Because honestly? There wasn't. It was my mother, proving once again that whatever else was going on in her life was more important than her sons. I didn't even know what she did or where she lived, only that it mattered more than me.

Another text. I sighed. It was from Price to me.

PRICE

Give him some time.

> Are you kidding me?

PRICE:

He's just as hurt as you.

I snorted.

> Doubtful.

I pocketed my phone and ignored the next buzz. I wasn't interested in hearing Price defend Will.

Daisy came up and snuffled her muzzle into my hand, then looked up at me pleadingly. She had what looked like icing on her fur, and she was definitely wet. With what, I could only guess. But I hoped it was water.

"You ready to go, girl?"

She gave a plaintive woof. I didn't blame her.

I looked over to where Devon stood, still in conversation with Miss Betty, and ignored the way my stomach twinged. The text from my mother had reminded me that I couldn't let myself believe that anything permanent would happen with Devon. It didn't matter that I loved Devon. Because I did. So much. But when had my love ever been enough?

23

AARON

LATE SEPTEMBER IN Alabama was almost never cold. Not even close. But today? When I sat in my swim trunks in a dunk tank filled with frigid water? The temps were in the upper fifties and the sun was hidden behind a thick layer of clouds. Even the humidity had taken the day off. I glanced over at my brothers, both of them dry and fully clad in jeans and long-sleeve shirts, and hated my life.

The only bonus was I hadn't been dunked yet. I looked back at the woman holding the baseball and squinting in my direction. "Try all you want, Lacey, but we both know your aim has been terrible since grade school!"

Lacey Patterson made a face at me and her friends joined her. "Shut up, Aaron," she said. "I'm getting you this time."

She wouldn't. But that was the whole point of the firehouse dunk tank at the annual fair: we'd lure people over—okay, women, it was almost all women and the occasional jealous boyfriend or husband—tease them mercilessly while they threw ball after ball, and put the money we made toward the firehouse. My brothers and I were always in the rotation; Chief made certain to guilt us into it every year.

I didn't mind it. It was a few hours in the tank, and most years it was an almost pleasant experience. This year, though? One, it was cold in here, and two, I would much rather have spent my day off in bed with Devon, my face between her legs, listening to her moan as I brought her to climax. And once I'd made her come, I'd slide into her and watch the way her eyes widened as I pushed in. I'd been on-shift three of the last seven days and had not had nearly my fill of Devon's body.

Fuck. Now I was almost hard. I shifted on the unforgiving plastic seat and re-focused on Lacey. "You throwing that thing or what?"

Lacey wound up and pitched the baseball toward the bulls-eye…and missed. Again.

I laughed and shrugged at the glare she gave me. "That was your last one, Lace. Try again later!"

She shook her head and started to walk away. "Nah, but thanks for the view," she called. "It's always my favorite part of the fair." She winked, then left with her friends.

I focused back on the front of the line and stopped. Devon had appeared out of nowhere, jaw-droppingly gorgeous in leggings and a sweater that very helpfully showed off her ass and a thin strip of her stomach. She adjusted the brim of her baseball cap, then held up a ball.

"Pretty sure you're not allowed to cut in line," I called to her.

She tossed the ball back and forth. "I bought my way in," she said, grinning mischievously. "Hell of a line you've pulled over here."

"They come every year," Will said, wandering too close to the booth for comfort.

"Do *not* get closer, asshole," I warned. I knew exactly what he was up to.

Devon kept tossing the ball between her hands. "Did I tell you I played softball growing up?"

Shit. "Really?"

She nodded. "Really."

"What position?"

"Third."

Shit. I didn't even remember the private school having a softball *or* baseball team. "Guess I'm getting wet."

As she laughed, I caught movement out of the side of my vision. "Don't you dare," I said and pointed at Will.

Will shrugged.

Devon got into position and peered at the target. "I'd say I was sorry for this, but I'd be lying." She wound up and threw.

And missed.

I crowed. "Ha! How long's it been since you threw a ball?"

She stuck her tongue out and readied to throw again. "Shut up and prepare to be dunked."

She missed again.

"So your team," I called. "Did you all win when you played?"

She pursed her lips. "Oh, you think you're funny."

I laughed and spread my arms wide. "Last ball, babe. Come and get it."

"I'm getting you this time," she said. She steadied herself, looked hard at the target and then behind me, and threw it.

The ball went wide, but it didn't matter. Price charged toward the tank, bolting to the arm and slamming his hand into it like he was giving it a high five.

I fell in, all of me instantly freezing and shriveling even though the water only came up to my chest. The line cheered as I glared at my brothers. "You two suck," I said.

They laughed good-naturedly, both of them backing away. "Come on, Aaron—we're doing it for the ladies."

"And *you*," I said, pointing to Devon as she neared the tank, "have terrible aim."

She laughed, her face lit up under the brim of her hat. "Didn't matter."

"Stick around for a few minutes?"

"Wouldn't miss this show for anything," she said, smiling wide.

I chuckled, then pulled myself onto the seat and up and out of the tank. I nodded at Mike, who'd been waiting to take my turn and who'd smartly donned a wetsuit. "The line will not approve of that get-up." I took the towel he held out and wiped the water off my chest.

"Yeah," he said, his eyes twinkling, "but my wife and my balls do."

I laughed. "Have fun up there."

Howls of protest came from the line as he climbed in, and I turned to Devon for a kiss. More howls, this time accompanied by whistles and cheers, erupted.

Devon broke the kiss and smiled. "You're cold."

"And you are unbelievably sexy in that outfit," I said, leaning in for another kiss.

"Break it up, you two," Jodi said, walking up with Ceci and the twins. "Children are present."

I shook my head as Devon laughed. "First you annoy us about getting together, and now you annoy us about staying away from each other. What's it gonna be?"

Jodi twisted her lips and shrugged. "We're complicated women. What do you want from us?"

"Besides, we're here for more than bare-chested firefighters," Ceci added.

Jodi snorted. "Speak for yourself. Where's Zach?" She peered around, looking for one of the probies.

Ceci and Devon snickered and Devon said, "Nice try."

Jodi's cheeks pinked, but she kept up the farce and studiously avoided looking in Price's direction.

Ceci turned to the twins. "We need caramel apples, kettle popcorn, bouncy houses, petting zoos, all of it. Right, kids?"

The twins roared enthusiastically.

"Guess it's my cue to be the best aunt on the planet and take you to the bounce house," Devon said. She got a second roar of approval as they each grabbed her hands and tried to run off. She laughed, then turned back to me. "I'll see you later?"

I leaned for another quick kiss, inhaling her vanilla scent and wanting nothing more than to take her into the small tent behind the tank and have my way with her. "Absolutely." I all but growled it.

I watched them go, then headed to the tent to change. Right as I emerged and was about to go find Devon, Will called me over to where he and Price stood.

"I'm watching the time and I know when you two are up," I warned as I approached. My smile faded when I saw how serious they looked. "What?"

"Mom texted," Price said.

"She's coming next week," Will said. "Dinner. You'll be at my house."

I bristled. "I know you didn't *command* me to come to dinner."

Will's eyes flashed, then Price jumped in. "Give her a chance," Price said.

I glared at him, my body heating with anger. "Why? She never comes when she says she's going to. And in case you've forgotten, she was the one who left us in the first place. We were *kids*. I was ten years old."

Will held his hands up. "Settle down. Do you need a hug? Maybe a caramel apple?"

"I'm not joking, asshole."

Price swatted Will. "Quit it." He turned to me. "She swears she's coming this time."

I scoffed. "Sure she is. Same as she swore the last time and the time before that. Can't wait to hear her excuse for when she doesn't show up." I turned to go.

Will grabbed my arm. "Hang on."

I swung back. "No," I said, struggling to keep my voice low. I stepped closer. "I'm sick of this shit. Why do you two keep giving her a pass?"

"We're not," Price started, but flattened his mouth into a line when Will shot him a warning look.

"What the fuck?" I gestured at their silent discussion. "So it's just me? I mean, I noticed when I was a kid but looking back I figured I had it wrong. But I didn't: she wanted you two. She sure as hell didn't want me." I clenched my hands into fists, trying to keep steady.

"Are you serious?" Will asked.

"*Yes* I'm serious," I shot back, incredulous.

"It's not like that," Price said.

"Oh no? Then how come when she *was* around she made it to whatever sport you two were playing each season, but when it was my stuff she was too tired, too drunk, or had something else to do, or who knows what. No apologies, nothing." I shook my head. "So yes, it *was* like that. But of course you two didn't notice. Why would you have." My chest was tight and I took a deep breath, trying to calm myself down.

Price ran his hand down his face, then met my eyes. "We're not trying to excuse her behavior. And I...shit, man, I didn't know you felt this way."

My mouth opened. "Are you fucking kidding me?"

Will spoke. "You've never said anything. You just get all sulky and quiet whenever the topic of her comes up."

I opened my mouth to say he was wrong, but shut it. *Is that what I did?* "Maybe," I conceded. Because unlike my mom, I knew how to acknowledge my mistakes. "But now you know."

Price clapped me on the shoulder and beamed, happy no one was yelling anymore. "So you'll come for dinner at Will's when she visits?"

I rolled my eyes. "She's not coming."

"She's coming," Will said forcefully, a determined glint in his eyes. "I'll make sure of it."

"Alright, man," I said, feeling the tension start to drain out of my body. I hated arguing with my brothers. They were the only family I had. "I'm not sure I believe you."

"You'll come?" Price pressed.

I shrugged. "I'll come."

"Good," Will said. He headed to the tent.

A splash and cheers rose up behind me. Mike had been dunked, by none other than his wife. I chuckled as she spun in a circle with her hands up in victory. From the tank, Mike smiled at her, his face full of open adoration.

I swallowed and looked away, suddenly feeling as though I'd seen something private. Their love seemed easy, effortless. I wanted that so badly. Always had, if I was honest with myself. But it wasn't anything I'd ever let myself really think would happen.

But now? With Devon? It felt...possible. Improbable, maybe, and she wasn't letting me all the way in yet, but it felt possible. And wasn't that the damndest thing. Even with the specter of a possible dinner with my mother looming over me, just thinking about Devon put me at ease.

"Dude, what's with the stupid grin on your face?" Price asked.

I slid my eyes over to him. "Nothing."

"She's not even around and you look like that. You got it bad, huh?" he asked knowingly.

I thought about lying, but Price would see right through me. He'd always known when I wasn't being truthful. "Yeah," I drew out.

"You happy?"

"I am. Still scared shitless she'll leave, but...she's worth the risk." I was a fool, but I was a fool in love. Not that I was telling her I loved her anytime soon. I wasn't *that* stupid.

He nodded. "I get that," he said, a thoughtful look on his face.

My phone buzzed and I pulled it out from my jeans.

DEVON

Is it bad that all I want to do is take you home
and fuck you?

I coughed. Holy shit.

"You okay?" Price asked.

I mean, if getting hard at the county fair was considered 'okay' then, "Yeah, I'm good." I looked back at the screen, careful that no one else was near to see it. Yep, that's what it said.

"See you later," I told Price. "I've got a blonde to catch."

24

DEVON

3 MONTHS, 21 DAYS TO GO

I WAS EASILY ten people back in the line at Daily Dose, and it wasn't even the morning rush. It was after lunch, a time in normal coffee shops when the lines got short or nonexistent, but not here, apparently. Jodi needed to hire additional help, but I knew she also needed to make those new payments she was staring down.

I cringed, thinking of my own dwindling savings and the steady decrease in funds that Gigi had earmarked for the house. Adulting was the worst. I'd gotten the electrician hired to start next week, and almost immediately, a leak had started in the ceiling of one of the guest bedrooms on the top floor. An investigation revealed that not only did that corner of the house need repairs done, but the whole house needed a new roof.

Finally I got to the front of the line. Jodi smiled, no trace of the stressed-out woman I'd talked to the other night for an hour on my front porch. "Hi, friend. Your usual?" I nodded and she rang me up. "How are things with Aaron?"

I smiled at her. "Good. Really good."

"Yeah?"

"It feels…right. Like I'm exactly where I'm supposed to be."

This past month or so with Aaron had been honestly wonderful. I didn't itch anymore. Wasn't worried that I had zero job prospects and my meager savings were dwindling right alongside the money for house renovations. And that had to be worth something. Was I all better? No. I still couldn't face the idea of working at the middle school, and I was still coming to grips with knowing Jason had died with our argument in his head, without me ever letting him fully in, and never truly knowing him in return. But the guilt about it was easing. And that was amazing.

Jodi's eyes shone bright as she clapped. "That makes me so happy!" She turned to grab my coffee and pushed it forward with a wink. "Wish we could talk more, but..." She gestured to the line of people behind me. "Enjoy!"

I made my way to my favorite overstuffed chair, took a sip of the delicious brew, and opened my laptop to pull up the minutes of the Town Council's last few meetings. After learning about the residency requirement from Miss Betty at the birthday party, I'd done some digging and finally gotten my hands on the minutes. They weren't hanging out on the website, ready to be read by the public. Never mind that they were supposed to be.

A few pages in, I saw something. The date of the meeting was on the 10th, and they'd enacted the resolution on the 14th, but they were supposed to enact it on the 15th. Would that be enough? Would twenty-four hours be the loophole that I needed? I wasn't sure. But maybe? I scribbled down some notes.

It shouldn't have been this way. The house I loved had turned into a too-expensive weight around my neck. Instead of memories everywhere I looked, I saw repair bills. Couple that with this rule that if I didn't live there, the house could be automatically donated to the historical society, and I was beginning to wonder why I was fighting this in the first place.

I took a sip of coffee and sighed. I wanted to stay now. But I wanted it to be on *my* terms. This kind of force by the Council didn't sit right with me. It was one thing for Gigi to have concocted a way to make me to face her *and* Jason's death. I understood that now, and yeah, point for Gigi, taking care of me from beyond. The thing was, the more I stayed here and worked on this house, the more I realized that I really didn't want to stay in the house. Stay in town? I didn't know yet. But stay at Gigi's? No. It was too big.

Still, I couldn't let Mrs. Withers win. It was petty. I knew it, but I absolutely would not let it happen. Let a decades-old feud go up in flames after mere months? Not on my watch.

But maybe it was time to stop being petty. Or try a different tactic: pretend to go belly-up and let Mrs. Withers get her hands on it, have the society dump money into the house to fix it, and once they were done, swoop in with this surprise about them enacting the rule one day too soon, and voila! Take *that*, Mrs. Withers!

Yeah, right.

The door jingled and I looked up to see a firefighter come in, clearly fresh from dropping his turnout gear at the station. His face and hands were streaked and dirty, and he walked straight to the counter without bothering to stand in line. "Four alarm," he said.

Jodi nodded and got to work without another word. The line stood back, and Lon, a woman I went to school with, piped up. "Everything okay, Mack?"

The firefighter turned to her and nodded wearily. "Nearly lost one of our own, but yeah, we're all okay."

My heart thudded and I sat up straight.

Mack continued. "Craziest thing, too. Will was right behind us, until he wasn't. We'd been on the second floor and gotten the fire out, so we headed down the stairs, which we'd checked for integrity. But Will fell through, and the oxygen rushed the hole." He shook his head. "His damn brother ran in like a godforsaken idiot."

"Price?" Lon asked.

"Aaron."

My world narrowed into tight pinpoints of near-black. Aaron had run into a burning building to save his brother? He was the fucking *paramedic*. There were a million regulations that should have kept him from doing what he did.

I jumped up from my chair, papers flying everywhere, my hands shaking. I looked around, caught Jodi's eye, and fled.

Out the front door I went, heading straight for the firehouse. I couldn't hear anything over the roar in my ears. He had to be okay. I needed him to be okay. There was no choice.

"Please please please," I whispered, my feet eating up the block of concrete.

The two trucks weren't packed away neatly like I was used to seeing them. Instead, they were pulled out of the bays, blocking the sidewalk ahead of me, being tended to by a handful of firemen I knew by sight but not name.

The smell hit me and I drew up short. Fire. Smoke. The particular scent of a life demolished. I choked back a sob and stood, rooted to the ground, unable to walk any farther. My heart kicked into high gear and I breathed shallowly, clenching my fists.

A dingy yellow fur ball raced past me and headed straight into the station. Samson. He'd not showed up this morning, and I'd wondered about him, but maybe he'd been taking care of these guys instead.

I forced a deep breath into my lungs, but all it did was push the odor of destruction farther into me. I'd never be okay with this. It was too much. Not today. Not ever.

I unglued my feet from the sidewalk and pushed forward, twin furies of anger and worry spurring me on. I swept into the engine bay and looked around, focusing on my breathing and not on the way it seemed nothing had changed in the bay.

"Devon?"

His familiar voice cut through my haze and I snapped my eyes up, meeting the very pair of warm gray-blue eyes I'd been searching for. "Aaron," I breathed.

Thank fuck. He was here. Whole. *Alive.*

He walked to me, his face streaked with black, and pulled me into a tight embrace before I knew what was happening. For the briefest of moments, I let myself melt into him, feeling the strength of his arms and banishing the memory of Chief telling me about the last person I'd loved and lost.

Then I pulled away and shakily wiped at the traitorous tear that ran down my cheek. "How *could* you?"

Aaron's look of concern was immediately replaced by one of understanding. "Sweetheart, I'm okay. Look, not a scratch on me." He held his arms out for my inspection.

I wasn't having it.

"No." I pushed at his chest, but of course he didn't move. "It's bad enough you're a paramedic with the fire department. But now you're running into burning buildings? *No.*" I pushed at him again. "You don't get to do that."

He grabbed my arms as I pushed at him again, aware we had an audience and not caring. "It was my brother, Devon," he said gently. "I had to."

"No, you didn't," I growled, still shoving against him even as he held my arms. "There were other firefighters! That's *their* job, not yours."

He sighed. "I couldn't do it. I couldn't stand there. Not when I could hear what was going on." His voice broke and my heart stuttered. "He's my *brother*, Devon," he repeated.

"I lost the love of my life in a fire, Aaron!" The words tore out of my throat as I shoved him again.

He blanched.

"You don't get to say it wasn't a big deal. It's a goddamn miracle nothing happened. Do you understand?"

He searched my eyes and nodded tightly.

I kept shoving. He kept on not moving, absorbing every blow I delivered. "I *buried* him, Aaron. I can't bury you, too. Don't you get that? I can't do that again."

He stayed quiet.

I shoved my hair back with a shaky hand. "What if it happens again? Can you tell me you'll stay outside?"

He opened his mouth, then shut it again.

"Can you?" I pressed.

"Not if it's one of my brothers."

"I can't do this." I doubled over, cold as ice, and sobbed the next words. "I'm not. No."

"Dev—"

I felt his hand on my back and wrenched away. "*No.*"

"Devon, wait!" He moved in front of me and held his arms up.

I stopped, my breaths ragged. "There is nothing you can say right now."

"Please. Please don't leave like this," he begged. "Can you come upstairs? Or my truck? Something. *Please.*"

With tears in my eyes, I took him in. I couldn't make him choose between his brothers and me. Not when I wasn't even sure where the next few months would take me.

Looking at him, knowing how loyal and good and strong he was...I finally understood that *I* wasn't strong enough. I was a fool for thinking I was. It was all too hard, and I was tired of hard. The thought of losing Aaron, the terror that'd gripped me...it was too much. I'd lost my parents. Then my husband. Then my grandmother. I wouldn't lose another person. I had to stop this before it got too far.

"You should go check on your brother," I said.

His shoulders dropped, and I left.

25

AARON

DEVON IGNORED MY calls and texts all day yesterday. I was still on shift, so I couldn't go to her house and make her talk to me. Make her understand the knot of ice that'd wedged inside me when I heard that Will had fallen into the stairs. Hearing the chatter between Chief and the others, knowing that Price was too far away to do anything...I had to do it.

I'd do it again, too.

Was it bad that, for a moment, I'd actually been ecstatic about how mad Devon was at me? It'd finally felt like she loved me, even if she'd simultaneously reminded me that the love of her life was dead.

I texted her again.

> Please talk to me, Devon. Come over tonight and let me make you dinner.

I stared at the phone, willing her to respond, but after five minutes, I gave up and headed to the weight room.

I found Will and Price already down there, Price acting as

spotter while Will benched more weight than anyone needed to. Dude was bent on being massive.

Will sat up, then grunted when he saw me.

"You're welcome, asshole."

Price flicked the back of Will's head. "Be grateful." To me, he said, "Even though you were an idiot, and it's a miracle you didn't get hurt."

I gaped at them. "Really? How about 'thank you for saving my life' and 'thank you for saving our brother's life'? Is that too much to ask for?" I threw my hands up. "You two are the only family I have, so excuse me for trying to keep you around!"

Will arched his eyebrow. "Mom doesn't qualify as family?"

I scoffed. "Please."

"Can we keep the drama to a minimum for one day?" Price said, doing his best to sound like a beleaguered parent.

Will shot a look at Price before turning back to me. "Aaron. You know I'm grateful."

"Could have fooled me."

"Fine. Thank you," he grumbled.

"That's marginally better."

"And don't ever do something that stupid again."

I rolled my eyes. "Your thank-yous need a hell of a lot of work."

Price waved a towel at me. "He's right. You're not a firefighter."

I wasn't going to get anywhere with either of them. "Whatever. Let's just drop it."

Will grunted again and Price smiled. "Deal."

"You done?" I nodded at the bench.

Will stood. "All you, man."

I pulled some of the weights off—no one needed to be as massive as Will —and Price spotted me. We all made our way through the room, and by the time we were finished, I had a text.

DEVON

When are you off shift?

I stared at the words, not knowing how to feel. Glad she'd finally responded, but apprehensive nonetheless.

A few hours. Meet me at my house?

The dots appeared, then disappeared, then came back again.

DEVON

Sure.

I blew out a breath.

I HAD JUST ENOUGH TIME AFTER WORK TO GET HOME and shower before she arrived. My heart surged at the small smile she had for me as I opened the door.

"Come on in," I said, stepping aside to let her in.

She nodded down at the dingy yellow dog at her feet. "Samson caught a ride from Wanda with me. She really is the only game in town for Uber, isn't she?"

"Others come and go, but Wanda is forever. Chief says she used to be the only cab driver in town, and once Uber became a thing, she moved to that."

"I thought I recognized her. Anyway, Samson seemed to think Daisy would be around for him to play with."

I watched as the dogs sniffed a hello and took off to play. "He's changed since you got here. For one, he used to never come in this house."

"That's what everyone keeps telling me," she said, not quite meeting my eyes. "I think it's a town-wide ploy to get him out of everyone's hair."

"I think he just wants to be yours." *Like me.* "Want some wine?" I asked, leading her to the kitchen. "I've got stuff here you can eat, too, if you're hungry."

"Wine sounds good, but no." She sighed. "Doctor's orders. I'm still not healing properly and there's some residual pain, so he put me on some medicine that I can't combine with alcohol."

"So no end in sight to the wires?" I kept my eyes on her, but she slid her gaze away.

"No." Her voice was low.

"Devon." I reached for her hands. "I'm sorry I scared you. The last thing I want is to do that."

"I know."

I pulled her to me, tucking her head beneath my chin to hold her close. At this point, the contact was something we both needed.

"I'm sorry, too," she said, her voice muffled against my shirt. She tilted her head up to look at me. "You literally rescued your brother. You shouldn't feel bad for that, and I'm sorry I made you feel that way." She smiled again, and my chest started to loosen. Maybe I'd blown things out of proportion. Maybe the fear I had of her leaving was just that: fear.

I forced myself to focus on the now, and set about pulling a simple dinner together for us: a protein smoothie for her, and a turkey sandwich and apple for me. Afterwards, we went to the back deck. I lay on the couch and pulled her down with me. She shivered, and I grabbed a blanket from the nearby chest. I threw it over us as she curled against me, resting her head against my shoulder.

We lay in silence, listening to the sounds of the autumn night around us. She snuggled deeper beneath the blanket, then I felt her hand skim the waist of my jeans.

"I don't think I've ever seen you in jeans before tonight," she said, her voice low.

I looked down at her. "No?"

She shook her head and pushed her hand up beneath my shirt, running it over my stomach and chest. "And I have to say, they are very, *very* flattering."

I grinned, thoroughly enjoying her hand on my skin and more than happy at the turn of events. "Oh, really?"

She nodded. "Really."

I tilted her chin up for a kiss, wishing like hell I could take it deeper. I wanted this, wanted her, forever. I slid a hand up her shirt and she arched against me.

"Please, Aaron," she said, her voice urgent.

I switched our positions, putting her back against the couch so that I lay on my side against her, and she clutched at me, almost frantic. I kissed her neck as I pushed up her shirt, then groaned at the red lace peeking out at me in the dim light. I wanted to slow this down.

"Off," she said, as if sensing my desire and having none of it.

I snapped the back of the bra to open it, then pulled it and her shirt off, letting her breasts fall free. God, they were tremendous. I leaned to kiss one, then the other, even as she continued to writhe beneath me. Her energy was frenetic. I pushed my free hand into her panties and slid a finger into her. She moaned and I pushed another in. Her walls clenched and I lost myself to her. Listening to her moans, my god, she would be the ruin of me. No one would ever measure up to her.

I rained kisses down her throat as her hips thrust against me. "Aaron, yes," she hissed.

I pulled her breast into my mouth again, sucking hard as I let her guide the now-punishing rhythm she was setting.

"God, Aaron, I'm—" she broke off, then shuddered as the orgasm took over.

"There we go," I whispered. "I've got you." I brought her down from the climax, kissing her forehead, then temple, cheek, and finally her lips.

Stay with me. I love you. I looked into her eyes, a dark blue in the night. "I would do that for you every day," I said, my voice thick, "if you would let me."

She swallowed and closed her eyes, breaking eye contact. "I know," she whispered. "Hold me, Aaron."

So I held her. And when she asked me to take her to bed, I did that, too. I gave her everything she wanted. And with each kiss, each stroke, I gave her every part of me, seeking a connection she seemed determine to withhold. We brought each other to climax after climax, but it wasn't enough.

Afterwards, when she thought I was asleep, she slipped out of the bed. She pulled up her jeans and threw on her shirt, then leaned down to grab her bra and underwear. She tiptoed out without a second glance.

The front door clicked shut, and a few minutes later, I heard a car approach and the door open. Probably Wanda. Woman never slept. The door shut, and as the headlights swept across the top corner of the ceiling, I pretended the hollow feeling in my stomach would go away.

26

DEVON

3 MONTHS, 13 DAYS TO GO

I F THERE WAS a worse word in the English language than coward, I didn't know what it was.

What was I doing? I'd bolted from Aaron's bed like a criminal, and why? Because it felt so good to have his arms around me, to feel the weight of him on top of me, and to finally breathe again even as he took my breath away?

No. Not because of that. But because I didn't deserve any of it. Not really.

I'd been in love before. Obviously. Whatever this was with Aaron, it was…different. I might have loved him, but if it was love, then why couldn't I open up all the way?

Whatever it was, it hurt. It felt like something was squeezing the air out of me and the only time I could really breathe was if I were near him. And that didn't feel like love. I'd felt love, and it'd been tender and sweet. The way I felt with Aaron wasn't like that. It was heated, laced with something I couldn't name. Desire, knowing.

A knock sounded at the door, followed by a familiar woof. I wrapped Gigi's robe tight around me—this old house was drafty as hell—and headed to the front door. "Mrs. Withers?" There was no keeping the surprise out of my voice.

The woman stood on the porch, clad in a coat with a scarf wound around her neck to ward off the cool, not cold, morning, and stared up at me with something approaching…kindness? Curiosity? Whatever it was, it wasn't her usual sneer of dislike. Even still, I couldn't bring myself to invite her inside, so I stepped outside. I rubbed my arms against the chill. "How can I help you?"

"Have you been taking care of this dog?"

Straight to business, naturally. No *hello, how are you*, none of that. I took my time answering, bending to scratch the little dog's head as he pawed at my kneecap. "Samson? Yes. He won't leave me alone, so really, I've had no choice." A thought occurred to me. "Is he yours?"

A rueful smile crossed her face. "I don't think Samson's in the market for anyone to 'own' him, but I did raise him from puppyhood for a while."

I couldn't help the delighted laugh that bubbled out of me at the idea of a puppy Samson. "I would never have guessed he was yours."

She tittered. Actually *tittered*. "Well, no one told *him* he was owned by someone, that's for certain. He took off and ingratiated himself into the community, and never looked back."

I wanted to look around to see if I was being pranked. In what world did Mrs. Withers show up on this porch and good-naturedly laugh about a puppy?

Samson turned his attention to Mrs. Withers, allowing her to pet him before finally dipping his head to the nearly empty water bowl on the porch. I knew he'd unleash those big brown eyes on me for his breakfast in a few moments.

"No one seems to know he's yours. Is…is that why you're here? Do you want to take him home?"

She waved her hand in the air. "Oh, gracious no. He's not

mine. He's no one's, really, but he does seem to have taken a liking to you," she said wistfully. "But he's not why I'm here."

I stiffened and waited for her to turn back into the mean old lady I'd known my whole life.

"I'm here to check on you. How *are* you?" Her eyes held nothing but open curiosity and kindness as she spoke. No narrowing of her mouth, or hardening of her stance.

"I...I'm fine," I stammered, defaulting to my normal answer. If I hadn't reached out to my own brother to admit near-defeat, then I had no business blurting my issues to Gigi's oldest enemy.

"Good," she said softly. "That's good. I've heard that this house is giving you quite a run for your money, and I'm guessing that's not at all what you expected."

I blinked away the tears that'd popped up at her kindness. "Um. Well, yes. It's a lot."

She nodded. "You probably think I'm here to gloat, but I'm not. I realize that I've put you in a terrible position, and I want to apologize for that, and at least explain why I've done what I've done. If you'll allow it."

I swallowed the lump in my throat. I should invite her inside, I knew I should, but the ghost of Gigi still wouldn't let me, apology or not. "Thank you. Sit?" I gestured to the rocking chairs that remained in desperate need of a fresh painting.

Mrs. Withers settled herself and sighed. "Did you know I used to live next door?"

"Where Mrs. Savage lives?"

She shook her head. "No. To the right."

I let out a low whistle. The property next door was beautiful, two full stories with intricate wooden details on the outside of the house. The yard was immaculate. A white, wooden picket fence stood guard all around the front, and thick hedges shielded what I assumed was a perfect backyard.

"How long ago?"

"When I was a child. Your grandmother and I were best friends."

I stifled a snort, then immediately felt bad. "Sorry," I murmured.

She tittered again, the noise sounding less alien this time, and folded her hands across her thick puffy jacket. "Seems impossible to you, I'm sure, but it's true. We wore a path between our houses. Probably would have stayed best friends, too, except for me stealing her boyfriend."

I whipped my head back to study her. "So the rumors are true? When was it, like in eighth grade or something?"

She raised her eyebrows above the thick glasses. "Do you really have such a poor opinion of me that you think I'd bother with a pre-pubescent boy? No, dear. College. I stole her boyfriend the summer after our freshman year of college."

I tried to imagine Mrs. Withers being young and plucky enough to go after Gigi's boyfriend, but came up empty. "She never told me."

Mrs. Withers laughed. "Of course she didn't! She didn't treat Gary right, but for me? He was perfect. We married, raised our children, and lived a good life." She paused. "He had a massive heart attack when he was fifty-eight."

I gasped. "So young. I'm so sorry."

She nodded. "Yes, well. Shirley and I had managed an uneasy truce after her second marriage, but to not even call or come by after my Gary died? It was unforgivable."

"So the two of you, what, declared war after that?" I prompted. "But I still don't understand what any of that has to do with now."

She took a deep breath and seemed to gather herself. "When a woman's husband dies, it's…it's unimaginable."

I looked at her. "No shit," I said flatly.

Her eyes widened, then she recovered. "I wasn't finished. Do you remember me coming? To the visitation?"

I searched my memory, trying and failing to recall the old woman anywhere. The entire week of Jason's death was hazy. "I don't. You were there?"

She nodded. "I was. You were in such a state, poor dear. To lose him so young, in such a tragic way, it was...well, like I said, it was unimaginable."

I swallowed hard. When I spoke, my voice was thick. "Thank you for being there. I'm sorry I don't remember you."

She waved my apology away. "Shirley was furious I'd come. Thought I was trying to make the whole thing about me, which I honestly didn't understand. But the point I'm trying to make is that I had to sell. My dad passed shortly after Gary, and my mom went into hospice, and there just wasn't any money to pay the bills. So I sold it."

Realization dawned. "The house."

She nodded. "Broke my heart, losing it. Went through owner after owner, none of them treating it right until finally the owners who have it now. But they're older, their kids are grown...this whole neighborhood is full of old people or nearly old people."

I chuckled and gave her a pointed look. "Got something against old people, Mrs. Withers?"

She laughed, a sweet, tinkling sound that I would have bet my life savings I'd never hear out of her. "No, but I think this neighborhood deserves younger people. Like you."

"So that resolution," I started.

"Was designed to ensure that you would stay. No matter how bad things may get, you always have a home," she finished.

I sat back in the chair, letting her words sink in. "I thought this was some hare-brained scheme to get control of the house so you could do who knows what with it."

She harrumphed. "No. If anything, this was the only way I could figure to apologize to Shirley in a way that she might finally forgive me."

Oh, *wow*. I reached my hand over to grip hers.

Before Mrs. Withers could respond, Betty's voice floated from next door. "Is that cantankerous old woman bothering you? One word, Devon, and I'll call Sheriff Peterson to get her off your property."

Mrs. Withers rolled her eyes. "I honestly don't know how I have the reputation I have."

I raised an eyebrow. "Mrs. Withers."

She gave me a knowing smile. "Okay, maybe I do. But calling the sheriff on me?" She sniffed. "Completely unnecessary."

Betty made her way down the steps and over to the yard. She clomped up the stairs, her gardening clogs wet with morning dew, and glared at Mrs. Withers. "You have some nerve showing up here and harassing sweet Devon. What's next? You formulated a plan to kick her out and wanted to tell her in person?"

Mrs. Withers stood and faced Betty, her spine ramrod straight and her jaw tight. She was clearly ready to do battle.

I stepped between them, trying to contain my amusement. "Ladies, back to your corners." Both of them muttered, and the laugh burst out.

Betty wrung her hands together. "Guess you don't need my help anymore. Is she your best friend now?"

My god, she was precious. I bit back another laugh and reached to squeeze her hand. "No, Betty. And as for Mrs. Withers," I glanced at her and found she was still glaring at Betty like her very life depended on it, "she was explaining some things to me." I squeezed Mrs. Withers' hand as well. "And I'm grateful for it."

Betty's shoulders dropped a smidge, but she held Mrs. Withers' glare and gave as good as she was getting. Finally, Betty turned her gaze to me. "You sure you don't need me to give her a good wallop?"

I snorted, then covered my mouth. "No, Betty. No. Thank you."

Mrs. Withers stepped forward. "Devon." Her voice was soft, kind. "Promise me you'll stay."

Instantly, panic flared inside my chest. "I—I can't promise." As good as it was to understand the reason behind Mrs. Withers and the historical society's efforts, it didn't make staying any easier. And I still didn't agree with them, either, no matter their good-hearted intentions.

Her eyes widened. "But if you don't stay, then what was all of it for?"

"I didn't ask for any of it," I said, trying to stop the shaking in my voice. "And I can't promise to stay."

She searched my face. "Okay. Will you at least promise to consider it?"

She looked so earnest, so hopeful, that I nodded. "Yes," I lied.

"Thank you," she said, smiling gently. "Then I guess it's time for me to go. Thank you for hearing me out. It means a lot. Now *move* out of my way." She said that last bit to Betty, who hadn't stopped glaring suspiciously at her, and maybe moved an inch as Mrs. Withers passed her if she moved at all.

We watched her get into her purple Ford Fiesta—because of course it was a purple Ford Fiesta—and putter off. I gave my attention to Betty, who'd remained remarkably quiet during that last exchange. "You want some coffee?"

Betty shook her head, then sniffed in the direction of the departed Fiesta. "No, thank you. What was all that about?"

I thought, trying to put it in words. Finally, I gave up. "That old Mrs. Withers is complicated."

Betty *tsked*. "As a snake, maybe."

I grinned. "She's got a few more layers than we were giving her credit for," I said. "Samson was hers when he was a puppy."

"With her for an owner, it's no wonder the poor thing fled," Betty shot back.

"Did you know she stole Gigi's boyfriend in college? And *married* him?"

Betty rolled her eyes. "Gary? Old news."

I poked her, grateful for how clearly she was letting me off the hook. "No one told *me* that old news."

"Oh, please," she countered. "If you don't know the decades-old gossip, it's not my job to educate you."

I threw my hands up in mock exasperation. "Who else is my Yoda if not you?"

She narrowed her eyes. "Did you just compare me to a three-foot-high green creature with no teeth?"

My abs were getting a workout with all the laughter I was holding back. "No?"

"That's it. Time to change my hair color. Pink isn't cutting it anymore." She turned to clomp back down the stairs, but stopped when she got to the bottom. "But really. Is there anything I can do?"

My heart squeezed. "No, Betty. I'm good. Thank you."

I watched as she made her way across the yard, leaving a trail in the dewy grass. We waved at each other once she was on her porch, and together, we went inside our houses.

Well, Gigi's house. It still didn't feel like this place was mine. I was beginning to think it never would. All the love I'd had for it, all the memories, felt tarnished and out of focus. I slumped onto the couch and pulled the quilt that lay on the back of it over me.

How was my life being batted around by two old women, one in the ground and one very much not? Since when had this become my life?

And Aaron.

I pulled the comforter over my head. It wasn't going to work. All the joy and warmth and safety he gave me, it wouldn't last. He'd proven it when he went after his brother. Even as a paramedic, his job was risky. He'd get hurt, or worse, and I couldn't be here for it. Couldn't lose another.

The only question now was how long I was willing to stay in this town. This house.

I pulled my phone out of my pocket and opened the email I'd gotten the other day wanting to schedule an interview for a job in San Diego. It was time.

27

DEVON

3 MONTHS, 11 DAYS TO GO

"A WEEK?" JODI looked at me in the empty coffee shop, her mouth open in shock. "You're leaving in a week?"

I'd asked them to meet me here earlier, but it was closer to dinner time before Ceci could get away. Meaning I'd had all day to stew about the job offer I'd taken. But I was certain it was the right thing to do.

Ceci was a millisecond away from smacking me upside the head before I ducked. She sat back, unsatisfied, and glared. "I'm going to say this with all the love in my heart, so you should take it precisely the way it sounds: Have you lost your goddamn mind?"

Jodi pointed at Ceci in a silent *what she said* gesture.

"I never said I was staying," I reminded them.

Jodi squeaked like she was about to say something, but then clamped her mouth shut.

"It's not even been three full months." Ceci's blonde hair swung as she spoke. "Are you really going to give up on the house?"

I nodded, resigned. "You and Rick have made it clear you

don't want it. And it's too much for me. Mentally *and* financially. It's not home anymore. Gigi made it home, and without her, it's not worth it."

Ceci shook her head. "I thought this time it'd be different."

"What about Aaron?" Jodi's voice was low.

I looked at her, my chest aching at the mention of his name. "He knows it's coming."

"Have you actually told him?" Ceci asked.

"No, but it was always a matter of time. I'm certain he knows that." I sipped the cold coffee in front of me.

"You're certain he knows?" Jodi repeated, her voice rising as she spoke. "You're certain. You haven't even told him, have you?"

I didn't answer.

She shook her head, disgusted. "You are *such* a coward."

My eyes wide, I started to protest, but she wasn't done.

She took a deep breath and narrowed her eyes. "This isn't okay, and for once I'm going to say something."

"Jodi, it really is for the best," I said, reaching for her.

She jerked her hand out of my reach. "No. No, it's not. It's as far from being for the best as it could possibly be. I thought you'd grown. I thought you understood, but it turns out you're as emotionally stunted as you've always been. You were a coward to run five years ago after my brother died, and you're a coward now, running away because another man who is far, *far* too good for you loves you." She shook with barely contained anger.

"Jodi, I—"

"No. You don't get to speak." She held up her hand and stood up, her face blotchy and her voice beginning to shake. "I already texted Aaron and he's going to your house. Because knowing you, you'll think telling the two of us is good enough. God forbid you talk to your brother, who, you know, you barely talk to anyway since you probably think talking to his wife is good enough. News flash: it's *not*. Must be nice to be able to choose not to talk to your brother. Your *brother*, who is *alive*. But what do you care, huh?" She spun on her heel to walk away, then spun back. "Get out of my shop. Go home. Tell Aaron to his face. You owe him that. That is the absolute barest of what you owe."

She turned, her skirt swinging, and speed-walked into the back of the shop.

Ears ringing and face burning, I looked at Ceci, who stared back with an expression that told me she agreed with everything Jodi had said.

Wordlessly, I swallowed, nodded, and scraped back my chair.

I SAW HIS TRUCK IN THE DRIVE AS SOON AS I TURNED the corner. Samson did, too, and bolted down the sidewalk to Aaron without sparing me a second glance. Aaron paced the porch, lit up only by the street lights. His movements were tense, his body rigid.

I shook my hands, trying to get rid of the nerves that shot through me the closer I got to him. I hadn't worked out what I was going to say.

If I were honest, I thought that maybe Jodi was right. Maybe I *was* going to just leave. Maybe I would have left him a letter.

God.

They were right. I *was* a coward.

He looked up as I turned onto the walkway and approached the porch. His jaw was tight and his eyes searched mine. "Is it true?" he asked.

I wanted to speak, but the words clogged in my throat. I motioned to the front door as I passed him, mute and clawing at the urge to cling to him and beg him to tell me it was all going to be okay.

"All" being everything I'd fucked up.

Samson trotted in first, fully expecting to be fed and watered. I was next, with Aaron behind me. I went to the kitchen, needing to buy more time. Every sound I made, from picking up the bowls to getting fresh water to opening the bag of food and pouring the kibble in, seemed magnified.

I set Samson's bowls down and he dove in. Nothing to do but face Aaron.

He leaned against the island and stared at me, his arms crossed over his chest. "Is it true?" he asked again.

"I was—"

"Were you really going to leave without talking to me?" He was stiff, absolutely nothing about him relaxed.

"No!" Even if maybe I was lying. "This is all happening too fast."

"Whose fault is that?" he demanded.

"Will you *wait* a minute?" I choked. "Give me time to gather my thoughts."

He shook his head. His eyes were the color of cold metal in winter, glinting harshly in the kitchen light. "Time is all I've given you. Time and patience and understanding…and for what?" His voice broke on the last word.

My heart broke right along with it. "Aaron," I said.

He wiped a hand down his face. "I'm an idiot. You were never going to stay and I let myself believe that you would. That what I thought we had was worth exploring. That I was enough. But instead, you're doing exactly what you've been doing for five years and I knew—I fucking *knew* and I let myself believe you'd stay." He pushed off the island.

"I'm sorry." Pathetic words. My mind whirred, filled with nothing but static. I didn't know how to explain. And even if I did, what good would it do?

"You're sorry," he repeated flatly.

I nodded and fought the tears that stung the backs of my

eyes. "I just…" But nothing would come. I was flailing, scrambling for purchase.

"You just. You *just*," he said, his voice getting stronger. "You just *what*, Devon? Just thought some plan would fall in your lap so all of this would be easy? Just thought you'd let me fall in love with you and then leave?"

I jerked my head up. "What?"

He threw his arms out. "Of course I love you, Devon! That's been the whole point!"

Shit. The tears fell freely now, but my head still buzzed. I couldn't think. He loved me? He *loved* me?

But of course he did. Everything he'd done for me, every glance, every touch. It had all been out of love.

He circled the island and faced me again, pressing his hands onto the countertop. "Do you know what's funny about all this? Gigi planned the whole thing. All of it. She fell down a few stairs a couple years ago and I answered the call, and we got to be friends."

I stared at him. *What?*

He kept going. "Yeah. May as well get it all out. And to think I was scared to tell you. God, I'm stupid."

"Aaron."

"Almost every week I'd come over. Play cards, talk, whatever. Me, her, Betty sometimes. Gigi was a hopeless romantic, and she read way too many romance books, because she concocted this whole scheme. She was convinced you and I were meant to be together." He laughed bitterly. "Well, you showed us, didn't you? Nothing can touch you, Devon. God forbid we touch on something deep."

"Wait a minute," I said, straightening. "That's not fair."

"Isn't it?"

"No!" I shot back. "I lost my *husband*, Aaron."

"You did. But he wasn't the love of your life."

I narrowed my eyes, my chest squeezing. "What?"

He spoke with conviction. "You lost *a* love, Devon. Not *the* love. You can fight it all you want, but what we have?" He pointed at his chest. "It's everything. It's scary, but it's exhilarating. I never know what's coming next, but I knew as long as I had you, I'd be okay."

Chills raced across my skin.

He sighed. "There's more than one love out there, Devon—there has to be. Look at Betty: she had four husbands. Four loves. Hell, look at Gigi! She had three."

My brain twitched. Someone else had said something similar. "No." I shook my head.

He rolled his eyes. "Yes."

"She never...no," I repeated.

"Believe it or don't, Devon, but she did. Maybe if you bothered opening that wedding album in the living room, you'd know."

The blood drained from my face. "Did you—did you *look* at that? When?"

"When Gigi showed me, Devon." He paced around the kitchen. "I don't even know why we're arguing about that. You still haven't admitted it."

"Admitted what?"

"That you love me!" he exploded.

I jerked my head back. My whole body tingled. And I... couldn't say a goddamn thing.

He sighed into the silence, leaning onto his elbows and dropping his head. When he spoke, his voice cracked. "You love me, Devon. You don't say it, but you do. The way you look at me when you manage to get out of your own way? It's love. But it's not enough, is it? Because it's never enough." He lifted his gaze to mine, his eyes growing colder by the second. "And there you stand. Nothing to say for yourself."

"What do you want me to say?"

He straightened and his voice rose. "Give me an explanation, Devon! The real one. You owe me that, at least."

"I don't owe you anything!" The words tore out of my throat, unbidden.

He reeled back as if I'd punched him, his face a mask of hurt.

Immediately I wanted to take it back. Even with these godforsaken wires, it seemed I still needed to shut my mouth. Of course I owed him an explanation. The problem was, I didn't have one. Not one that was actually worth something. So I stared at him, trying to keep the tears at bay, and honed in on the other piece of information he'd thrown out.

"Have you been in on this the whole time?"

"On what, Devon?" he asked, resigned.

"Did you and Gigi concoct this whole thing? She pulls me back here for six months and you just happen to run into me? Has any of this even been real?"

He gave a hollow laugh. "Of course that's what you focus on."

I crossed my arms. "Answer the question."

His face closed up and his eyes shuttered. "No, Devon. I didn't. She brought it up, and I told her I wouldn't be a part of it. I didn't know she'd done it until you were already in town."

I nodded, unable to swallow the knot in my throat.

"But while we're on the topic. She was convinced you and I could have something together. She only ever wanted you happy. Couldn't figure out why you wouldn't come home. But I guess you didn't owe her anything, either."

He walked out without so much as a backward glance.

Samson followed and slipped out the door with him.

I looked around the kitchen, numb. Unsure of what, precisely, had just happened.

Except...not really. I knew exactly what had happened. And as always, I wasn't willing to inspect it.

I walked into the dining room and pulled out a bottle of

Merlot, twisted the top off, stuck a straw in, and drank straight from the bottle. Eventually, I'd have to face it. Face myself.

Tonight was not that night.

And if I had anything to do it, that night would never come.

I flopped onto the couch, the wedding album directly in my line of vision. I toasted it with my bottle and chugged.

My phone buzzed with an incoming text.

RICK

What the fuck, Devon? You're really leaving town?

28

AARON

I WOKE UP to Daisy whining and licking my face, her paws on my chest. I groaned and pushed her away, but she wasn't having it. It didn't help that I was on the couch, making it that much easier for her to get to me. Paws back on me, she panted and looked at me expectantly.

"This is why I should have gotten a cat," I muttered, sitting up as Daisy turned in circles, eager to go outside. I pulled myself up to standing, crumbs from last night's pizza falling to the floor, and walked to the kitchen to let her out. The deck practically screamed at me, reminding me of the last time I'd been out there with Devon.

"I don't owe you anything."

The words had pinged around in my head for two days and were already at it this morning.

It was exactly what my mother had said. Word for word.

Well, fuck me.

I flung myself back on the couch and closed my eyes.

Banging on my door brought me back to consciousness. Judging by the way the light slanted through the curtains, I'd slept past noon.

"Aaron!" Will's voice boomed. "You in there?"

"Keep your panties on," I yelled, pulling myself up to deal with an unwanted interruption for the second time that day. I yanked the door open and glared at him. "What."

"You're late for your shift, that's what." He pushed past me to walk in. "Jesus Christ, man. The fuck is wrong with you?" He gestured to the place, then pulled his shirt up to cover his nose.

I kept glaring. "None of your fucking business."

He rolled his eyes and spoke through his shirt. "Nice try, asshole. Spill it or I'll give you a noogie."

I scoffed. "You can't give me a *noogie*, Will. We're grown-ass men."

He lunged.

I ducked.

He was faster.

"Ow! Dammit!" I yelled, flailing and slapping at nothing, thanks to my brother's superior head-locking skills. Which I would never admit. "Get the fuck off me!"

"Now that's the brotherly love I like to see," came Price's voice from behind me.

At least, I assumed he was behind me, seeing as how my brother had gone full twelve-year-old and was, as threatened, attempting to saw through my skull with his bony knuckles.

I changed tactics and went for his pants, jerking them up and grabbing his leg hair.

"Mother *fucker!*" Will said, letting go of me and hiking his knee up to rub at his shin. He looked at Price. "He pulled my *leg hair!*"

I stood triumphantly. "Served you right."

Price laughed.

"Also, you stink," Will said, waving at the air in front of his nose.

I shrugged. "Maybe don't go giving noogies and you won't be subjected to other people's smells."

"You look like shit," Price declared. "Also, what is that on your face? You know you need to go through puberty before trying to grow a beard, right?"

I rubbed at the scruff that'd grown over the past few days. "Fuck off."

Will stepped past me and went to the kitchen door to let Daisy in.

Price took in the scene around him and swung his eyes to me. "Seriously, man. What's going on? You're not answering texts and you were due at the station this morning."

I sat on the couch and leaned forward, my elbows on my knees. "Devon."

"Ah."

Will walked back in. "You're welcome for feeding your dog. She's acting like she hasn't been fed in days."

"Go easy on him," Price said. Then he looked at me. "What happened?"

I shook my head and flopped back onto the cushions, closing my eyes. "We broke up. She's leaving. Or she's left. I don't know."

"Shit, I'm sorry," Price said.

Will grunted, which in Will-speak was the equivalent of saying he was sorry, too.

"Yeah, well, another one I couldn't make stay."

"Better than Will here," Price said. "This loser can't even get a woman to look his way."

Will punched Price. "Shut up. And at least I try, which is better than we can say for your emotionally stunted ass."

"Ooh, burn," Price said, waggling his eyes.

I was too tired for this shit. "Could you two leave?" I asked. "I'll go to the station. Just…leave."

Will studied me, and damned if he didn't look like he actually cared. "Really?"

I sighed. "Yes, really."

"And you'll clean up this disaster of a house?" he prompted.

"Eh."

"Will you at least shower before you come in?" Price asked.

I shrugged. "Sure."

"Call it a win," Price said to Will. "Let's go. I want ice cream."

"Seriously?" Will followed Price out the door. "You haven't even had lunch yet."

"So?"

They kept it up as they left, and I sagged in relief at the silence that followed. Daisy looked at me, her brown eyes assessing whether I was going to actually move.

Broken heart or not, I had a job to do. One that sometimes dealt with literal hearts. I hauled myself up and got in the shower.

29

DEVON

3 MONTHS, 4 DAYS TO GO

I T'D BEEN A week.

The longest week of my fucking life.

Seven days. Seven nights.

I'd wallowed. Done nothing else. Just...wallowed.

I had managed to get myself to the appointment I'd forgotten about in my haste to skip town, so here I was, mouth slightly open as Dr. Osmond cut the last of the wires out of my mouth.

"All done." Dr. Osmond smiled triumphantly. He held up the final piece of wire and it glinted in the fluorescent light, shining like a combination torture device and second-place medal at the same time.

Eleven weeks. Eleven tortuous, life-altering weeks, and I was unwired.

I opened my mouth and moved my jaw around gingerly. *Freedom.* "Oh my god. I can open my mouth." A smile ghosted across my face. "And I sound completely normal again."

The nurse raised me up, and I looked at the doctor. "I'm done, right?"

He looked over his shoulder at the new person who'd walked in. "Well, you're done with me." He gestured at the woman.

"This is Emily, your physical therapist. She'll take it from here. And don't forget: your stomach hasn't dealt with solid food in a long time, so you'll need to ease back into it."

He left and I looked at the therapist. "Hi." I tried to offer a smile.

She gave me a sympathetic one in return. "I'm Emily. And these," she said, brandishing a stack of popsicle sticks, "are about to be your best friends—or worst enemies. It'll probably depend on the day."

The nurse took that as her cue to leave, and Emily schooled me in the finer points of popsicle stick physical therapy. "Your goal is to be able to stack three of them, sideways, on top of each other. That's a little more than two inches wide."

We tried for one, and that wasn't so bad. But trying to open my jaw much more than that was a joke. After getting all the instructions from Emily and signing a million pieces of paper, I finally met up with Ceci in the waiting room.

Ceci stood when I finally walked into the waiting room. "Let me see that wire-free smile!"

I flashed her the pearly whites.

She reeled back. "Jeez. If that's your version of a smile these days, then don't do it again." She jangled her keys. "Let's get out of here!"

I followed her outside. It was the third week of October, and fall had come. The sky was a pale turquoise and crows cawed in the distance, likely bullying some poor robins or cardinals out of a tree.

I took a deep breath and blew it out, testing my jaw. "I needed this."

"What, being able to open your mouth?" Ceci joked as she unlocked the minivan.

"No—well, I mean, yes. But really this." I gestured to the air. "Thank you for bringing me."

"It's the least I could do since you stayed," she said. "I mean, you've not done anything but melt into the couch, but at least you're here."

"Damn, Ceci. Taking shots at me already?"

She pursed her lips as she stopped at a red light. "You can take it, Devon. You're stronger than you were three months ago, for one, but also, I'm a mom. It's my sacred duty to push buttons. So this is me, pushing yours."

I considered her. "I think I'm touched."

"You should be," she sniffed haughtily, trying to inject some levity into the conversation. "I only push you because I love you."

I flushed with warmth. "I love you, too."

"Good. And here's the next part: How are you going to fix things with Aaron? I mean, you *did* get your jaw unwired, after all." She leered at me.

I groaned. "I don't know yet." I massaged my jaw muscles, which were already sore from the talking. "Can we not talk about it?"

She glanced at me. "We have to talk about it, Devon. It's the only way you're going to fix it."

I slumped down in the seat and fought the tears. "He probably hates me. I broke his heart, Ceese. He can't want anything to do with me."

She hummed thoughtfully. "We'll see."

SAMSON WAS WAITING FOR ME ON THE PORCH WHEN I got home. He pranced around, licking my outstretched hands and bolting inside when I opened the door. I followed him, angling for the kitchen even as I catalogued the work that still needed to be done.

Not counting the week of wallowing, I really had been making progress. With everything that I'd been dragging out of the house, from clothes to unnecessary junk, the house was beginning to feel lighter, as though everything I'd pulled out had been weighing it down.

But for as ruthless and efficient as I'd been with everything—and as meticulous, because I was looking at every piece of paper and ephemera—there was still one glaring weight that practically screamed at me every time I passed by: the wedding album. It sat in the living room, where I rarely went, taunting me.

It was entirely possible that Gigi planned it this way.

Well, she *had* planned it this way, all the way down to meeting Aaron, or at least hoping I'd meet him. I couldn't even be mad at her for it. More than anything, I felt like I'd let her down.

Gigi had always understood what I needed to feel better. Whether it was a skinned knee from a bike fall as a kid, or the heartache of an unrequited crush as a teenager, Gigi had been a continuous source of wise comfort. So why, then, had I steadfastly refused to come home for half a decade?

The truth was, I didn't know. Maybe I wanted the pain. Maybe I felt I deserved it, since Jason had died after an argument.

In the kitchen, I eyed the giant, beautiful bag of Doritos I had waiting for me. I'd blown my life to smithereens, definitely, but I'd promised myself weeks ago that Doritos would be the first thing I'd eat when I got unwired.

I opened the bag, and the smell of processed cheese and spices wafted up at me. I grabbed a chip and took in its orangey perfection. A triangle of crispy, salty, flavorful, crunchy deliciousness.

Hell yes.

I debated taking a little bite, but no. I opened my mouth as wide as I could—which was only enough to slide the entire chip in—and bit down.

It was practically a religious experience. The sensation of

biting down and chewing was its own revelation, but feeling the flavors burst on my tongue was ah-maze-ing.

I giggled, overwhelmed with the silly happiness of it all, and popped another chip into my mouth.

"Oh, god," I moaned. "So gooood."

Samson hopped and circled on the tile floor beside me, and I shrugged and gave him a chip. No need to keep the glory all to myself. "Don't get used to it," I warned him sternly, instantly regretting giving it to him as he turned his big brown eyes on me, licking his chops and panting.

RICK BARGED IN LATER THAT NIGHT, SENT BY CECI and demanding I tell him the whole sorry story, including the Mrs. Withers part and breaking up with Aaron part. Because apparently Ceci thought he should hear it all from me.

Recapping it felt like giving him a highlight reel of all my screw-ups.

"So you don't want the house, either," he said.

"That's your take-away?" I asked. "No wonder I don't talk to you more."

"Be serious," he said, unimpressed with my pathetic attempt at humor.

I buried my face in my hands. "I don't know, Rick."

"Seems like you need to know," he said, taking a drink of the beer he'd brought with him and popped open the second he'd walked in.

"Thanks, Captain Obvious."

He caught my gaze and held it. "Stop that. Stop throwing up shields. I'm not the one who's made a total mess of things, little sis."

My instinct was to tell him I'd done no such thing, but that was a lie. Of course I'd made a mess. Like I always did, if I were being honest.

And Rick wasn't about to clean it up for me.

It was the one thing he'd steadfastly refused to do. Not once, when we were growing up, did he clean up whatever mess I'd created for myself. But he'd always taken care of me. He was only four years older than me, so we'd been nine and thirteen when our parents had died. And even though I wanted to spend a week straight in bed, he forced me to act human: eat, take baths, brush my teeth.

"How'd you do it?" I asked him now.

He peered at me. "Do what?"

"Take care of us for that week after Mom and Dad died."

It was almost imperceptible, but I saw the flinch. "I didn't have a choice," he responded, looking away from me. "Gigi couldn't get to us at first."

"Why didn't you ask anyone for help?"

"Says the woman who refuses to do the same," he said pointedly.

I ignored that. "Did you ever wonder why it took Gigi so long to get up there? To Seattle?"

He heaved a big sigh. "Because she was burying her own husband."

I straightened. "What?"

"She was burying her husband," he repeated. "Did you forget?"

I shook my head. "I didn't *know*."

"What do you mean you didn't know? Do you not remember the guy who looked like Santa Claus? Like, literally —twinkly eyes and a round little belly, the whole thing. Warner?"

I sat up, parsing through my memories. There was a vague recollection of…well, Santa Claus. "That was her husband? I thought he was just a friend."

"Nope. Husband. Why do you think we took forever to get home once she picked us up?"

"Her love of road trips," I said.

He snorted. "Hardly. She hated road trips."

"She loved them! We went on them all the time!"

"*You* loved them," he corrected. "And we wanted to do whatever kept you happy."

I frowned. "Why did it take us so long to get here, then?"

"Because she needed time. Time to process losing her son and daughter-in-law, and her husband. And you needed it, too." His tone was gentle.

"What about you?"

He shrugged. "Someone had to be strong."

"But you were just a kid, " I said, and realization finally dawned. "My god, Rick. How are you even normal?"

He laughed. "You can thank Ceci for getting me straight all those years ago."

I leaned back on the couch. "I fucked up."

"No shit."

"No, I mean…" I struggled to force the words out. "For years. I've been fucking up for years."

His face softened. "Ah, Devon. That's just who you are."

"Um, harsh, bro."

"Some of it's my fault, I think. After Mom and Dad died, the way you were…it scared me so bad. When Gigi finally showed up, I was at the end of my rope. She saw the state you were in, and panicked. She and I spent so much time making sure you were never like that again that I guess maybe it backfired."

I considered his words. "So all those road trips…"

"…and everything else you wanted," he finished. "Yes."

It was as if I was on a tiny boat in the ocean, being rocked around by waves that didn't mean to overturn the boat, but were going to anyway, because they were huge and it was their nature.

I guessed that's what the truth felt like, though. Big enough to drown you, but not intentionally.

Might as well keep pressing forward, I thought. "I have a question."

He snorted softly. "What now?"

"Why did Gigi leave me the house?"

He heaved another sigh. "Honestly?"

I nodded. "Honestly. Pretty sure we've moved past sparing my feelings."

"She wanted you home. It was as simple as that. Here, with me and Ceci and the kids. And besides, I...shit."

"Spit it out."

"I fucking hate this house."

I stared at him. "Bullshit."

He shrugged. "Hate it. Hated it when we moved in, hated it the whole time we lived here, because Gigi turned me into her personal handyman...hated it because it wasn't home."

"Who *are* you and what have you done with my brother? Like, seriously."

He stared back. "Devon, it's as though you've forgotten entire swaths of our childhood or something. The first year we lived here, it was torture for me. And I get it—you were a little kid and wouldn't have paid that much attention—but everything we did was for you. Never for me. Gigi finally figured it out after I lost it on the anniversary of our parents' death, but this house was like a prison to me."

I blew out a breath. "Fuck, Rick. I had no idea."

He nodded. "Yeah, well, like I said. Pretty sure at least some of that is my fault."

We sat in silence, each of us lost in our own thoughts. How self-absorbed must I have been to never notice my brother's pain? To never notice Gigi's? Good god, I was so oblivious I didn't even know she had more than one husband, and yet here I was finally understanding she had *three*. Three!

Our life here had been good, considering what we'd lost. And beneath all of that, Gigi was nursing the loss of multiple husbands. Or at least two. I was still confused about the first one. I searched my memories, trying to recall conversations with her about any of them.

I was a horrible granddaughter. To me, she'd always been just Gigi. I knew implicitly that I'd had a grandfather, but I couldn't put a finger on anything other than that.

"Just how self-absorbed am I?"

Rick sipped his beer and looked at me with compassion. "I'm not in a position to answer that."

Wow. That bad, huh? I tried a different path. "When was the last time we talked about anything that went below surface level?"

"You mean other than right now?"

I nodded.

He scratched his chin thoughtfully. "I don't know. Maybe at your wedding? Before I walked you down the aisle?"

I shook my head. "All you said was that I looked beautiful and that Mom and Dad would've been so happy to see me happy."

"And that was true."

"And I was—happy, I mean." I'd been so happy. Jason and I had a perfect romance. No bumps in the road, everything moving along exactly the way it was supposed to. But I'd kept our love surface-level. And when Jason wanted more, I pushed him away. I lost him before I could get my shit together.

Is that what I wanted to happen again? Push away another man who loved me? Who made my whole body and soul come to life every time I was around him?

I'd spent this whole week in a state of limbo, afraid to make a decision. Afraid, period. Afraid of letting go of the guilt over Jason. Afraid of losing Aaron. Afraid of staying still.

"Aren't you scared?" My voice was quiet.

"Of what?"

I raised my hand and let it fall to my lap. *"Life.* Losing the people we love. We've already lost so many." I paused. "What would you do if Ceci died?"

"Truthfully, I don't know." He looked around, considering, then met my eyes. "Here's what I know. Yeah, we lost our parents. I miss them all the time. They didn't get to see you get married, or me get married. They don't know their grandchildren. They've missed out on our whole lives. But we've *had* lives, Devon. We have been given the gift of these messy lives, and we have to *live* them. What you've been doing these past five years? It's not been living."

I heaved out a breath. "It's been longer than that, Rick. So much longer."

Without another word, he opened his arms. I scooted into them, closing my eyes and letting the tears fall. I needed to admit that I'd kept myself closed off ever since Mom and Dad had died. Rick and Gigi had done their absolute best, and Jason had tried, too. But maybe they had protected me too much. Let me run too much.

And now I was faced with losing Aaron, and it was because of my own stupidity. My own fear. He'd asked me to let him in, and he'd waited patiently for me to do it. And I'd refused.

"You'll be okay, little sis," he said quietly. "But you have to put in the work."

He was right. "What am I going to do?"

"About which part?"

I sniffled and laughed miserably as I sat back up. "How do I get Aaron back?"

"For starters, you have to stick around. Act like you wanna be here. Do all the shit that shows him you're permanent."

I swore softly. "This digging deep shit is the worst."

He tipped his beer at me. "That it is, little sis. That it is."

30

AARON

THE RIG HAD never, and I mean *never*, looked this good. Then again, I'd never been an absolute robot with nothing to do but slog through my days in a fog of despair. I threw the rag into the hamper and heaved myself up the stairs into the firehouse.

How had I lost myself so completely to her, so quickly? Especially when I'd known the end result?

The days were colorless, blurring into each other. The only indication that time was passing was the twice-daily feeding of Daisy and Samson. Samson seemed to have decided his loyalties were with me, which was irony at its fucking best.

Inside the firehouse, I made my way to the couch and slumped down. Samson hopped on and wedged himself against my leg and Daisy lay her head on my knee, while I stared blankly at a football game I didn't give a shit about. I wasn't on shift, but no way was I going home. Everything there reminded me of Devon. Once my brothers had forced me out, I'd been there as little as possible.

"Aaron," Chief boomed. "My office. Now."

I fought the urge to roll my eyes and stood up. I wasn't in

the mood for one of his famous talks. I didn't know if I'd ever be again. I dragged my feet, and when I got there, I leaned against the doorjamb and shoved my hands in my pockets.

Chief looked up over his glasses from his chair. "Get in here. Shut the door behind you." He motioned impatiently. "This year."

I did as he asked, but slowly. Sullen teenagers had nothing on me.

He reclined in his chair and folded his hands over his slight belly. "I heard."

I clenched my jaw. "Of course you did. I'm sure it's all over the Facebook group."

He waved my comment away. "It's not your fault, you know."

I huffed out a sad laugh. "Chief, it's *always* my fault."

He looked at me quizzically.

Fuck it. "They never stay. Literally none of them. Or haven't you and everyone else realized that? It started with my mom and it's been downhill since."

"What are you talking about?"

I grunted. "You heard me. They leave. I'm not good enough to keep them."

Chief leaned forward. "Listen here, son. You are the best among us. And I can't speak for what happened with you and Devon, or even any others, but I can sure as shit tell you that your mom didn't leave because of you."

"You can't know that."

He raised an eyebrow.

I narrowed my eyes. "What are you saying?"

"I'm saying your brothers owe you an explanation."

A faint buzzing sounded in my ears, and my fingers and toes tingled. "What are you talking about?" I pushed.

He shook his head. "Not my story to tell. Never has been,

and they've been idiots to keep it from you. Go to the Daily Dose. Your brothers are there."

I furrowed my brow. "What the hell is going on? Why do I need to meet them there?"

"I've said enough. Go find them."

I stood and opened the door to take my leave. Chief wasn't making any sense.

"Aaron."

I looked back at him.

"I meant what I said. You're the best of us. Your mom leaving? Not your fault. Remember that."

I headed down the stairs and out of the firehouse, both dogs at my heels. Minutes later I stepped inside Daily Dose and scanned the room, looking for my brothers. I froze. They sat in the back on opposite sides of a table, and our mother was with them.

All three turned to look at me as I crossed the room, but I only had eyes for Will. I knew he'd orchestrated this. I pulled out the remaining chair, still looking only at Will, and sat. "Why is she here?"

"Because it's time you heard the truth," he said evenly.

I'd had enough. "What truth? The one where she ignores me my whole life? The one where she leaves and doesn't bother with an explanation? Or maybe it's the one where she never manages to visit her kids after she leaves? Or after her husband dies? She's never bothered to give us shit. You honestly think it's going to start now?"

"Yes," Mom said from across the table.

Finally, my stomach in knots, I let myself look at her. She'd aged in the three years since I'd seen her, the lines around her eyes and mouth growing more pronounced. Her hair was completely gray. But her eyes, the ones with my and my brothers' exact coloring, looked different. Brighter. Less troubled.

"It's so good to see you," she said, a tentative smile spreading across her face.

I shook my head. "Enough with the pleasantries. Just get out whatever it was you came to say so you can leave again and not come back for, what, another three years?"

"Aaron," Will chided.

Mom flicked her gaze to him and lay her hand on his wrist. "I deserved that." To me, she said, "Your brothers thought it was time I tell you. About why I left."

I twisted the cap off the water that sat in front of me and took a chug, feeling the coolness of it wash into my chest and wishing it'd wash everything else away with it. I studied her face, how worn it looked despite the clarity in her eyes.

"I guess I should start by saying I love you."

I flinched. "You've got a hell of a way of showing it."

She nodded. "I know. And the second thing to tell you is how sorry I am." She looked at the table and traced a pattern with her finger. Finally, she met my eyes. "I was depressed. Clinically. I'd fought it since I was in my teens, and it got worse with each pregnancy."

My chest tightened. Great. So this really *was* my fault.

Price kicked my foot and shook his head. "Not your fault, man. Listen to her."

How the hell did he always know what I was thinking?

I shifted my eyes back to her and nodded tightly.

She smiled sadly. "No, my depression is definitely not your fault. Never was. It took me years to get diagnosed, and it was way after I'd left here."

"Still doesn't explain why you left," I said. Mental illness was terrible, full stop. But there had to be more to the story than that.

"No, it doesn't," she agreed. "My parents never took me seriously. They'd never wanted kids, and when I came along, I was far too dour for them to deal with. They decided I was a moody teen, and once I went to college, they were done with me. I wasn't welcome in their home after that." She wrung her hands. They were aged, worn. Her nails were short and uneven, but clean. The sweater she wore looked old, as well, but taken care of.

"I didn't finish college. Met your father when he was in Tuscaloosa visiting some friends, fell head over heels for him, and followed him here, back to his home."

My lips tipped up at the memory of Dad telling the story. How he'd seen this dark-haired, gray-eyed beauty and couldn't believe his luck when she smiled at him.

"Just being around your father was enough. For a while, anyway," she continued. "But with each pregnancy, my symptoms got worse. And your dad, he wanted me to talk to someone. But instead of talking, I drank."

I laughed harshly. "No shit."

"Yes. No shit," she repeated softly. "And as my depression got worse, so did my drinking."

"And then you laid in bed all day, managing to rouse yourself for Will and Price, but not for me," I said. "I remember."

She raised her eyebrows. "I deserve that."

I let out a breath. "Look. I appreciate what you're saying here. And I'm glad you've finally gotten help—I really am. But you still haven't explained why you left, or why you stayed away for over twenty years. *Twenty-two* years, Mom, if we're counting. And I am."

Tears sprang to her eyes. "I know. I'm sorry."

Price swatted my arm. "Be patient."

I looked at him. "Really? While she's getting around to explaining her side of things, how about you two explain to me how much of this you've known and kept from me?" Heat coursed through me and I gripped the plastic bottle so hard that water spurted out and ran down my fingers.

Will leaned forward. "Quit being an asshole, Aaron."

"I don't have an excuse for leaving the way I did," Mom said, shutting all of us up.

I sat back in my chair and waited.

She fidgeted with her hands. "I checked myself into a clinic in Tennessee. I needed to get far enough away that I couldn't run home when it got too hard." She met my eyes. "Your father knew. He decided it was best if we didn't tell you boys anything."

All the air left my lungs. *Dad* was the reason we never got an explanation?

"After everything I'd done, the way I'd behaved. I didn't think I deserved to fight him on it. It was...shameful. The way I'd let you three down. You, Aaron, especially."

I ground my teeth. "Still not making this any better. I'm trying to understand why it's *now* that you're finally here."

"Let her finish," Will growled.

I rolled my eyes.

She sighed. "So I got help. But I was still so ashamed of how I'd behaved. All I could hear was the disappointment of my parents all those years before, then the look in your dad's eyes. All your eyes, really. Then I'd grab a drink and fall off the wagon." She looked up again. "It was a cycle. For a long, long time. Whenever I showed up here, it was because I was trying to get better."

"Why didn't you say anything?" I asked. "When Dad died? We could have helped. We could—"

"No," she interrupted, sitting up in her chair. "You couldn't. The only person who could help me was me. I never wanted to put the burden on you boys. It was the only thing your dad and I managed to get right."

I shook my head, unconvinced, then looked at Will and Price. "When did you find out?"

They glanced at each other.

"Oh, fuck you two. Always the pair of you, thinking you

know best, treating me like I'm incapable of handling things. I lost my childhood after she left. Not that the two of you noticed," I said, the bitterness of it coating my tongue.

Will clenched his jaw. "Since I was nineteen."

"Jesus. I was in fucking high school, Will. That not old enough for you? What about you?" I looked at Price.

"Come on, man," he said.

"Hell no. Answer the question."

"Same time Will learned," he muttered, darting his eyes away.

I looked up at the ceiling. "Unbelievable. Really unbelievable."

No one spoke. The silence stretched until I looked back at the three of them. "So to be clear, it's been over fifteen years. And you never thought I should know?"

"You never wanted to talk about her," Price said.

My blood boiled. "Oh, hell no. You can't use that as an excuse. I would have wanted to hear *this*, for fuck's sake. I'm not a little kid anymore—I haven't been for a long-ass time. And you," I said, locking eyes with Mom, "you never thought I deserved to know? Do you even remember telling me you didn't owe me an explanation? Why was I so unworthy?"

"That's not what it was," she said.

"Then what the fuck was it?" I asked, struggling to keep my voice down. "Because from where I'm sitting, I don't see any reason I shouldn't tell all three of you to go fuck yourselves."

"Watch it, Aaron," Will said, his eyes flashing.

I scoffed. "Or what, Will?"

Price held his hands between us. "Come on, guys."

"It's my fault." Mom spoke up. When I turned to her, still seething, she said, "I asked them not to tell you."

"Why?"

"Because you were the youngest. You were supposed to stay

innocent. Supposed to, I don't know, not have to deal with any of it."

I stared at her in disbelief. "You're serious, aren't you?"

Her eyes reddened, but to her credit, the tears didn't come. She lifted a hand and let it fall. "Somehow I thought...that it was better for you to be mad at me instead of disappointed. The way you looked at me, Aaron—like you could see everything. I couldn't bear your knowing." She took a deep breath, clenching her hands on the table. "I see now that I made a mistake by not telling you, and by asking your brothers not to tell you."

What was I supposed to say to that? "Yeah, you did."

"Okay, that's enough," Will growled. He hunched over the table and whisper-shouted. "Get your head out of your ass, Aaron. She's got a disease. Two of them, actually, and she's spent the last two years working her ass off to get sober and stay that way, to finally come home and sit here and tell you what's been happening."

"And when she canceled on us again?" I asked, still not quite ready to give in.

"I was helping a friend through a relapse," she said quietly. "I didn't want to say what it was, because you'd want more explanations and I needed to tell you to your face." Her face was open and honest. "I am so sorry," she said. "I've made so many mistakes. But I love you. I have always loved you. I wanted to tell you everything. And I know I have so much to make up for."

Fuck. I sagged in my chair, all the fight finally out of me. Between this and the ache in my heart that began and ended with Devon, I didn't have the energy for it. I met her eyes. "You're right. You do."

She smiled tentatively and reached for my hands.

I pulled away. "We aren't fixed. But having you here, telling me all this. It's a start."

～

Jodi caught my eye as we left a while later, headed to Will's place for dinner. I managed a smile, and she waved me over.

"Hey," she said, a worried look on her face. "You okay?"

I lifted my shoulders. "Yeah. No. Maybe?" I took a beat. "I'll get there."

"I bet. Listen, um." She scrubbed the clean counter with an equally clean cloth. "Have you talked to Devon? Since…?"

I looked away. "No." I wanted to. God, I wanted to. I spent every night wanting her in my bed. Every morning wishing I could see her face, the way her eyes glittered when she smiled.

Jodi's face fell. "Oh. I thought maybe…well. Never mind."

I studied her. "Maybe what?"

She waved it away. "Nothing. Go. Be with your family. See you later?"

I turned into Will's driveway and sat, the engine idling. Chief's words came back to me. *You're the best of us. Your mom leaving? Not your fault.* So he knew. Of course he knew.

I wanted to talk to Devon, to tell her everything that'd happened and work through what I was feeling with her. Even though she was gone. Even though she'd probably run screaming at the hint of a deep conversation. I couldn't help it. I missed her so much that my chest physically hurt. It hadn't stopped hurting since I left her house that night.

I didn't know where she'd gone. She hadn't posted anything to her social media, because I'd looked more times than I cared to admit. The last photos were of the two of us, on her porch and up on the mountain.

Fuck. I squeezed my eyes shut and gripped the wheel. I had an explanation for my mom leaving and staying gone, and that should have made me happy. Or at least marginally better. But all I felt was a sadness so deep it was a pit that would never be filled.

31

DEVON

NO MORE COUNTING DOWN. I'M STAYING.

I T'D BEEN TWO weeks since my argument with Aaron. One week since the talk with my brother. And with every passing day, every painful session with those godforsaken popsicle sticks, missing Aaron hurt a little more. I'd thought it would be easier, now that I'd decided to stay.

It wasn't. Not even close. No matter the progress I made in other areas, the days were dulled around the edges, and the hole in my chest throbbed and ached. I missed the safety of Aaron's arms, the sense of knowing I was home inside of them. I wasn't sure if he even knew I'd stayed. I didn't see him the few times I'd gone to the coffee shop, and Jodi—who was still pretty salty about my attempted escape, but was slowly coming around— would only say he looked as sad as me.

I had no idea if he'd forgive me. But if I wanted a second chance at him, I had to get myself set to rights first.

So I put my head down, and move forward. The lights upstairs finally worked, for one. The electrician had rewired the entire house, and in doing so, had relieved me of the last bit of Gigi's funds. I'd filled up the dumpster outside and already had a fresh one halfway filled. I'd aired out old quilts and made beds with fresh linens. I wasn't going to stay in the house, but I'd make an effort while I was here.

I'd also reached out to the elementary school about being a substitute teacher while I re-upped my teaching license. I wasn't ready to go back to the middle school, but this was a step.

I was doing the work. Like I'd promised Rick. And like I'd promised myself. But I still had one gauntlet to run: the wedding album.

I hadn't touched it since the day it opened to my and Jason's wedding. And even after hearing of Gigi's husbands, I still hadn't been able to open it.

Today was the day.

I grabbed it and got comfortable on the couch. The smell of old leather wafted up as I opened the book, its spine cracking.

The pages were black, and there, on the very first page beneath a yellowed sheet of tissue paper, was a black-and-white photo with scalloped edges tucked into four black picture corners. In the frame stood a very young Gigi, clad in a smart-looking cream skirt and jacket and a tiny cream fascinator placed jauntily on her head. Beside her, dressed in what I thought was an Army uniform, stood a man I didn't know. They smiled happily at each other on the steps of the town's courthouse, their hands clasped and their bodies pressed against each other. A yellowed piece of paper below the picture captioned, *Shirley and Herman, April 9, 1952.*

I did the math. She'd been all of seventeen years old. So young. They looked so happy. I could only assume something happened to Herman while he was in the service. Korean War, maybe? I ran my fingers over the image, trying to imagine what it must have felt like for Gigi to lose her love like that. I remembered the way she'd comforted me after Jason's death. *Losing someone in a tragedy is the worst kind of loss. Even if you know there's a risk, you think it won't happen to you. And when it does, it takes your breath away.* I didn't know she was speaking from experience.

Heart heavy, I flipped the page. There was a photo of my great-aunt Donna marrying her husband, Henry. They'd moved up to Yazoo, Mississippi after the wedding, so I never met them, but Gigi had regaled me with stories on our road trips about their adventures growing up.

The next page had a picture I recognized, at least partially. Gigi and the man who was my grandfather, Robert. They'd gotten married at church, and Gigi's dress was a stunner, plain white silk that hugged all her curves and ended in a train that floated down the steps of the altar. They were flanked by groomsmen and bridesmaids, none of whom I knew but whose names were listed on the card below the frame. *Shirley and Robert, June 1955.*

The next couple of photos were of people and weddings I didn't know, but then I got to the one of my parents. Instantly, tears sprang to my eyes. I remembered this picture on the mantle at our house in Seattle, the way my mother teased me for always grabbing it and looking at it. It was a close-up shot, waist up, and they smiled brightly at the camera, hugging each other, as if neither one of them could bear to be apart from the other. So full of love and life. *Laura and David, 1990.*

The next page held Gigi's third wedding photo. *Shirley and Warner, 1994.* A heated flush of shame washed across me as I took it in. There he was. Santa Claus. How did I not realize they were married? I peered at Gigi's hand and saw only a tidy gold band. I flipped back. The same kind of band she wore with Grandpa. I flipped to the front, but Herman's hands covered hers. I turned back to the one of her and Warner. No way she wore the same gold band for all of them, right? Either way, I'd always assumed the ring she wore when I lived here was the one Grandpa had put on her hand. That might have been wrong.

I knew the next page was my and Jason's, so I flipped past it to see if I could find Rick and Ceci's. I turned the page and choked out a laugh. True to form, the image was a bit chaotic.

The photographer had tried to get us all in line and smiling, but Rick had already snuck shots to all of us and we were more than a little tipsy. Rick and Ceci were mid-laugh as the rest of us attempted to get into position. I'd never seen this image, and it was sheer perfection. *Rick and Ceci, 2015.*

Taking a deep breath, I went back a page. There we were: me on Jason's back, both of us laughing, surrounded by our friends and family as we wove through a sea of bubbles on the way to the car. We'd been so happy. So full of promise.

I closed my eyes, waiting for the familiar onslaught of guilt and pain to hit. But it didn't come. After a moment, I released the breath I'd been holding and opened my eyes.

I was finally getting better. I hadn't told Jason I loved him on that last day, but it wasn't eating me up like it used to. We'd fought, but we would have made up. We would have worked through it. I had to believe that. And I had to believe that he would have helped me become a better person. I'd always be grateful for the time we had together, and I was finally able to move forward. I'd lost *a* love of my life when Jason died, but he wasn't my one and only. My story couldn't end with losing Jason. In fact, maybe it was just beginning.

I loved Aaron. Deeply. But I'd never told him. What kind of cowardly move was that?

I sat up and closed the wedding album. Enough of this. I still had a chance. I had to try. I *had* to, because he was alive. And I'd lost enough people in my life. It was time to put the rest of the plan into action.

I grabbed my phone and called Betty. When she answered, I asked, "How mad do you think Mrs. Withers would be if we really did turn this house into a bed-and-breakfast?"

32

DEVON

T HE DAY WAS appropriately overcast as I thanked
Wanda and stepped out.

"You sure you don't want me to wait?" She looked
at me skeptically. "Not confident any of these folks still have a
valid driver's license."

The corner of my lips lifted at her light-hearted humor. "I'm
sure. Thank you."

"Okay. Well, you got my cell so you holler when you're ready
for a pick-up." She rolled her window up and did a U-turn in the
parking lot.

I rubbed my arms to ward off the late October chill. No
amount of layers were going to keep me warm.

Looking up at the wrought-iron gates, I took a deep breath.
Nothing to do but get on with it. I walked into the cemetery,
muscles straining with the effort of not turning and bolting for
the hills.

I wound through the walkways, doggedly heading for Jason's
grave. It came into sight quickly, because it was a small cemetery, intended only for the local police, firefighters, veterans, and
their families. My steps slowed, faltered, then stopped

completely in front of it.

The gravestone still looked so new and bright, its raw marble untested by decades of weather. A firefighter's helmet was carved at the top. His name, birth and death dates were beneath it. *Beloved son, brother, husband* under that.

I hated it.

"I never apologized, did I?" I said, lowering to my knees in the grass. "Not really. Not for what mattered."

The breeze was cool against my bare neck. I flipped the flannel's collar and squinted into the sky.

"So." I paused, searching for the words. "Jason, I'm sorry. I'm so sorry. I'm sorry I never let you in. You were so good to me, and I repaid you by never loving you as much as I could have. Never letting you love me the way you wanted."

The grass was too well-kept and soft beneath my jeans, and I wanted it to poke through, spike into my knees. Provide some kind of punishment. I needed it.

Why?

I looked around, searching for the source of the question. But of course, no one was there. And it's not like it was Jason's ghost asking me. Still, I thought about it.

"Because I'm still here and you're not. Because I can't stop thinking that you left home that day knowing I was mad at you. But even though I was mad, it was because I was scared. I loved you. Of course I loved you. That was never the problem."

I pulled at the surrounding grass, rolling it in my hands.

"We were good, you know? You and me. Storybook stuff. The teacher and the firefighter. College sweethearts. The whole thing. We weren't supposed to end the way we did."

I took a breath.

"There's a guy," I blurted to the helmet. "His name is Aaron Joseph and you knew him and I think that's good, right? That you knew him. He's so good, Jason. I bet you really liked him. And I"—I sighed—"I love him. So much. It's terrifying. *He's* terrifying. I messed up, though. I'm trying to fix it, but..."

I swallowed and forced back the tears.

"The way he looked at me, Jason. Like I was the oxygen he needed to breathe. Did you ever look at me like that?"

I glanced past the headstone. Focused instead on the oak tree that towered five yards away.

"I don't know if you did. Even if you did, I don't guess I was in a place where I could have seen it and appreciated it." I lowered my voice. "And I don't think I looked at you that way, either."

I inspected my hands. "I loved you. I still do. But I don't think I could have loved anyone fully back then because of what happened to me as a kid. Still. You'll always be my first love."

I pulled out the small trowel I'd grabbed from Gigi's set of garden tools, and moved close to the headstone. I dug a small, deep hole right beside it. When I was satisfied, I pulled the black velvet box out of my purse and rolled it around in my hands. Finally, I flipped it open.

I'd never had a diamond. Jason was never the showy type, and that had always been just fine. He didn't really propose to me, either—at least, not in a big, romantic way. We'd been on inner tubes, going down the Cahaba River on a lazy Sunday afternoon, and he'd said, "We should get married." Six months and two golden bands from the pawn shop later, we were.

And now I looked at those rings as they lay against the velvet. I'd regretted not burying these with him almost as soon as they lowered him into the ground. The regret was immediately chased away by guilt. How could I not want them?

But I didn't. It'd felt right that they should be with him. Because he'd always have a piece of me, and the rings represented that.

I picked them up and pushed them onto my first finger's knuckle, then brought them to my lips. "I love you."

I returned them to the box, snapped it shut, and lay it carefully in the hole. The tears came then, mixing in with the dirt. When it was filled, I tamped the too-nice sod back into place, then emptied a bottle of water on top.

Satisfied with my work, I wiped my eyes and stood.

"Take care, Jason."

A sudden breeze caressed my cheek in response.

33

DEVON

IT TOOK ANOTHER week to get everything in order. Turns out, dealing with things like loans and banks took longer than I realized, and apparently I was supposed to be grateful that it happened as quickly as it did. I'd barely slept, and I probably looked more than a little ragged. I'd managed to shower today, though, so I was calling that a win.

Jodi waved me to the counter as she stepped out from behind it. "Are you sure about this?"

"It's been three weeks without him. I've never been more sure about anything in my life."

"Not about Aaron—I know that." She worried her bottom lip and gestured to the crowded coffee shop. "I mean the loan to me. It's a lot of money, Devon."

I smiled. "Jodi. You had faith in me when I didn't have any in myself. You've been nothing but supportive for years and years, even though I've been a self-involved brat. Loaning you the money for the shop is a small way of saying thank you. I owe you much more than this." I shrugged. "Besides, it's not really me you have to thank. It's the bank for agreeing to hold off, *and*

Price for agreeing to buy the house. And Will, too, but saying his name doesn't make you blush."

She blinked the tears back and swatted at me. "Shut up," she muttered.

Laughing, I pulled her to me for a hug, one that *I* actually instigated for once. As she sniffed against me, I squeezed her hard. "You mean the world to me, Jodi. I'm grateful I got you as my little sister. I love you."

She pulled away and wiped her eyes, then smiled teasingly at me. "Look at you, saying those three little words. You warming up?"

I laughed nervously. "Something like that."

Ceci swung over and wrapped her arm around my shoulders. "How are you?"

"Queasy," I said. "I should have just done this at his house."

"What? No way," she said. "Besides, it was a great excuse to convince my husband we needed a sitter for many, many hours." She winked salaciously at me.

"Okay, now I'm *really* queasy," I answered. "How many times do I have to tell you to keep that mess to yourself?"

She laughed and snuggled into Rick, who'd chosen that exact moment to walk up.

The bell over the door jingled and Will and Price walked in. Instantly I stopped breathing. Forget queasy. I'd just expire on the spot.

Price broke into a wide smile and made his way to us. Behind me, Jodi squeaked, making me grin a little. Her obsession with Price was so obvious.

"He's there," Price said, oblivious, as always, to the way he affected Jodi. "Chief is about to send Daisy and Samson our way." He nodded back at Will, who waved new Halloween-themed dog toys in his hands.

"You ready?" Price asked.

I forced the air into my lungs and shook my hands out. "As I'll ever be."

He pulled his phone out and texted Chief.

I shivered and wiped my clammy palms on my pants. This had to work.

Rick stepped close and squeezed me tight with a burly arm. "You've done great, little sis."

I looked up at him. "Yeah?"

He nodded and smiled. "Yeah." He gave me one last squeeze and let me go.

Miss Betty and Mrs. Withers were up next, giving twin hugs and wrapping their arms around me in a puff of baby powder.

"Good luck, Devon," Mrs. Withers said.

"She doesn't need luck!" Miss Betty snapped.

"Easy, ladies. We're all on the same side here. For once," I added under my breath.

I felt for the thick piece of paper in my back pocket and tried to breathe normally. Will opened the coffee shop door and stepped halfway out, the toys in his hands. "C'mon, Daisy! Samson!" He whistled and waved the toys.

"We should never have trusted him with this part," Price mumbled. "He is the least warm and fuzzy man on the planet."

But I heard the scrabble of nails on sidewalk, and in seconds, the dogs were in the shop, fresh toys in their mouths and running around like they'd just won the lottery.

"He's coming," Will said, stepping inside and letting the door shut behind him.

Breathe.

It felt like an hour, but finally the door flung open and there he was. "Will, what the—" he stopped, his eyes roaming the very filled, but very quiet, shop.

I can do this. I can do this. I can do this. I kept repeating the phrase as I drank him in.

His face was paler than normal, and there were dark circles under his eyes. But god, he looked good. Wide shoulders and thick chest barely held back by the tight, navy-blue tee shirt he wore. Dirty blond hair that I wanted to run my fingers through. Lips I wanted on mine. And eyes that caught mine now in a question.

I swallowed. "Hi."

Price rubbed his hands together. "This is gonna be so good!" he said.

Will had moved back with us and he thwacked Price on the chest. "Shut up. For once in your life, *please*, shut up."

Price scowled at Will and rubbed where he'd been hit.

Aaron still stood at the front of the shop, both dogs at his feet with their new toys. Suddenly, it seemed utterly stupid that I'd planned on doing this in front of everyone.

"Um," I said, sliding my eyes to Jodi and Ceci.

"Right." Ceci nodded. With a louder voice, she said, "Okay, everybody, act like we have things to do."

Everyone jumped into motion and started talking. I couldn't help but laugh a little, because it was ridiculous. This entire thing was ridiculous. But it didn't matter, because the man I loved was in front of me.

I took a tentative step forward, then another. After a moment of hesitation, Aaron met me halfway. He smelled so good. It took everything I had not to wrap my arms around him and bawl. But I had things I needed to say, and judging by the wary look in his eyes, I needed to get to it.

"I thought you'd left." His voice was flat.

My heart squeezed. "I couldn't."

We stared at each other. My pulse had skyrocketed, and now my breath skittered out of me.

He frowned. "Your heart rate." His hand twitched, the professional paramedic making an appearance as he closed in and pressed two fingers to the vein on my neck. "It's racing."

I huffed out a laugh, grateful for the touch, no matter how clinical it was. "Because I'm nervous, Aaron."

His eyes widened as he inched back and dropped his hand to his side. "Your mouth."

I was desperate for his touch again. But I managed a tentative smile. "Yeah." I waved my hand at the shop. "You're probably wondering why I did all this."

"You, uh, could say that."

"Can I..." I started. "Um." *Spit it out!* "Fuck, this is hard." But then I met his eyes, and I knew exactly what to say.

34

AARON

GOD, SHE WAS beautiful. It was only now, in the face of her, that it felt like I could breathe again.

Devon looked nervous, twisting her hands and shifting her weight from one side to another. I wanted to grab her and pull her into my arms, tell her that whatever was going on, that it was okay, that I wanted her back. But what if this was one big set-up to let me down?

Finally, Devon lifted her eyes to mine, their turquoise depths calm and steady. The world fell away, leaving only the two of us.

"Aaron, I love you."

Her words hit deep, filling my chest and wrapping around me. She loved me. She loved me, and she was saying it out loud, around all these people.

She reached for my hands, bolder now. "I love you," she repeated, her voice clear and even. "I love you so much. And I've been a complete coward. I've been afraid of so many things, but especially going below the surface. You have absolutely *terrified* me this whole time, because you," her breath hitched, "you are definitely below the surface."

My heart was coming back together with every word she

spoke, the pieces locking into place one by one. I was pretty sure I was smiling. "Does this mean—"

She shook her head, tears springing to her eyes. "I need to finish."

I pulled her closer, still holding her hands but bringing our arms flush against each other.

"You brought me to life. Not even back to it, but *to* it. You always saw all of me. Who I was, who I could be, and that scared me. When Jason died and I left town, I shoved you out of my head so far that I nearly forgot you." She stepped even closer, her gaze steady and warm, never leaving mine. "And seeing you that first time a few months ago? It was no surprise I literally fell at your feet. You have been so patient with me. So kind, and understanding, and always giving me what I needed, even when I didn't know what that was. I didn't deserve it, and I still don't deserve you. But," she said and swallowed, "I'm hoping maybe you could find it in your heart to give me another chance? Because I'm staying."

"You're staying?"

She nodded. "Yes. You are *every*thing to me, Aaron. I want to be with you, here." She took an uneven breath. "Will you please forgive me?"

"Devon." I wrapped her in my arms, crushing her against me and breathing her in. "I love you, too," I whispered roughly. She squeezed me back, and I felt her sob.

I pulled back to look at her. Tears streamed down her cheeks, and my own eyes stung.

"But do you forgive me?" she asked, her voice small, her smile unsure.

Her *smile*. The wires were gone. "Yes, baby. Yes, yes, yes." I punctuated each word by kissing away her tears.

Dimly, I was aware of squeals and clapping around me. It didn't matter. The entire world could be watching and I wouldn't have changed anything, because I was finally whole.

"Kiss me?" She smiled through her tears. "Like, *really* kiss me?"

I took a deep breath and cradled her head, then tilted her chin as I dipped my head to hers. I tasted her chapstick. I'd missed the softness of her lips, the tiny noise she made every time we kissed.

She opened her mouth, inviting me in. Time slowed as my tongue swept against hers, and I tasted the promises she'd made. Here, in her arms, was exactly were I was supposed to be. I deepened the kiss slightly, still letting her guide me, my head full of sunshine, my senses full of Devon, only Devon. The sweet taste of her mouth, the vanilla scent of her, the feel of her arms wrapped around me.

I didn't care who was watching, didn't care how long the kiss was lasting, but I was quickly approaching rock-hard status, and if I didn't stop us now, I was going to scandalize a lot of people.

Devon whimpered as I pulled away, opening her eyes and meeting my gaze unflinchingly. As always, I could read everything in those beautiful blues, and right now, they spoke of forever.

Her arms around my waist, she said, "I know I have a lot to work on. Being more open and not being as afraid, for one. But I'm trying. Just keep being patient."

I leaned close, my words only for her. "Remember what I said that night at Gigi's? 'Whenever, wherever, however.' I'm all yours, Devon. Always."

Relief spread across her face. "There's more," she whispered, a leftover tear streaming down her face.

"More?"

"I'm selling the house."

I furrowed my brow. "That…is not what I expected you to say."

She hurried to say the rest. "And I'm going to substitute

teach at the elementary school. I'll start next semester. I've already found buyers for the house."

"You're really staying," I said.

She nodded, laughing. "I said that."

"Say it again."

"I'm staying, Aaron. I'm staying and I love you."

I crushed her to me once more, my knees nearly buckling in relief.

"Does this mean you two are back together again?" Price called. "Because it'd be great if he stopped moping around the place. It's not a good look."

Devon laughed against my chest as I shifted to look at him, one arm still holding Devon against my chest. "Fuck off," I said, grinning like an absolute fool.

Price laughed. Beside him, even Will was smiling, his usual judgy scowl on hold.

Chief, of course, beamed. "I knew it was only a matter of time for the two of you," he said, tucking his thumbs into his belt and rocking back on his heels. "We'd have her back, and you'd both settle down."

Devon giggled. "Chief, hold your horses. Give us some time, will you?"

I looked at Devon. *The* love of my life, without question. "Did you really need all these people to tell me you loved me?"

Her eyes shone. "Absolutely. I needed Jodi for the location and Ceci for moral support. She and Rick used the excuse to get a sitter for the twins and they're going on a date any minute now. Chief, Price, and Will for the dog shenanigans. Miss Betty because no way she would miss it, and Mrs. Withers because, well, she wouldn't have missed this, either." She paused. "Although I don't know who the rest of the people are."

I chuckled as I looked around at everyone in the shop, friends, family and smiling strangers, and kept her tucked against me. "Fair enough. But Mrs. Withers?" I looked over to where she and Miss Betty stood, each of them with a plate of cookies in one hand and a cup of coffee in the other. "I thought you two were mortal enemies."

She shrugged. "That's a story for later. It turns out her heart was in the right place, but her execution was seriously flawed."

"And you're really selling the house?"

She nodded and pulled a bundle of paper from her back pocket. "I am. This is proof. Miss Betty, Mrs. Withers and I cooked up a scheme to turn it into a bed-and-breakfast."

"Sounds like another plot right out of one of Gigi's romance books."

Devon grinned. "It does, doesn't it? I have to finish out the six months like Gigi's will says, but I think Gigi would be just fine with how everything has turned out. Don't you?" She winked. "Also, your brothers are the ones buying the house."

I blinked. "I misheard that."

"You didn't." She smiled broadly now.

"You're shitting me."

Price closed the distance to us and clapped his hand on my shoulder. "Bet you didn't see that coming, did you?"

I looked between my brothers, unable to process. Out of everything, *this* might be the craziest thing to happen today. "Whose idea was this?"

Will tipped his chin up. "Mine."

"He needed a partner, and I couldn't pass up the opportunity to find a new way to drive my big brother insane," Price quipped.

"Ahem," Mrs. Withers said, joining our circle. "I'll have you know that I was the one to suggest they buy it."

"True, but can we all agree that I was the knight in shining armor?" Price asked. "Per my usual?"

I shook my head again. "Unreal."

But as I looked around at everyone who'd shown up for Devon and me, I realized it was real. So incredibly, perfectly real. I had the woman of my dreams in my arms, and she was staying.

She tipped up on her toes to whisper in my ear. "Just so you know, I've been working hard to get my jaw open."

My fingers tightened on her waist.

"And I can *definitely* fit your dick in there."

35

DEVON

A ARON HAD US out of the coffeeshop in three minutes flat.

I laughed openly, my whole body tingling and more alive than I've ever felt. "Guess that worked."

He squeezed my hand as we turned behind the station toward his truck. He only let me go to climb in and start the engine, and then his palm was on top of my leg, its heat searing into me. My pulse kicked up as I did the same, dragging my fingers up his thigh and giggling as he jerked in surprise.

"Oh, you are going to pay for that," he growled playfully.

"I hope so," I said, inching my hand closer to his crotch.

He punched the gas.

MY BACK SLAMMED AGAINST THE INSIDE OF HIS FRONT door as he pressed against me, relieving me of my jacket and sweater before I could catch a breath.

"Fuck, Devon," he said against my neck, his hands gripping

my breasts over my bra. "I didn't think I'd ever get to do this again."

I inhaled sharply, the pleasure of him squeezing my nipples spiking through me. "Bedroom," I said. He grabbed for my ass as I wiggled out of his embrace, and I shrieked, laughing, and darted away.

I made it to his room just ahead of him, and was already undoing my jeans and stepping out of my shoes when I turned to him.

His face went slack as he studied me. "Holy. Fucking. Shit," he croaked.

I spun slowly, letting him take the outfit in. I wore navy blue, cotton cheeky panties with a matching bra. It was simple, but showed off every curve I had. His eyes were dark with lust as I faced him.

"Undress," I commanded. "Except your underwear."

He raised an eyebrow and smirked, but obeyed, reaching back to pull his t-shirt off in one smooth motion and leaving my mouth dry in the process. The man's chest was the stuff poetry was written about. I licked my lips, and he huffed out a pleading groan. "Fuck me."

I laughed and motioned for him to keep going. "Believe me, that's the idea."

He gestured helplessly. "I mean, your outfit, and now you—your lips…fuck." He finished undressing within seconds, and stood before me, clad in black briefs.

"Sit," I said.

He complied, and I walked to stand in between his legs. He looked up. "Kiss me," he said. "I just want you to kiss me. Please."

The craving in his voice. It nearly undid me.

I leaned to him and fused our lips together, opening for our tongues to meet in a tangle of hot, wet heat.

We both groaned as he wrapped his arms around my waist,

pulling me close.

I whimpered. My god, his tongue. In my mouth. The delicious, soft scrape of whiskers against my skin. So. Good. I tried to push him back, but he resisted, surging up to stand instead, his tongue pushing further in as he palmed my waist, branding me with his warmth.

He growled again, and I grinned against his lips before pulling away, kissing his stubbled jaw, his neck, then making my way to his chest and stomach before dropping to my knees on the carpeted floor in front of him.

"Devon," he whispered, looking at me.

I met his gaze without hesitation, welcoming the intensity of it—of him—and I held it as I pulled his briefs down just enough to lick at the divots of his hips. He pushed my hair away from my face, then his eyes rolled back as I let the waistband snap into place. Opening my mouth a little, I breathed against his cock, then lightly bit down on him through the cotton.

"Shhhhhhhhiiiiit," he exhaled, his legs shaking.

I looked through my lashes. "You like that?"

"Apparently," he rasped.

I did it again, nipping softly up and down his shaft, listening for his moans and gasps to guide me. I scraped my nails across his thighs, hard enough to leave marks, then pushed inside the briefs to clamp my hands on his ass, nails first.

"Fuck," he grit out, his hips pulsing involuntarily.

Taking the elastic band of his underwear in my teeth, I pulled them down to his knees, delighting in the look of awe on his face as he watched. I straightened and pushed them the rest of the way off, then blinked at the cock jutting into the air before me. Guess we were about to find out just how well I'd done my physical therapy exercises.

"I have wanted to do this for *months*," I murmured.

"Devon, you don't—"

I took his cock into my mouth.

"Jesus fucking Christ. Oh my god."

I hummed against him, testing my jaw. So far, so good.

Moving slowly, I sucked him in deeper, then eased up. As I continued, he responded to every move, his hips flexing back and forth. I pulled back, letting my mouth take a rest while I swirled my tongue around the head, tasting his precum, then licking its length from root to tip and swirling around the top again.

He gazed at me, his eyes molten. I turned my attention to his impressive dick again. Using my tongue was amazing, but it was the ability to open my jaw that I'd been waiting for.

A loud groan escaped him as I took him into my mouth again, one hand at the base and the other cradling his balls. "Devon. *Fuck*."

I looked up at him as I worked him over, licking and sucking, and his eyes briefly widened and then shut. "You," he grunted. He let his head fall back. "My god. There is no way I'm lasting."

"Good." I loved the power of having him at my mercy. Ignoring the dull ache in my jaw, I took him again all the way inside my mouth, letting the tip of him hit the back of my throat. His legs began to quiver as I continued, and soon he grabbed my hair. "Devon," he warned. "You don't—I can't—"

I knew what he was saying, but no way was I stopping. I moved faster, humming and gripping him. Seconds later, his legs stiffened and he groaned, emptying into my mouth.

"Fuck." He was hoarse. "That was too much. Holy shit."

I scraped my nails up his legs and he moaned softly, then fell back onto the mattress. "We're putting this day on the calendar."

"Why's that?" I asked, still tracing my fingers up his thighs as my eyes honed in on the divots in his hips. Christ almighty. I used to think those only existed on the statue of David. "Because it's the day we got back together?" I shifted up, kissing the soft inside of his thigh and working my way up to the bed.

"Because it's the day you ruined me," he said, arms splayed, eyes closed, as I hovered over him.

I straddled him and bent to kiss him, gently. As I straightened, I rubbed the muscles beneath my ears.

Aaron's eyes narrowed thoughtfully. "Are you okay?"

"Just sore from overuse," I said, grinning. "Totally worth it."

He laughed, bouncing me as I sat atop him. "I love you, Devon."

I hummed. "I love you, too, Aaron."

The force of his smile was almost blinding. "I'm gonna need to hear you say that again."

"I love you." I ran my hands over his pecs and followed with my mouth, finding a nipple and swirling my tongue over it. He grunted in pleasure. "I love you." I continued down his chest, letting my fingers run along the ridges of his abs. "I love this chest, and I love you."

He growled and flipped us, staring at me with a passion and lust that seemed limitless. I welcomed it. I wasn't scared of what his eyes promised anymore. I wanted it. I wanted everything. But I especially wanted him. "I love you," I said again. "And I'm never leaving you. You're stuck with me."

The ghost of a grin passed over his face. His eyes darted to my mouth. "Can I?"

I nodded, and with another hungry growl he pressed his lips against mine, pushing his tongue into my mouth, hot and needy, as I opened for him. I lost myself to the kiss, felt nothing but his mouth on mine, our tongues dancing, our lips fused. My nipples stood at full attention as he held me to him, my breasts tight and aching.

"You can't possibly know how long I've waited for this," he said, his rumbling voice raking across my skin. He kissed my neck, his lips so hot it made my eyes roll back in my head. "Tell me you're mine." He pulled my ear lobe into his teeth and bit down.

Goose bumps raced over me as I gasped. "I'm yours," I said, my voice not my own.

He continued his path down the column of my neck and back up to my other ear, nibbling and sucking, while I gulped one breath after the other. "Say it again." His voice was low, gravel at midnight.

I shivered. "I'm yours. I love you and I'm yours."

He lifted off me, holding my gaze while he reached behind me to unclasp my bra, pulling it off one arm and the next to release my breasts. "Please," I whispered, aching with desire.

He barely shook his head, his eyes so dark they barely held color, as he pushed my panties down and off.

He kneeled between my legs, an absolute specimen of a man. Inside as well, but I was focused only on the physical right now. I trembled, needing his hands, his mouth, his skin, my god, *anything*.

"*Please*," I said again, unafraid to beg.

His eyes roamed every inch of my skin as I lay before him, panting, legs spread, nipples peaked, palms up in supplication. My inner walls clenched, and I squirmed with the unbearable need for pressure.

"I need you. *Please*," I repeated.

He hovered over me, his eyes boring into mine. "Say it again."

The words came without hesitation. "I'm yours. I love you. I need you. Always. Please."

He fell onto me, his mouth capturing mine, and I lost myself to the way our tongues danced, slick and hot, and the scrape of his scruff against my skin. His hands moved, caressing my waist and hip, gripping my ass as I lifted a leg for him. His weight on top of me, the heat of him, skin on skin, the perfect fit, was its own fantasy. One I intended to have forever. His mouth moved to my cheek, then to the sensitive skin beneath my ear, one of his hands still skimming my body.

Then he pushed up onto both his hands to angle above me, his eyes traveling over each breast and down to my stomach and back again. "You are so unbelievably sexy." He kissed my neck. "I am the luckiest man in the world."

"You're mine."

"Fact." He grabbed a breast and squeezed. "Now," he said, the timbre of his voice falling and shooting straight between my legs. "Be a good girl and tell me what you want me to do to you, Devon. How do you want to come?"

I groaned and fought to keep my gaze on his. Shards of need spiked through me. I ached for him. "I want your mouth on my pussy and I want you to make me come."

He smiled wickedly, shifting back on his heels. "Good answer."

He moved again, sliding down and pushing my legs farther apart before settling back on the mattress, his head between my thighs. I felt his hot breath on me and trembled with anticipation.

His tongue flicked out, and I gasped with pleasure. "More."

His tongue was on me again, light, then hard. In seconds he had me writhing, my hand gripping the top of his hair as his tongue swirled around my clit. I moaned his name.

He answered my cries by humming and increasing the pressure. I circled my hips, unable to be still, sending a string of delighted curses into the air as he pushed his fingers into me. Aaron's tongue kept going, his wide shoulders keeping my legs apart as he took me to the edge.

Within moments, heat gathered and swirled, concentrating into a pinprick of pleasure, pulsing, then bursting across my body in a tidal wave of pleasure. I cried out, bucking and squirming, and Aaron kept going, pushing me higher and higher through the orgasm, until finally I collapsed, spent.

My entire body tingled, and I simply breathed, trying to

remember what reality was. After a moment, I managed to croak, "Your mouth. It's actually your mouth I belong to."

A low laugh escaped him as he kissed the inside of my thigh, his lips lingering. Then he scraped his teeth across my skin and bit it, sending another spike of want through me. He made his way up my body, his lips hot and wet against me, before pulling a nipple into his mouth and sucking.

I arched up and gasped. "Fuck."

He squeezed the other as he pressed his body to mine, melting me into the mattress. I wrapped my legs around his and gathered him closer, feeling him hard and ready against me. I arched my hips into his. "Aaron."

He lifted his mouth off my breast and crashed his lips onto mine. I opened for him, tasting myself on his tongue. His kisses were soul-melting, pulling my every emotion to the surface, and I welcomed it.

"Please," I whimpered. "I need you inside of me."

Wordlessly, he rolled off me and stretched toward the bedside table.

"No." The word shot out.

He stilled.

My hands gripped at him, pulling him back and meeting his lust-blown eyes. "I'm on the pill. I want all of you, Aaron. Nothing between us."

He returned, settling between my legs. "Devon," he whispered reverently.

I gathered him to me, bringing his lips an inch from mine. Our breaths mingled as I felt the tip of his cock breach my entrance. "Now, Aaron."

He pushed in, and my eyes rolled back as he filled me. Tears pricked at my eyes. This. This was...my god.

He groaned and stilled above me, letting me get used to him. "Sweetheart." His voice was thick.

I rolled my hips and he pulled back, then slowly pushed in again, filling me even more.

I was going to explode. His cock. He moved in and out of me, almost too slowly, and I gripped his ass to push him down. He understood, and pushed in hard. I sighed in relief. I licked the hollow of his neck, and he shivered and pushed in harder.

"Yes. *More.*" I gave myself to him completely.

He shifted and pulled my leg up to tuck the knee against his side, kissing it as he pushed into me. "Tell me what you want, baby."

Three weeks I'd been without this man's cock. We could be gentle later. Right now, though? "Fuck me, Aaron. Make me forget my name."

He smirked, then exploded into action, his hips pistoning into me at a punishing rate. I felt him deep inside of me, hitting exactly where I needed, over and over. Sweat beaded on his forehead.

"Baby," he grunted. "Fuck."

"More." The word tore out of me.

He shifted, and I saw stars. My god.

I held onto him, unable to do anything but take what he gave. I felt the heat of another orgasm gathering. I surged, meeting him thrust for thrust, needing to feel every inch of him as he filled me and surrounded me with his body.

He crashed his lips onto mine and lost the rhythm above me, and I whimpered. Then he wrenched his mouth away and met my eyes again. "Come for me, baby. Because I—"

I shattered, tipping over the edge and into near oblivion as I felt him stiffen above me.

He groaned, his cock jerking inside me with his own climax, my walls squeezing him tight. He buried his head in my neck and I wrapped my arms around him, both of us holding onto each other for dear life as we rode out the waves of pleasure.

I whispered a curse, squeezing him hard with all of me. "I..." But I had no words.

"That..." he whispered as he fell on top of me, spent.

I shivered at his breath on my skin. "Exactly."

After a minute, Aaron shifted onto his side, propping his head in his hand to gaze down at me.

I smiled contentedly. "Can we do that again?"

"Oh, I plan on us doing that again," he leaned to kiss me, "and again," another kiss, "and again."

"No plans on stopping?"

"None."

EPILOGUE

ONE YEAR LATER: Devon

For once, I wasn't running late. I was a solid ten minutes ahead of schedule, and thank goodness, because the caffeine gods were beckoning me to Daily Dose.

Never mind that Aaron had set the coffee pot to go off at 5:30 a.m., with the precise intention of the aroma luring me out of bed since he was already on shift at the firehouse. And it had worked. But Jodi had asked me to come by with the promise of the perfect oat milk lavender latte, and besides, I'd discovered that copious amounts of coffee were needed when it came to dealing with the students of Talladega Middle School.

Bless their hearts.

Actually, no. Bless mine. And their parents'.

In fact, let's bless everyone, everywhere, who has to deal with kids going through puberty.

I put my new-to-me Subaru Outback into park and smiled contentedly. I'd never loved a car more. I'd purchased it with part of the modest profit off the sale of Gigi's house, which of course I'd split with Rick over his objections. I'd kept chanting "twins, twins, twins" and "college fund" as I shoved the check at him. He'd eventually relented. And Jodi had already paid back a lot of the loan I'd given her, too.

I grabbed my purse and headed into the shop. As always, Jodi was behind the counter alongside Darius, who she'd brought on full-time. Jodi flitted from one station to the next, brewing coffee, pouring espresso, creating the perfect latte and then swiveling to nab a pastry and place it on one of the mismatched plates she used. She saw me and waved, her matte red lips parting in a smile.

I gestured with a silent *Should I wait in line?* question, and she beckoned me forward.

"Step over there and I'll get your drink." Then she turned to serve the next customer in the long line.

I looked around. It seemed more crowded than usual in here, but maybe that was standard for an early Wednesday morning. I was rarely in here on a weekday morning any more. After I'd sold Gigi's house, Aaron had convinced me to move in despite my misgivings. Only they weren't of the 'will I get the itch to leave' type—they were 'will he change his mind about me' type. But he'd persevered, and the mornings he wasn't at the station were mornings spent rolling around in bed with him.

The past year hadn't been the easiest, because it turns out we had a delightful set of issues to work through with each other. But slowly, I'd managed to lay down most, if not all, of my fears, and he'd done the same. We weren't perfect, and we probably never would be. But we kept on showing up for each other, and that's what mattered.

"Here you go!" Jodi said, stepping around the counter and handing it to me.

"Thanks. What's up? Did you need to talk to me?"

She nodded. "Come over here." She led me to the corner of the shop I'd come to think of as mine. It's where I always gravitated, whether talking to Jodi and Ceci, sharing a decadent slice of cake with Mrs. Withers, grading student papers, or having a coffee with Aaron while he was on shift.

I tucked myself into the plush velvet chair and took a sip of the latte. "Delicious, as always."

She squeezed her hands together and bit back a smile. "Thanks."

I peered at her. "You're acting weird."

"Me?"

I nodded. "Yeah. You." I leaned forward and lowered my voice. "Are you finally going to say something to Price?"

Her cheeks burned as she bit her lower lip. God, she was the cutest.

"Well?" I prompted.

"He's never going to see me that way, Dev." She shrugged and looked at her watch. "Oh, lookathatgottago," she said, stringing her words together and bolting away.

I scooted to the edge of the chair and looked around. What was going on?

The front door opened and Samson came in, heading straight for me, his paws skittering across the wooden floor's varnish.

I bit back a smile. Samson hadn't been at the house this morning, and I'd figured he'd gone with Daisy and Aaron to the firehouse. And maybe he had, but wherever he'd gone, he'd gotten his little tuft of mohawk dyed a fire engine red.

Tongue lolling, he leapt into my lap and wiggled, licking me on my cheek. I laughed. "Hey, buddy," I said, trying to calm him down. "Where've you been?"

He sat on his haunches for all of a second, but it was enough to let me see the rolled piece of paper that was attached to his collar. I ducked the attack of licking he was determined to give, and pulled the paper off.

Good morning, gorgeous. Come to the firehouse this morning. And don't worry about being late to school.

I looked at Samson. "What's he up to?" I asked him.

In response, Samson licked me and scampered off my lap to head to the door. Once there, he looked at me expectantly.

I stood, curiosity getting the better of me.

As soon as I opened the door, Samson bolted outside, then stopped to make sure I followed.

I laughed again. "What is with you? First you get your mohawk dyed red, and now you're acting like you're trained for the first time in your life."

He barked.

I shrugged and followed in the direction of the firehouse. Ahead of me, one of the rigs blocked the sidewalk, its engine running. Samson ran around it and disappeared from view. The truck pulled farther into the bay, and I stopped dead in my tracks.

Oh. My. God. Standing on the sidewalk, hands casually in his pockets as if the very sight of him hadn't just incinerated my panties, stood Aaron. He was devastatingly handsome, dressed in a navy blue suit with a crisp white button-down and a thin navy tie, his hair slicked into submission. He smiled shyly.

"Hey, gorgeous," he said.

I swallowed and squeezed the to-go cup in my hand. "Um. Hi." I remembered I had legs and used them to walk to him. "You look...wow."

He smiled, the corners of his gray eyes crinkling. "Wanted to increase my odds."

I tilted my head. "Odds of what?"

He turned and whistled, and Samson came trotting back out, his collar weighted down with a black velvet box.

Oh my *god.*

Aaron sank to one knee and unhooked the box from Samson.

"Aaron." My breath caught, and my heart fluttered.

Samson took off and Aaron shifted his attention to me. "Devon."

I stared at him.

He quirked a smile. "Baby. Breathe for me. I'd hate to see you faint right now."

I sucked in a breath and exhaled, but I was still light-headed.

He spoke again. "You were the woman of my dreams from the moment I first laid my eyes on you. I was a goner. But it was impossible, so I tried to shove it down. Way down. And when everything happened, something inside of me flared to life. It didn't matter that you were gone and seemed to have no plans to come back. It refused to go away, and so for five years, I fought. I fought the voice that told me to reach out, and I sure as hell told Gigi where she could put her ridiculous plan."

I choked out a laugh, tears already streaming down my eyes. "I guess all those romance novels she read were good for something."

He smiled. "They were." Then he opened the black velvet box. Nestled inside, catching the sun's light and sending it back out, was an emerald in a princess-cut solitaire, flanked by triangles of tiny diamonds on either side.

My breath caught again. This time, I remembered to breathe.

"Devon Gillian Rayne, will you marry me?"

"Yes!" I said through my tears. I pulled him up to kiss him.

Cheers went up us as he slid the ring onto my finger. I looked around, and we were surrounded by everyone. Jodi, Ceci and Rick, Miss Betty and Mrs. Withers, Will, Price, Mike, and Chief. And of course, Samson and Daisy, who yipped and pranced around us happily.

Aaron pulled me into a tight hug, lifting me off the ground and squeezing. "Thank god you said yes."

I laughed against his neck. "Would've really disappointed everyone otherwise."

"Exactly," he said, letting me slide to the ground. "Kiss me, Devon."

I lifted my head as he brought his lips to mine, and my heart burst wide open. It'd taken more than one try, and more than one chance with Aaron, but I'd found my forever.

COMING NEXT IN THE "GUIDED TO LOVE" SERIES:

THE BARISTA'S GUIDE TO THE PERFECT STEAM

CHAPTER 1: JODI

A trickle of sweat makes its way down the center of my back as steam from the frother billows into my face. I step back, wipe my forehead with my arm, and keep moving. The early-March air that gusts in with every swing of the door isn't anywhere close enough to cool me off.

I shake cinnamon onto Mr. Steele's latte. He keeps telling me to call him Henry, but the man was my high school principal, so, no way. I push the drink to him and glance around the shop. The line isn't getting any shorter, which is good. Great, even. But at the same time, it would be awesome if people could time their need for caffeine in a way that made my mornings a little less insane.

I'm grateful; don't get me wrong. Of course I'm grateful. I'd have lost the shop way before now if these glorious customers weren't lining up for their daily dose.

That's the name of the place, incidentally. Daily Dose. I've owned it since I was twenty-three, a whole four years now. You know that saying, *Ignorance is bliss?* Yeah, that was me. Blissfully ignorant, thinking *how hard can it be to run a coffee shop?*

Ha.

It's hard.

Suck the marrow from your bones hard.

Beg the town bank to take pity on you and restructure your loan because you had no idea what a balloon payment was when you signed the initial loan papers hard, and thank your lucky stars your best friend loaned you money *and* is a hard-core coffee drinker because you're now giving her free coffee for five years hard.

But at the same time, it's pretty badass to own a business this young. To have managed to haul myself up after my firefighter brother died in a fire and go for my dream? Epic. It's the only time I've really done...anything, really. My badassery got even badder after my dad hightailed it out of town in the wake of my brother's death, closely followed by my baby sister taking off to chase singer-songwriter dreams in Nashville. Then, finally, the money shot: my mom sold my childhood home and moved in with *her* mom in Charleston.

Meanwhile, I managed to not only healthily grieve my brother's death, but move forward in the same damn town, a freaking block from the firehouse where my brother worked. And not a soul gives me credit for it. Especially not my family.

"Love of my life, sweetness and sunshine, your ass is so glorious *but could you please move.*" Darius growls that last part at me.

I shimmy my glorious ass, as Darius so eloquently puts it, out of his way. He's my only full-time employee and according to him I pay him a pittance, but I like to remind him that his goal is to be a published fantasy author, not a barista, and that usually shuts him up. For about five seconds.

We move around each other, a dance borne from two years of coffeeshop-counter choreography, and keep the line moving.

"Mrs. Withers!" I beam at the crotchety old lady as she steps up to the counter. "Your usual?"

She smiles at me, and I nearly trip on the floor mat. I keep forgetting that she isn't as cranky as she used to be. She and my best friend/ex-sister-in-law, Devon, sold the house Devon inherited from her grandmother, and Mrs. Withers turned into a fluffy little kitten overnight. It isn't right. Frankly, I'm worried her new attitude is going to mess with the Earth's rotation.

"Yes, please. The lavender latte with two shots of vanilla syrup." She insists on repeating her order to me every time she's here, even though I know hers, and everyone else's, by heart.

"Coming right up," I say. A glance at Darius tells me he's halfway through making her order already.

"When are you going to take me up on my offer of selling my famous lemon squares?" She peers up at me from behind her thick glasses. And I'm only 5'2", so you can imagine what it takes for someone to *peer up* at me.

I smile politely. "Because then I'd have to hear about it from Miss Betty, who swears *she's* the one with the famous lemon squares. And I'm not getting in between the two of you." There's been enough animosity between old ladies in this town, thank you very much. I'm not about to be the start of another one.

But I'm gonna be honest: Mrs. Withers' are better. I think it's all those years of being sour.

Mrs. Withers sniffs like she knows I'm bullshitting her—she probably does—then pays and moves to the left to pick up her drink.

Next is Sarina, who owns the burger and beer joint on the other side of the town square, then Rebecca, the best hairstylist on the planet, then Brook, who owns Brook's Books. And more after that. Then it's nine a.m. and the rush is over.

And then.

Sweet mother of all that is holy.

The Brothers Joseph walk in.

Two firemen and a paramedic walk into a coffeeshop.

It's as if the movie of my life has gone into slow-mo as three fine-as-hell walls of navy-uniformed muscled goodness walk in, joking and laughing with each other. There's Aaron the paramedic, the blond baby of the bunch who's engaged to Devon and is smiling like he's stupid in love. But he actually *is* in love, so he doesn't make me want to barf. Then there's Will Joseph, the oldest and the darkest and the beefiest, who always looks like he's disappointed with the world and gives off this Very Stern vibe.

But then.

Then there's the middle brother. Price. Melter of panties and primary provider of my alone-time fantasies. His dark blond hair flops deliciously over his forehead and he sports a perfectly-maintained beard that's thick but still manages to look like it'd be soft if he graced you with a kiss.

I have crushed on this man since I was twelve. Is it healthy? Probably not. Do I place the blame for my persistent virginity at his likely-pedicured feet? Damn straight I do.

"Ahem." Darius hip-checks me and lowers his voice. "Try not to let the drool get into the steamed milk."

I glare at him before turning my signature matte-red smile at the trio. "Good morning, guys. To what do we owe the pleasure of all three of you at once?"

Oh, god. That sounded dirty. I can feel the splotches of red on my chest and neck, and I'm a ginger, so it's not a subtle look on me.

Will barely looks at me, but Aaron tilts his head a little and leans in. "You okay? You look a little flushed."

Aaron and I have been, if not friends, then at least acquaintances, for a long time. We weren't in the same grade growing up, but it's a small town and there were only two schools, so, close enough. And right now, if it wouldn't mean that Devon would have lost *two* great loves in her life, I would murder him in his sleep. "I'm fine," I grit out.

The espresso machine chooses this moment to hiss at me, and I flinch.

Aaron narrows his eyes, and all my prayers to the coffee gods that he lets it drop must get answered, because he smirks and lets it go.

"Hellooo, Jodi!" Price bounds to the front and smiles at me.

See, this is the thing. Price likes people to think he's like an overgrown Mastiff puppy. And generally, that works for him. It has his whole life, from what I can tell. He was far enough ahead of me in school that I don't think he ever never knew I existed until I started making him lattes. But I knew of him pretty much from the time I started noticing boys, and these days, I choose to believe there's more to him than he's letting on. I give him a warm smile. My warmest of smiles. I'm very smiley right now. "Hi, Price. Your usual?"

He nods and winks at me. "You know my weakness."

You have no idea how much I wish I were your weakness, I think. But I don't say it out loud. I would never. Instead, I chirp, "One vanilla oat-milk latte coming right up."

Darius gives me a Look and I give him one right back. His says *girl*. Mine says *what do you want me to do about it—tell him?* And his replies *Yes, yes I do*. And I laugh. Because right along with death and taxes, there is one absolute certainty in this world: Price Joseph will never look at me as anything other than the coffee girl who makes a killer vanilla oat-milk latte.

ACKNOWLEDGMENTS

Sitting down to write acknowledgements for the first full novel I've published in a 20+ year writing journey is wild, y'all. So the first thanks I'll give is to you, the reader. Thank you for giving this book your precious time. I hope it brought you as much joy reading it as I had writing it.

Thank you to my husband. Your unwavering support and belief in me has been the foundation I've built this dream on. You make all of it possible. Thank you for holding down the fort while I spend countless hours at the laptop and coffee shops. Maybe one day you'll read my books, and maybe you won't, but I always know you have my back. You're my happily ever after. I love you. #TeamVforlife

To my kids: you won't read my books—ever. But maybe you'll see this. The light and joy you bring to my life is limitless, as is my love for you. Thank you for your support, even when you didn't fully grasp the dream I was chasing.

Thank you to my family. From Tennessee to South Carolina, from the Bronx to Florida, you have cheered me on every step of the way. Not every romance writer has the luxury of their family's support, and having yours means the world to me.

Thank you to the Queenies, most especially my agent, Tracy Crow, who championed my writing way back when we were fellow grad students. Thank you to my early teachers, notably Pinckney Benedict, whose "dreaded letter" exercise probably still terrifies students and changes their lives simultaneously like it did for me, and to Elizabeth Strout, whose gentle guidance and quiet brilliance put this baby writer at ease and made her believe she could do it. Thanks to Fred Leebron, who personally called to admit me to the program way back in 2003. Pretty sure romance writing was the last thing on anyone's list when I matriculated, but I guess that final class I taught on "How to Write a Sex Scene" should have been a clue. Thank you to Jeff Hess, the first one to put me in print. Thank you to Erin McReynolds, Kevin Jones, Melanie DeCarolis, and so many others. My years with you, both in school and outside of it, have shaped me in countless ways.

There was a moment when I wrote books for kids. They might eventually see the light of day, but until then, I have these amazing humans to thank for all they taught me about writing for children (who are, for the record, the hardest audience on the planet for whom to write): Ashley Martin for plucking me out of the PitchWars submission pile, Claudia Pearson, Randi Pink, Kaitlin Hundscheid, Tay Berryhill, Cathy Hall, Jo Kittinger, Sharon Pegram, and many, many others in SCBWI Southern Breeze. When I told you I was switching to romance, every one of you smiled and said, "That makes sense."

PitchWars Class of 2017! I came in as a Middle Grade writer and took a left turn into romance, and you've cheered me on the whole way.

To Kat Saturday, Alicia Wilder, and Ivy Fairbanks: the best critique partners a writer could ask for. Your insights and friendship are precious to me. All the Doritos for you!

Thank you to Danika Bloom and the Author Ever After community for holding me accountable and cheering me on.

Finally, thank you to this book's muses: Ashley and her husband. Thank you for letting me take parts of your life and turn them into a story. You got your HEA, and so did Devon and Aaron!

xo,

Valerie

ABOUT THE AUTHOR

Valerie Pepper is an incurable optimist and a firm believer in the girl getting the guy, or the guy getting the girl, or the girl getting the girl, or the guy getting the guy, or basically any way it needs to happen to make a real-life happily ever after, even if it takes more than one try.

When she's not writing, you can find her reading, hiking, listening to whatever music suits her mood, and hanging out with her family. She's fascinated with the idea of a capsule wardrobe, but loves clothes and shoes and boots far too much to make a real go of it.

She's currently living out her own happily ever after with her husband, kids, and dogs, and maaaaaybe too many shoes. She lives in Birmingham, Alabama, and is the recipient of the Contemporary Romance Writer's 2021 Stiletto Award. Follow her on social media @AuthorValeriePepper, and learn more at www.authorvaleriepepper.com.

Made in United States
Troutdale, OR
08/14/2023